The Body in the Boot

Also by Patrick C. Walsh

The Mac Maguire detective mysteries

The Dead Squirrel

The Weeping Women

The Blackness

23 Cold Cases

Two Dogs

The Match of the Day Murders

The Chancer

The Tiger's Back

The Eight Bench Walk

Stories of the supernatural

13 Ghosts of Winter

The Black Vaults Experiment

All available in Amazon Books

Patrick C. Walsh

The Body in the Boot

The first 'Mac' Maguire mystery

Garden City Ink

A Garden City Ink ebook

www.gardencityink.com

First published in 2015

A CIP record for this title is available from the British Library

ISBN 9780993280016

Cover art © Seamus Maguire 2015

Garden City Design

CC source image courtesy of Lars Plougmann

https://www.flickr.com/photos/criminalintent/4389864598/

"The worst sin towards our fellow creatures is not to hate them, but to be indifferent to them; that's the essence of inhumanity."
— George Bernard Shaw, The Devil's Disciple

For Kathleen and Patrick

Monday 5th January

The meeting had been a total and utter disaster and the salesman just hadn't seen it coming. He'd been so sure when he walked into the room that it was all in the bag but now, he was sure of nothing. Nothing except for the fact that his job and his future were both on the line.

His head was buzzing, trying to come to terms with the catastrophic loss of an order that he'd long considered a done deal, an order that would have provided his firm with work for years to come. Then he thought of the massive mortgage he'd just taken out on the back of it and it made his stomach churn. He knew that he needed to get his excuses lined up for tomorrow's inevitable inquest or he'd be for the chop.

Things just couldn't get any worse, he said to himself.

Although it was still only early afternoon the sky had darkened and it was spotting with rain as he approached the traffic island. It's never a good idea to have your mind filled with such concerns while trying to cope with the complicated task of driving and, because of this, things did indeed get worse.

Afterwards the salesman had no answer when he was asked why he hadn't noticed the other car. The light hadn't been that bad and, even if it had, the other car's sidelights had been on. He could only conclude that, somehow, he just hadn't looked to his right at all as he drove into the traffic island at speed. Whatever the reason he found himself coming to an unscheduled and very abrupt stop. His head whipped forward and he felt as though he'd instantly pulled every muscle in his neck and shoulders. The teeth clenching noise of metal on metal echoed around and around his head. For a second, he thought that something had happened to his vision but it was just his windscreen that had crazed over, shattered by the impact. He climbed out of his car and shakily stood up. He saw that he'd hit the other car right on the passenger door.

His first hope was that this was some bad dream and he'd soon wake up, his second was that the people in the other car hadn't been injured or worse by his own massive stupidity. With overwhelming relief, he noticed that there was no-one in the passenger seat.

The engine of the other car gunned as it tried to move off but the metalwork behind the front wheel had crumpled and somehow welded itself to the salesman's car. Then, in a sort of delayed reaction, the boot lid of the other car slowly popped open. A few seconds later the salesman was amazed to see the other driver abandon his vehicle and run off at considerable speed towards the town centre.

He shouted at the fleeing figure, 'Mate, you don't need to run. It was all my fault.'

The man didn't even look back and soon disappeared around a corner. The salesman was confused and not quite sure what to do next. Although a jam was building up behind him the salesman didn't hear the blaring of their horns as the traffic weaved around the collision. For some reason he felt it was important that he should shut the boot on the other car.

In the open boot he saw something that was wrapped in a blanket. He pulled at the blanket and an impossibly white hand with long, delicate fingers fell out, touching his hand as it did so. He felt the hand's coldness on his skin and he jumped back in horror. He stood there in a state of shock, staring at the pale unmoving hand.

All he knew was that it belonged to something human and something very dead.

Chapter One

Tuesday 6th January

Mac smiled as he read the legend on the shiny brass plate out loud, 'The Garden City Detective Agency.'

It sounded very grand but at that moment the agency consisted of just one detective, himself. He looked up and down the street. No-one was nearby so he gave it a quick polish with the bottom of his jacket sleeve. A sudden ray of winter sunlight caught the brass plate and made it sparkle.

He smiled again and, thinking positively as he'd been told he should do, he put it down as a good omen. He made his way down the hall to his office. The top half of the door consisted of a frosted glass panel with the words on the brass plate emblazoned in gold and black lettering. Mac had thought it an extravagance but his friend Tim had insisted on it. He said that all the best detectives in the movies had office doors just like this. Just to be really authentic Tim had also placed a bottle of whiskey in one of the desk drawers.

The office was somewhat minimalist at the moment containing only a hat stand, an old desk big enough to play table tennis on and three chairs, one for him and two for the clients.

Clients, he thought, now that would be a fine thing.

He'd been a policeman for the better part of thirty years but this was all new to him. If he was honest, he'd also have to admit that recent events had knocked his confidence somewhat. He'd always been so sure of himself before but now?

He just didn't know and that scared him. It was only eight thirty in the morning and the office was eerily quiet. After half a year of not working this all seemed so strange to him. Perhaps it was strange because his old workplace had been nothing like this. Just six months before his office had been a desk in a large room where he sat with his team of detectives. He could go there any time of day or night and there would always be someone working and something going on.

Mac felt a pang of self-pity as he sat there and allowed the silence to close over him. A familiar deep tiredness began to seep into his veins and the insidious thought of going home to his bed and diving back into the darkness that had engulfed much of the last six months ran though his head like a siren's song. He jumped when his mobile phone rang.

'Dad, are you alright? I tried calling you at home, are you at the office?'

It was his daughter Bridget and she sounded more than a little concerned. Mac collected himself and tried to sound upbeat.

'Yes, I'm here, sitting and waiting for something to happen.'

'Don't worry dad, something will turn up. You just have to be patient,' she said trying to sound hopeful.

'I wish I was as sure as you are about that,' he replied glumly.

'It's going to take a little time but hang on,' she pleaded. 'You need to be working, you can't...well you need to be doing something.'

She hadn't said it but he knew what she meant. He'd spent too long moping around the house feeling sorry for himself. He knew that he needed to be doing something too, yet he felt so tired and useless. Some days a major victory was just getting out of bed.

'I know Bridget, I'll do my best, I promise.'

'Don't forget that Tim said that he might have a client for you soon and you said that you'd do some

4

research on the internet to keep yourself busy in the meantime,' she reminded him. 'Have you changed your pain patch?'

'Yes, I put a new one on before going to bed last night.'

Mac wouldn't be able to function without the small, square pieces of clear plastic that he stuck onto his shoulder every couple of days. One side of the patch was sticky, spread with a glue that contained a powerful analgesic, powerful enough to temporarily push back the constant pain that gnawed at his lower back.

'That's good. Anyway, as it's your birthday soon, I think you should look in the bottom drawer of your desk. I hope that it cheers you up a bit. Sorry but I have to go now, good luck dad.'

He opened the drawer and pulled out a hat box. He opened it and smiled. It was a new charcoal grey fedora hat. He looked at his old one and thought that it reminded him of himself, old and creased and battered by life.

In a sudden surge of determination, he threw his old hat into the waste bin and put on his new one. It fitted perfectly. He went over to the window, now rain-streaked from a sudden winter shower, and looked at his half reflection in the glass.

He smiled. He'd always worn a fedora. He'd got his first one when he made detective and kidded himself that it made him look a little like Humphrey Bogart. His wife Nora always used to tease him about it. The smile left his face and his eyes misted up as the memory washed over him.

His reverie was interrupted as his eyes focussed on what was happening on the other side of the glass. The window looked out from the back of the building onto a large car park. It was early January and, although not actually freezing, it was cold enough. Rain was falling on a middle-aged woman who was standing unmoving and blank eyed just a few yards away. Her long hair now resembled rat's tails and her make-up was running. The tweed jacket and skirt she wore were sodden and shapeless.

Mac opened his back door.

'Can I help you?' he shouted into the icy rain.

A gusty breeze splashed his glasses with rain. The woman didn't move.

'Please come in, you're getting very wet out there,' he said.

The woman seemed to awake as if from some sort of trance. She looked around her, nodded wearily and made her way into the office. Mac got a large wad of paper towels from the washroom and gave them to her. He then made them both a cup of tea. She drank her tea in silence while Mac busied himself by polishing his rain-spattered glasses. He put his glasses on and looked over at the woman. He hadn't been interested in anything much lately but he found that he was interested in this strange woman.

He guessed that she was in her forties but she still had a good figure. Although her clothes were wet through, he could see that they were obviously very good quality as were the shoes. Around her neck was a single lustrous string of pearls. He was fairly certain they were real. He gave her all the time she needed as she attempted to dry herself with the paper towels.

Eventually she looked sheepishly up at him and said, 'Thank you...er ...'

'Maguire, Mac Maguire.'

'Thank you, Mr. Maguire. I don't know what came over me, I don't normally...' she said with a shrug.

'Don't worry about that, we all have our moments,' he replied with complete sincerity. 'I can see that you're troubled. Is there any way that I might be able to help?'

'I don't know...' she said, looking around the room for a clue. 'What do you do here?'

'I'm a private detective,' he replied, feeling slightly silly.

'A detective?' she said in wonder. 'I'm not particularly religious but perhaps God has sent me here. Oh, Mr. Maguire, I'm in such pain!'

She burst into tears and Mac held her hand while feeling a strong temptation to join in. When she'd quietened down a bit he went and got more paper towels.

She dabbed at her eyes as she said, 'I'm so sorry for the exhibition Mr Maguire, it's so unlike me.'

'Don't worry about that. You said you were in pain, what kind of pain?'

She took her car keys out of her bag and laid them carefully on the desk. On the fob was a small picture of a young girl in a clear hard plastic holder. She caressed the picture with her finger.

'That's the reason I was so upset, it's a picture of my daughter Hetty, my only child. She was ten when this was taken but she was a bit of a wild child even then. She's twenty-two now...no, she was twenty-two is probably more correct. Late yesterday evening, after a phone call from the police, I drove to Luton and saw my daughter lying on a slab. She was dead. I identified her and afterwards I drove home, had a cup of tea and a biscuit, brushed my teeth and went to bed.

I slept well and woke up at six thirty, as always, and had my usual breakfast while watching the news. I decided that I needed some shopping and so I thought I'd come into Letchworth. I parked the car but after locking the doors I dropped my keys. As I picked them up, I saw her photo. It's been on my key ring for years but, in that moment, it was as if I'd seen it for the very first time. I remembered in that split second how much I loved her and all the dreams I had for her and then I realised that I would never ever see her again. My daughter was dead. It was just too much for me, I'm afraid.'

She started crying again but more gently this time. Mac held her hand and waited.

'Mr Maguire, no parent should see their child dead, should they? I have no-one now. My husband died when Hetty was nine, not long before this photo was taken. I've often wondered if she'd have gone off the rails so spectacularly had her father been alive.'

'Tell me about Hetty,' he asked gently.

She made an attempt to pull herself together.

'Oh dear! I haven't even introduced myself, how rude. My name is Janet, Janet Lewinton and I live just off Turnpike Lane in Ickleford. We've lived there ever since David, my husband, got a job at the bank in London. He hated the city and so he used to drive to Hitchin Station at seven every morning and catch the train. We were living there when Hetty was born, seven pounds and six ounces she was, and such a beautiful child. The happiest moments of my life were in that house but there's just me there now.'

She shook her head as if she were trying to clear it.

'Anyway, you wanted to know about Hetty. She was wild alright and scared of nothing. In a young child that can be an endearing quality but in a young adult it can be…well, dangerous I think is the word. She was clever too. She got good grades in all her exams and then went to university to study psychology. She'd always been interested in it. I've heard it said that many people who study psychology do so not to understand other people better but to understand themselves. I think that might have been true for Hetty. I don't think she ever understood why she did certain things, certainly I didn't. Anyway, she went to the University of Bedfordshire in Luton which, all too unfortunately, was something I persuaded her to do.'

'Why was it unfortunate?' Mac asked.

'I didn't want her moving too far away, just in case, so I thought Luton might be a good choice being only a few miles down the road. She seemed to be doing alright but in her last year I knew that something was wrong. She'd stopped calling me and then she didn't come home in the holidays. She was only a few miles away but she might as well have been on another planet. She rang me when she got her results, a two-one, not a bad result really. When I asked her if she was going to come home, she just made some vague excuses. She told me that there were things that she had to do, although she didn't say what, and that was the very last time I talked to her.

She just disappeared Mr Maguire. I tried to find her and, although Luton's not such a big place, I never could. A friend of hers told me that she'd gotten into drugs in her last year, quite seriously into drugs. She'd spotted her one night in an area called High Town where she was selling herself. I couldn't believe it Mr. Maguire, my beautiful troubled daughter was a prostitute. I often wonder if it would have happened if she'd gone somewhere else. Was it all my fault that things turned out so badly for her?'

She dabbed at her eyes again with a paper towel.

'Anyway, I went there quite a few times looking for her but I never saw her again until yesterday. It's not right, her dying like that, tossed into the boot of a car like a bag of rubbish. And no-one cares, no-one but me. The police certainly don't, I even overheard a police-man say that she was 'just some prossie who'd over-dosed'. Just some prossie, yet they're all someone's daughter, aren't they Mr. Maguire? I'm never going to have any closure unless I find out what happened, how she died. I want to hire you Mr. Maguire. One can imagine all sorts of terrible things, even if you only

9

find out how my daughter passed, then that would be a blessing.'

She looked at Mac with such pain in her eyes that, even if he had wanted to, he couldn't have refused her.

Chapter Two

Luton Police Station was red brick and, like most police stations, stolid and quite unremarkable. Mac was grateful that there was a ramp outside leading up to the main entrance. Although he could do stairs if pushed, he preferred not to. He was never quite sure where to put his crutch and he was scared of tripping up as any type of fall might leave him in abject pain for weeks afterwards. Although it was only a short walk, he found that his back was grumbling by the time he reached the front door.

Inside a woman constable manned an enquiry desk and there was a queue. When it was finally his turn, he asked the policewoman if he could see Detective Inspector Carter. He gave her one of the 'Garden City Detective Agency' business cards Bridget had ordered for him. She took it and told him to take a seat.

He looked up at the clock on the wall, it was a quarter past ten. At eleven o'clock he was still waiting and he started to wonder if all private detective work was this boring. He had to keep standing up and shuffling around the confined waiting area every ten minutes or so to stop his back from stiffening up. By half eleven he'd read every poster on the notice board and was just about to call it a day when a young man tapped him on the shoulder.

'Are you the private detective who wants to speak to DI Carter?' he asked.

When Mac nodded the young man gestured for him to follow. Mac followed him down several corridors and was puzzled for a moment when the young man gave him a questioning look as he ushered him into an interview room. The room contained four chairs, a table, some recording equipment and a very grumpy looking policeman in his late thirties.

The policeman, who was rumpled and unshaven, waved at him to take a seat. He looked at Mac's card with clear suspicion.

'A private detective then, are we?' he said as he threw Mac's card back at him. 'Before we start, I'd just like to say that I don't particularly like people like you on my patch. You're all just bloody amateurs who've read a few magazines and then suddenly decide that you're a detective. If you've got any credentials, which I doubt, you probably got them by saving cereal box tops. I don't know what you want but we don't give information out or want to work with people who are...'

The DI's tirade was halted by the soft trill of his mobile phone. He read a message from the screen and glanced up at Mac. He leant across the table, picked up the business card and read it again. He dry-washed his face vigorously with both hands and then looked at Mac with a tired, resigned expression.

'It says on the card that you're from the Garden City Detective Agency which is all I read if I'm honest. It also says 'Contact Mac Maguire' in smaller letters.'

DI Carter cleared his throat and gave Mac a lugubrious look.

'Now that wouldn't be the same Mac Maguire who, until fairly recently, was a Detective Chief Super-intendent in the Met and head of the Murder Squad there?'

Mac nodded.

'It just isn't my day, is it?' DI Carter said with a glum shake of the head. 'I'm very sorry sir about my comments...'

Mac cut him short.

'If it's any help I also found that most private detectives I came across when I was in the force were a pain in the backside too. Shall we start again?'

'Please,' DI Carter said, managing a faint smile.

'I'm here representing Mrs. Janet Lewinton whose daughter, Henrietta, was found dead the day before yesterday in the boot of a car.'

The DI looked at Mac quizzically.

'Sorry, I've not been across that case. We've just had a major terror alert which thankfully turned out to be a damp squib. I could have well done without it though as it's taken the last two days to get it all sorted out. A body in a car boot?'

He gave it some thought.

'Oh yes, I remember now. It seemed to be more or less an open and shut case so I gave it to one of my new detectives, in fact it was the young copper who showed you in here a few minutes ago. I'll go get him and then, if it's okay, I'm going to go home and get some much-needed sleep.'

'Of course,' Mac replied.

Mac thought about the terror alert and what it must have been like. He thought of similar moments he'd had with his own team, working together for days on end, fuelled only by the odd pint, junk food and adrenalin. It could be gruelling and beyond frustrating at times, especially when you didn't get a result. Yet there was something glorious about it too, a team of different talents all working towards the same end, the thrill of the chase and the camaraderie. It was the camaraderie that Mac realised he missed the most. He'd never really known what loneliness was until this last six months.

His thoughts were interrupted by the door opening. The young detective walked in and sat on the other side of the table. He was tall and slim and looked to

Mac as though he should still be in school uniform. He placed a thin manila folder on the table.

'Good morning DCS Maguire, I'm Detective Constable Tommy Nugent,' he said respectfully as he pushed the folder towards Mac.

Mac was intrigued.

'Was it you who texted DI Carter?' he asked as he picked up the folder.

'Yes, but how could you have known that?' he asked as he gave Mac a mystified look.

'It was that look you gave me as you showed me into the interview room. I could tell that you recognised me somehow.'

'Well they used some of your cases in the training course when I was at the police college.'

'Really?'

Mac was absurdly gratified when he heard this. It made him feel as if he hadn't been totally forgotten.

'Is that how you recognised me?'

The young detective nodded.

'But I'd have recognised you anyway. Some years ago, my mother bought this book. She thought it was really good and so she gave it to me and said I should try reading it. I have to admit I wasn't into books that much but one rainy day I was bored rigid and gave it a go. I found that I couldn't put it down and, when I'd finished it, I went straight back to the start and read it again.'

'What was the book?' Mac asked, genuinely interested in what the answer might be.

'It was called 'The Perkis Investigation' and it was about how you caught Hugh Perkis. I thought it was brilliant, still do. After reading it I wanted to become a detective too.'

Hugh Perkis had been a particularly noxious and elusive serial killer. He'd preyed on young homeless boys and Mac had only caught him after he'd killed

14

eight times. He'd not only had the killer but his own department against him for much of the investigation. His superiors hadn't believed that the killings were linked and anyway rent boys hadn't been deemed much of a priority at the time. It had taken all his determination to solve that one.

A friend of his, who was also BBC reporter, had written a book about the case and to their surprise it became something of a best seller. Mac had always worried about whether the book might have trivial- ised police work in some way but, even if Tommy had been the only person inspired by it, he now felt that it had been well worth it.

'Good,' Mac said feeling embarrassed for some reason as he opened the folder.

There wasn't much in it, just a collision report, a statement from the driver who had discovered the body and some photos. He read the statement and report, which contained little of interest, and then looked at the photos. They showed the two cars from several different angles and there were several of the body in the boot. It was completely covered except for a long white slender arm which stood out in stark relief against the dark coloured blanket.

'Haven't forensics done a report or taken any photos yet?' Mac asked

The young detective shook his head.

'Their priority's been the terror alert and they were a bit backed up before that anyway. Want to go over to the morgue and see what's happening?'

'Will that be okay?' Mac asked with some surprise.

'Absolutely, DI Carter said to give you every possible cooperation.'

Mac made a mental note to thank DI Carter when they next met.

Tommy ushered Mac down a corridor into the car park and opened the passenger door of an unmarked police car for him. He wasn't overly familiar with Luton so he had no idea where Tommy was driving him. After fifteen minutes they drove into a car park at the rear of a hospital building. Tommy pulled up near a door that had a ramp leading up to it. A sign said 'Morgue – no entrance unless authorised'. Tommy opened the door for him and then rang the bell in the cramped reception area. A few minutes later a harassed looking young woman in a white coat came out.

Tommy showed her his warrant card and said, 'We're here about Henrietta Lewinton.'

'Is that one of the staff or one of the deceased?' she reasonably asked.

'One of the deceased,' Tommy confirmed.

'I'll just be a minute,' she said and disappeared through the double doors again.

'It's only temporary,' Tommy said while they waited.

Seeing that Mac clearly had no idea what he was talking about he continued, 'This, the morgue. I believe that we're pooling our resources with the Hertfordshire and Cambridgeshire forces so that we'll have a state-of-the-art facility someday. The only problem is it'll probably be miles away.'

Mac nodded and tried to think of something to contribute to Tommy's strained efforts at small talk. He was glad to see the young woman emerge again.

'It looks like it's your lucky day,' she said with a smile. 'Henrietta Lewinton is next up if you want to come and have a look.'

Tommy's face was a picture. Mac could tell that he wasn't looking forward to seeing a dead body cut open. After some thirty years he'd never quite gotten used to it himself.

They followed her down several very long corridors. Mac started saying a little prayer that, wherever it was they were going, it wouldn't be too far away. He'd already walked much further today than was advisable.

If he overdid it the pain was rarely immediate, it usually came some twelve to eighteen hours later. Thankfully she soon stopped, opened a door and ushered them into a darkened room. It had a large plate glass window that overlooked the autopsy room. Below them there was a stainless-steel table that had guttering around the edges so the blood could run off. The outline of a body could be seen as it lay on the table covered up by a white sheet.

'We use this for students mostly. You can see and hear everything the professor says,' she said pointing to a speaker on the wall.

'The professor?' Mac asked.

'Yes, Professor MacFarlane. He's Head of Life Sciences at the university, a very highly thought of pathologist too,' she said as she disappeared through the door.

'We might as well make ourselves comfortable,' Mac said grateful to be able to sit down at last. Tommy took the seat next to him. 'Good view from here, isn't it?'

From Tommy's expression it was clear that the view might be a bit too good.

'Is this the first time you've attended an autopsy?' Mac asked.

'No, this will be the second,' Tommy replied looking very ill at ease.

'How did your first one go?'

Tommy hesitated before saying, 'I threw up.'

'Yes, I did that too on my first one. I didn't even make it to the toilet.'

'Really?' Tommy said with a smile.

It was clear that Mac's confession had cheered him up a little.

'Yes really. It never happened again but, even after all this time, I still don't care for autopsies much.'

Two gowned figures strode into the operating theatre below and the loud speaker came to life.

17

'Right what have we got?' the taller one said.

Without waiting for an answer, he quickly read from a computer screen.

'Okay, Henrietta Lewinton, white female, aged twenty-two, dead at least a day. Known prostitute and drug user, found in the boot of a car, assumed to be a drugs OD. Why are we doing this one?' he asked his assistant.

'Because of the tox results,' she replied.

He spent a few seconds scanning the results.

'No trace of heroin, crack, the usual suspects...now that's a surprise. If she was a user it should show something. So, what killed her then? There are some odd peaks here though, I haven't seen those before. Right let's have a look at her then.'

He pulled the sheet down and started examining the body. He removed her dress with a pair of scissors.

'She has a thin dress on and no undergarments, so she wasn't exactly dressed for the weather we've been having lately. The dress is covered with hairs, dog hairs probably. Even more puzzling in view of the tox results is that she has plenty of needle marks, some of which look relatively recent too.'

He turned the body over and examined it for some time. He went back and looked at the computer screen again.

'She's supposed to have been dead for at least a day and perhaps more. Has someone made a mistake?'

'No, I remember her coming in. It was definitely yesterday evening,' the assistant replied.

'There's no lividity,' the professor said as he placed the body on its back.

He walked quickly over to a cabinet and started pulling instruments out until he found the one he wanted. It had a small mirror on the end of a long handle. Mac had seen his dentist use the same instrument when getting a filling. He wondered what the pathologist wanted it for.

The professor, instead of putting it in the mouth, held it near the mouth for at least a couple of minutes. Mac had no idea what he was doing.

Both he and Tommy jumped when the professor shouted, 'Christ, call an ambulance and get a blanket. She's still alive!'

Chapter Three

Mac managed to get a few words with the professor after the ambulance had gone. He looked quite shocked.

'I've heard of these things happening but I've never really believed the stories. I always thought it more likely that someone had cocked up.'

'Did anyone cock up here?' Mac asked.

'It doesn't look like it,' the professor replied in some disbelief. 'You see liver mortis only starts after four or five hours...'

The professor felt the need to explain.

'Lividity, you know black and blue marks in the lowest point of the body where the blood has pooled...'

He stopped, seeing from their expressions that Mac and Tommy already knew what lividity was.

'Sorry, I keep forgetting that everyone watches CSI these days. Anyway, someone would have given her a quick look over when she came in and, as you wouldn't expect lividity to necessarily show up so soon after death, they would just have checked for vital signs. There being none, they put her in the morgue pending.'

'Pending what?' Mac asked.

'Pending further action, if there was any that is. If we're really stretched, as we always seem to be these days, and it's obviously an overdose then we might not examine any further. It's funny though, we seem to have had quite a few overdoses in recent months.'

'You say that there were no vital signs, so how can she still be alive?' Tommy asked.

'Now that's a good question. I only knew that there might be a chance she was alive because of the lack of lividity. I held the mirror to her mouth and it fogged up but it took its time. I examined her as much as I could while waiting for the ambulance and, if I'm honest, I still might have pronounced her dead if I didn't know better. I eventually found a sort of a pulse but it's incredibly slow, almost undetectable and her body temperature is way lower than you'd expect for anyone who wasn't dead. It's like she's in some sort of hibernation, her body is only just about ticking over. In twenty-five years I've never seen anything like it.'

'What about the needle marks?' Mac asked.

'Yes, they're strange seeing as how she had no known drugs in her system.'

'Known drugs?'

'People don't spontaneously go into the state that young girl is in, something made her like that. Looking at the needle marks you can see than some are more recent than others. She's probably had a couple of injections a day for at least a couple of weeks. Hopefully the hospital should be able to identify what it is.'

The professor's assistant interrupted them.

'I'm sorry but you've got an urgent call from the Executive Dean of the University.'

'Well, I better not keep him waiting too long. I'm sorry gentleman but I have to go.'

'If you think of anything that might help...' Tommy said as he gave the professor a card.

'Of course,' the professor replied as he made to go.

He was halfway out of the door when he stopped and turned.

'You know, since seeing the tox results and the needle marks, there's an idea I just can't get out of my head. You don't suppose someone's been using her as a lab rat do you?'

Without waiting for an answer, he disappeared.

Mac and Tommy looked at each other, the distaste at the idea clearly showing on both their faces.

'Where have they taken her?' Mac asked.

'To the Accident and Emergency unit at Luton and Dunstable Hospital.'

'Isn't this a hospital?'

'Yes, but it's a mental hospital,' Tommy replied.

'Oh, I see. Take me to the Luton and Dunstable Hospital then.'

It took less than ten minutes before they arrived outside the emergency entrance. The hospital was like most Mac had visited, too big, too confusing and too impersonal. Tommy spoke to one of the women manning reception.

'She's in the EAU, the Emergency Assessment Unit which she said is down this way,' Tommy said, pointing to his left.

Mac followed Tommy into what seemed an endless corridor. His heart sank as he looked at the distance he'd have to walk. He stopped and leant against the wall.

'Just hang on a minute,' Tommy said noticing Mac's pained expression.

He returned a few minutes later with a wheelchair and a big grin.

'Tommy's Taxis, want a lift?'

Mac felt like a big girl's blouse but he still sat down and allowed Tommy to wheel him down the corridor.

'What exactly is wrong with you? I can see that you have trouble walking,' Tommy asked.

'They don't really know, it could be an old injury or some sort of slow bone disease. Whatever it is something has eaten away a good bit of my spine. The bottom three vertebrae are basically buggered as are all the discs in between.'

'They don't know?'

'Yes, you'd think with all the technology they have nowadays they'd have an idea. Anyway, I've had a CT scan, a bone scan and umpteen MRI scans and that's all they can tell me. Of course, my neurologist says if I really want to know he can open me up, the only problem is I might not be able to walk afterwards and the pain might get even worse.'

'Are you in pain all the time?'

'Yes, sometimes less, sometimes more, but it's always there.'

'Can't they do anything at all?' Tommy asked.

'My neurologist says that, although medicine has come a long way, they can't rebuild spines just yet.'

'How do you cope?'

Mac couldn't see Tommy's face but he could hear the concern in his voice.

'By taking it a day at a time, plus I use some really heavy-duty painkillers. There's a drug called fentanyl, a hundred times stronger than morphine, it's on a little plastic patch that I stick on my shoulder every couple of days. If it wasn't for that...'

Mac paused as he saw a sign for the EAU and stuck his hand out to indicate that they should go right. Another lengthy corridor faced them and Mac was even more thankful that Tommy had found the wheelchair. Halfway down the corridor they found the unit. They parked the wheelchair outside and went in.

Inside it was a hive of activity, nurses and doctors crowded around a central nursing station completing paperwork or looking at their computer screens. It all looked a little chaotic but Mac was sure there must be some underlying order to it all. He glanced at a large whiteboard which had the names of the patients scribbled on it and where they were located.

'Look, there's her name,' Mac said.

Tommy turned and saw 'Henrietta Lewinton' scrawled in capital letters. She was in section D, bed four. They looked around and saw that section D was just past the end of the nursing station. They had just started to go towards it when they were stopped in their tracks.

'And just where do you think you're going?' a middle-aged nurse asked as she blocked their way with her amply padded body. Suspicion was writ large on her face.

Mac suddenly felt like a schoolboy caught in some felonious act.

'Section D?' he asked tentatively.

'I'm afraid not,' she stated hands on hips.

She reminded him a little of the actress who used to play the matron in the 'Carry On' films.

'There are strictly no visitors allowed unless it's been previously authorised. This is an emergency unit,' she said sternly.

Mac was grateful when Tommy produced his warrant card.

'We're here to see what's happening to one of your patients, Henrietta Lewinton.'

The matron examined the card carefully and then pursing her lips she said, 'You can wait in the relative's room. I'll tell the doctor in charge when she's free.'

She led them to a small room containing a coffee table, with numerous rings discolouring its surface, and four hospital armchairs. Uncomfortable as they looked Mac was glad to be sitting down again.

'God she's a bit scary, isn't she?' Tommy said.

'Yes, I certainly wouldn't like to be in her bad books.'

The word 'relative' had stuck in his head. He thought for a moment and then cursed himself for being an idiot.

'Bloody hell, I'm nearly forgetting all about her mother.'

Mac took out his mobile phone and dialled Janet Lewinton's number.

'Mrs. Lewinton, it's Mac Maguire.'

'Have you found something?'

'I think you could say that. It's Hetty, she's alive.'

There was silence at the other end.

'Mrs. Lewinton are you still there?'

Another silence.

Then finally she said, 'Mr. Maguire, I think this is in very bad taste...'

'No really, she's alive, Hetty's alive. I know it sounds incredible but she's in some sort of strange hibernation. I'm in the hospital now waiting to see the doctor who's looking after her.'

'Where is she?'

Mac could hear the hope in her voice. He gave her the details and the phone immediately went dead.

'I take it that she didn't believe you at first,' Tommy said.

'Yes, it's understandable though. She's seen her dead and on a slab and then some old codger phones up and says that she's alive. What would you think? I just hope she doesn't drive too fast getting here.'

'What do you think the doctor will be able to tell us?'

Mac shrugged his shoulders.

'God knows, nothing probably. Her condition was certainly news to that professor and he seemed to know what he was doing.'

The door opened and an attractive blonde-haired woman came in the room and sat down. Mac thought that she must be a junior doctor until he noticed her name tag, 'Dr. Ludmilla Tereshkova, Consultant EAU'. Inside he sighed, everyone seemed so much younger than him these days.

'I'm Doctor Tereshkova, Miss Lewinton's consultant. How can I help?' she asked.

Mac was somewhat surprised that she spoke with a Scottish accent.

Tommy introduced himself and Mac before explaining how Henrietta Lewinton had been found and what had happened in the morgue.

'I'm afraid that I can't tell you much as yet. She's on a ventilator and we're trying to warm her up as she was very cold. In fact, she was colder than anyone I've ever come across who wasn't dead. There are also some unexplained peaks on the initial tox screens so we've put her on dialysis. If it is some sort of drug that's responsible for her condition then we're hoping that the dialysis might help reduce the levels of it in her blood. Until we get more information all we can do is treat the symptoms and hope. If I'm honest no-one's seen anything remotely like this before, we're not even sure where to start.'

'If it was a drug and we could find out what it was, would that be of any help?' Mac asked.

'If we knew exactly what the substance was then some sort of antidote might be possible. At the very least we'd have an idea of what we're up against. At the moment I can't give you any sort of prognosis. We've absolutely no idea how long she might stay in this state of hibernation, it could be days, weeks or even years.'

'Thank you, doctor. Would it be okay if we hang around for a while? Her mother's on her way, she should be here in a few minutes.'

'Yes, of course. Please make yourselves at home. I'll tell the sister that Mrs. Lewinton is on her way.'

After the doctor had gone Tommy said, 'Not much there then.'

'I guess that it'll probably take them some time to figure this one out. By the way Tommy, for the record, I'm just plain 'Mr. Maguire' now, I'm no longer a DCS.'

'Of course, I'm sorry Mr. Maguire,' Tommy said, looking a little crestfallen.

Mac laughed.

'No, I only meant when you introduce me to other people. You just call me Mac.'

'Yes, of course... Mac,' Tommy replied with a grin.

Mac stood up and gazed out of the window at a small unkempt courtyard. A bright, wintry sun had come out from behind the clouds. He and Nora had loved winter days like this. He remembered the time when, not long after they'd gotten married, they would walk the three miles or so along the canal into Birmingham city centre on a Sunday morning. Then they'd visit the museum or go for a drink and a bite to eat. The realisation again of how much he missed her hit him forcibly.

'Are you alright Mac?' Tommy asked. 'Is it the pain?'

'Yes, it's pain of a sort,' he replied softly.

'Is there anything I can do?'

'I wish there were...'

At this point the door burst open and a crying Janet Lewinton flew into the room. She wrapped her arms around Mac and gave him a huge hug. When she stepped back, Mac could see that, although tears were still falling, she had a huge smile on her face as well.

'I've seen her, she's alive just as you said. Only just perhaps, but even if she goes now, I'll be with her. Thank you, Mr. Maguire, thank you.'

'Er...Mrs. Lewinton?' Tommy asked hesitantly. He held up his warrant card. 'Would you mind if I asked you a few questions?'

'Of course,' she replied, sitting down. 'Just a few minutes though, if that's alright, I want to get back to her as soon as I can.'

'Have you any idea how your daughter might have ended up in the boot of a car?'

She was still smiling as she shook her head.

'None at all. I haven't seen my daughter for quite some time and I'm afraid that I've no idea what she's been getting up to.'

'However, you knew that she'd been working as a prostitute?' Tommy asked.

'Yes, that much I knew but I only heard about that from one of her friends.'

27

'Do you know if she's been taking part in any medical trials?' Mac asked remembering what the professor had said.

Mrs. Lewinton shook her head again.

'I'm sorry, I've no idea but I wouldn't put anything past her.'

Tommy gave Janet Lewinton his card.

'Please call me if you remember anything. I take it that you'll be staying here for a while?'

'I'm going to be by her side for every second of the day that I can,' she said with determination. 'When she wakes up, she's going to need her mother.'

'Please let us know if there's any change,' Tommy said. 'An offence has obviously been committed but, until we get some evidence, we can't be sure exactly what that offence might be.'

'I understand. I'll be in touch if anything changes,' she said as she jumped up and made for the door.

She turned just before she left the room and said excitedly, 'She's alive Mr. Maguire, she's alive,' as though she still couldn't quite believe it herself.

Mac followed Tommy out of the room. The 'matron' gave them a stern look. Mac went over and spoke to her. He motioned Tommy to follow him.

'She's not as bad as she looks. She said we could have a minute. I just want to see what she looks like.'

Hetty Lewinton lay motionless. Her long blonde hair had a wide streak of brown down the centre as her hair hadn't been coloured for some time. She looked beautiful, almost transparent, fragile and ethereal. Mac had a real problem picturing this girl selling herself on street corners. They were both silent as they made their way out of the unit.

'Okay, let's go. Now where's that taxi driver?' Mac asked as he seated himself comfortably in the wheelchair.

As Tommy drove them back to the police station he asked, 'Any idea what we should do next?'

'There's only the car isn't there?' Mac replied. 'Have forensics checked it out yet? Do we know who owns it?'

'I'll find out as soon as we get back.'

At the police station they learned that the car had been stolen sometime on Sunday night from outside a house in St. Neots. The owner hadn't noticed that the car had gone until Monday morning when he reported it as being stolen.

'St. Neots, that's in Cambridgeshire isn't it?' Mac asked.

'Well, technically in Huntingdonshire, but yes. We found who the owner was from the VIN number. The car had fake plates fitted.'

'Were the fake plates for a car of the same make and colour?'

'Yes, and it's been confirmed that the car with the real number plates never left Yorkshire,' Tommy said. 'The owner was selling it and had put an ad in one of the auto trader magazines which is presumably where our driver got the car registration from.'

'So, our man is careful, he spots the car he wants then makes up a set of fake plates before he steals it. I've been wondering if this might have been some sort of act of the moment. That perhaps our man had given her something, thought he'd killed her, and was just trying to get rid of the body. The planning beforehand now makes that scenario unlikely though. Is there anything from forensics yet?'

'There's an initial report on the car. They found loads of prints but haven't matched any as yet. They also found dog hairs, crisps, sweets and empty soft drinks bottles amongst other things.'

'I take it that the people who own the car have kids and a dog?'

Tommy nodded.

'What about the blanket?' Mac asked.

'That was also from the car. Lots and lots of dog hairs, apparently they used it to cover the seat when the dog was in the car.'

'So, that's where the dog hairs on her dress came from then. There's not much to help us there, we can only hope that we get lucky with the fingerprints. I take it that there was no CCTV?' Mac asked hopefully.

'No, the collision took place in a suburban area. Only one of the businesses on the road the driver ran down had CCTV and unfortunately they only had it inside the shop.'

'I take it that forensics did an initial report when she first came in. Was there anything in that?'

Tommy shook his head.

'They found nothing unusual and it will be a while before we get the results of any DNA tests. The initial look at the body, sorry she's not a body now, is she? Anyway, the initial look noted that she seemed abnormally clean and had probably been carefully washed. Forensics are going to take DNA samples and prints from the owners and from Miss Lewinton to see if they can narrow it down a bit.'

On seeing Mac's glum expression Tommy said, 'We've got nothing, have we?'

Mac shook his head.

'I'll bet a penny to a pound that forensics turn up nothing more. Our man's careful, he steals a car the night before, fits fake plates and I'll bet that he wore gloves all the time he was in the car. You're absolutely right, at this moment we've got nothing.'

Seeing Tommy's dejected expression, he added with a smile, 'Come on, chin up, we've only just started. Something will turn up.'

Tommy smiled as Mac said this but Mac found himself feeling a lot less sure than he sounded. He'd had cases in the past that he and his team had failed to crack and it had always felt like unfinished business to him.

He hoped that his first case as a private detective wouldn't prove to be one of them.

Chapter Four

Mac spent a little more time looking over everything Tommy could give him on the case but he still made no progress. He said a little prayer that the full forensic report on the car would give them a lead but he really wasn't all that hopeful. It was now well past five o'clock so, deciding that he'd better pace himself, Mac told Tommy he was calling it a day and would return early tomorrow morning if that was okay.

Luckily it was.

He called in at the hospital on his way home and they told him that he could go in and see Henrietta if he wanted to. He stopped and looked through the glass panel in the door before entering the ward. He saw Janet Lewinton sitting by her daughter's bed. She was stroking Hetty's hand and talking to her. It seemed such an intimate scene and Mac didn't feel it would be right to interrupt them so he went to the nurse's station instead. He asked if there had been any change. There hadn't. Mac asked if this was good news or bad news but they couldn't say. They still hadn't been able to identify what it was that had caused her condition.

Before he got into his car, he called his friend Tim and was grateful that he was able to meet him for a pint and for something to eat. All the way back to Letchworth Mac kept turning over the day's events in his mind. He was hoping for some new idea or take on the situation but nothing came to mind. He decided to talk it through with Tim and turned the radio on for the rest of the journey.

Tim was already in the Magnets when Mac arrived. He'd managed to get table thirteen. This was their usual table right in the corner next to the window overlooking the street. Of course, Tim had something less of a journey, around a hundred yards or so from his antique furniture shop just down the hill. It struck Mac as he waved to Tim through the window that he was a little like an older version of Tommy. He was tall and thin, his jet-black hair now greying in places but, unlike Mac, he still had a full shock of hair on his head. Mac's barber had once made a joke and said that his hair was waving, waving goodbye that is. For some reason Mac hadn't found it that funny.

Tim jumped up and headed to the bar while Mac seated himself. He returned smiling and carrying two pints of lager. A photograph of a grey-bearded George Bernard Shaw hung in the corner and, fully aware of the irony of having a teetotaller's picture in a pub, Mac raised his glass to the great man before taking a gulp.

'So how did the first day go? Any femme fatales? Did you have to smack anyone in the mouth with a forty-five?' he asked, trying to sound like Humphrey Bogart and doing it quite well.

Tim was a great fan of American film noir, especially gangster films. Mac's new office was next door to Tim's shop and was owned by Tim. Mac had tried to insist on paying rent but his friend had just pointed to the mental health charity shop across the road and said that he could give it to them as they'd both be requiring their services before long.

He'd laughed heartily at the time but afterwards he wondered if Tim hadn't come quite close to the truth. Since his Nora had gone, he'd been living in a black hole of depression and, if it hadn't been for his daughter and his best friend, he wasn't sure where he'd have ended up. He silently thanked God for having them both.

'I should be so lucky but I do have a client.'

Tim was surprised and insisted on Mac telling the whole story not once but twice.

'So, what do you think?' Mac asked.

Tim looked stumped.

'I don't know what to make of it at all. Obviously, the driver was up to something and that's why he ran off when he saw the boot lid open but what was it? I hope your professor isn't right though, just the thought of someone out there using people as lab rats is creepy enough. How could they possibly get away with it?'

'Unfortunately, it would be quite easy. These girls are looked down on by everyone, to their pimps they're property, just money machines, and I'm afraid that a lot of the police just see them as a lower form of life and so not deserving the same protection that everyone else gets. The rest of us just pretend they're not there, unless you're one of the many men who keep the oldest profession going that is. They're easy targets.'

'So how do you think they might have done it and why?'

Mac gave this a little thought.

'The how is probably the easy part. All you need to do is pull up in your car, stolen of course, and say you want a blow job. The girl gets in the car and you go somewhere dark, somewhere not overseen. When you're alone and she's in the act you inject her with something to knock her out then cover her in a blanket and pop her in the boot. If you want to get rid of the evidence after you've finished with her, knock her out again, pop her in the boot of another stolen car and take her back to the same area, again somewhere dark and secluded. Then position her sitting up in a corner and inject her with a lethal dose of say, heroin. Leave the syringe close by, making sure her prints are all over it, and then leave her to die. The day after, when its light, someone will find her but, as far as the police and forensics will be concerned, she'll be just another prossie who's overdosed, a casualty of the trade as it were. If there's any investigation at all it would probably just be a cursory one.'

'That sounds all too plausible and more than a little depressing,' Tim said.

'It is and I've seen too many women end up that way myself. Unfortunately, it's just a fact of life for a copper.'

'But what about the why? Why would someone want to go to all that trouble?' Tim asked.

'That's the question we need to answer but we've got nothing to go on so far. We've got no description of the driver and our only witness is in some weird sort of hibernation. There's nothing from forensics so far that might help either.'

'So, what have you got then?' Tim asked.

'What do you mean?'

'Well, you have this weird hibernation and, as the professor said, it must be caused by something so perhaps that's the place to start. Pity you don't know any doctors,' Tim said with a sardonic smile.

'Just the one,' Mac said.

Then he thought again.

'No, two actually.'

He'd been seeing a doctor for the last two years, ever since the pain had started getting worse. Mac had been surprised at being referred to a neurologist for back pain but Bridget had explained that the brain and spine were part of the same system, the central nervous system. She said that Dr. Wilkins, who worked at the same hospital that she did, was a very highly thought of neurologist.

As it turned out Mac never got to see his brilliance at work. After all the tests and scans all he could do was give Mac a mournful look and explain at length why nothing could be done for him. To give him his due though it was Dr. Wilkins who first prescribed the fentanyl pain patches and he knew he should be grateful for that at least. For some reason he thought a neurologist might be just the person to ask about the hibernation drug.

'Yes, I'll give my neurologist a ring tomorrow, Bridget too,' Mac said, grateful that there was something he could do that might push the case forward a bit.

'Bridget's a paediatrician, would she know about weird drugs and hibernation?'

'No, probably not but she works at the Royal Free in London and they do a lot of medical research there, in fact she went out with one of their researchers for a while. Oh, what was his name now?'

As always, when he couldn't quite remember things, he wondered if this was the first tendrils of dementia showing itself. He said a little prayer that, if his brain was going to degenerate, then it might be the bits responsible for pain that went first.

'It was Sammy something or other, I think. Anyway, from what she told me about him it sounds like he might be just the man to ask.'

'It sounds like it might be worth a shot then.'

As Tim spoke Mac's phone went off.

'That's probably Bridget now, wondering how I got on,' Mac said.

Tim could only watch as Mac answered the call. Mac's surprised expression made it clear that it wasn't Bridget on the other end of the call.

All Mac said was 'Really?' and then 'Yes' twice.

When he finished the call, Mac was thoughtful for a moment before he said, 'Now that was a real surprise.'

Tim's curiosity was getting the better of him.

'What's a surprise?'

'I'll tell you in the taxi.'

'Taxi? Where are we going?'

'We're going to Hitchin. I'm going there to meet an old acquaintance.'

'Anyone I know?' Tim asked as they downed their drinks.

'I hope not, he's not exactly someone you'd want to make friends with in my opinion.'

In the taxi Mac explained.

'That call was from one of Mr. C's minders.'

'Mr. C? He has a letter for a name?'

'It's just what people call him. His real name is Pranav Contractor. His family originally came from Gujarat, in the west of India, via Uganda. Apparently, amongst other things, they use professions as surnames so you could have a Mr. Doctor or a Mr. Engineer. Anyway Mr. C came here when he was a boy and he's done quite well for himself. He owns a string of brothels in North London, several casinos, a hotel chain and God knows what else. He's into prostitution, drugs, gambling, anything that will make money and he doesn't much care what he has to do to get it.'

'So, what's he doing here in leafy Hertfordshire and what does he want with you?' Tim asked.

'God knows but I must admit that I'm intrigued enough to want to find out.'

'I take it you ran into him professionally?'

Mac nodded.

'Yes, twice. Both were murder cases and both done by him. I don't mean personally, he'd never dirty his own hands, but I'm as sure as I can be that he gave the order.'

'I take it from your expression that he was never brought to justice?'

'We could never get anything on him, he was just too clever,' Mac explained. 'You know he never uses a computer for anything important, never writes much down, almost everything is done by word of mouth.'

'So, with all of those businesses, how does he keep track of things?' Tim asked. 'I have enough problems just running one shop.'

'He's got a phenomenal memory and, so I've heard, have his sons. Both are trained accountants and they keep all the figures in their heads, so there's no physical evidence.'

'When was the last time you saw him then?'

'God, it must be five or six years ago now,' Mac replied. 'We got a call when one of his competitors, a thug called Bobby Bosio, was found hanging upside down from a lamp post outside his own house. His tongue had been ripped out and his penis cut off. They'd put his penis inside his mouth and stitched up his lips, all done while Bobby was still alive according to forensics.'

'God, you're right, he doesn't sound like someone you'd want to say the wrong thing to. Why did he do that?'

'This Bobby Bosio got too full of himself and he probably mistook Mr. C's laid-back attitude for him being scared. So, Bobby thought he'd try and put the frighteners on him. He said he'd see Mr. C dead and that he'd personally rape his wife and daughter once he was gone. Now Mr. C really loves his daughter and someone even saying that they didn't like the colour of her dress might end up with a couple of broken arms and legs, so you can imagine who we went looking for when Bobby turned up hanging from the lamp post.'

'And?' Tim prompted, after Mac had gone silent for some seconds.

'Sorry, I just remembered something. The pathologist today said there'd been a lot of overdoses lately. I wonder... Sorry, anyway back to Mr. C. We went through the motions, we investigated and investigated but we found exactly nothing. There was no evidence linking Mr. C to the killing or anyone else for that matter.'

'What's he like? I've never met a real gangster before,' Tim said with a smile.

'You won't today either. He's made it quite clear that I'm to come alone. We're meeting in the Gate of Asia, so wait for me in the Vic and I'll come over after I've seen him. What's he like? He must be worth many millions but he certainly doesn't flaunt his wealth. He always dresses in a dark suit, nice but not one of those designer suits, white shirt and a black tie. He lives in a four-bedroomed house in North London and owns one car, an old Bentley. He's of average height, slim and he always wears rimless spectacles. If someone told you he was a bank manager or a doctor you'd believe it. He has this stare though, I can't remember ever seeing him blink although I'm sure he must. When he looks at you it's like he's looking through you. I mean, I've been a policeman for decades and seen a lot of stuff but even I find that stare a bit unsettling at times.'

The taxi dropped them outside the restaurant.

'Are you sure you'll be okay?' Tim asked, concerned for his friend's safety.

'I'll be fine. He wouldn't have asked to meet me somewhere so public if he had a problem with me. Don't worry, save me a seat and I'll be with you in a few minutes.'

Tim made off in the direction of the pub which was only a couple of hundred yards down the road. It was a proper January evening and Mac felt the cold through his jacket as he stood hesitantly on the pavement. He was hoping that what he'd told Tim would prove to be right because you could never tell with Mr. C.

The 'closed' sign was displayed in the window but Mac knew that one of the most feared gangsters in London was sitting inside. For a split second we wondered what the hell he was doing, then he girded his loins and opened the door.

Chapter Five

Inside it was lusciously warm and the complex aroma of Eastern spices made his mouth instantly water.

Mac had grown up in Birmingham, one of the best cities in the world for curries, and he'd always thought of himself as being something of a connoisseur. He had tried quite a few restaurants in the area and found them all wanting, all except for the Gate of Asia. There was nothing special about its location, sitting between a launderette and a Chinese take away, or indeed its décor. The food, however, was heavenly.

As he walked in, he wondered how Mr. C knew about the restaurant.

There were only five people in the room. Three extra-large men sat at one table, their suits barely containing their muscles. They all looked steadily at Mac as he walked in. Another muscleman locked the door behind him before patting him down. At the far end of the room a slim man sat at a table by himself.

Mr. C's face remained impassive as Mac took the seat opposite.

'On time Mr. Maguire, as always. Have you eaten yet?'

'No, I haven't.'

'Join me then. I'm only having some starters but what starters they do here! The only time I ate a better Bhaji was when my poor mother was alive.'

He raised his hand and two waiters quickly appeared followed by the restaurant owner. Mr. C ordered Onion Bhajis and Lamb Tikkas for them both.

'How do you know about this place?' Mac asked.

'I grew up not far from here, in Luton actually. They've got some good places there too but this is the best restaurant near where you live.'

'So, it wasn't just chance that brought you here then?'

'I leave very little in life to chance, Mr. Maguire. I have a problem and I dropped in here on my way back to London in the hope that you might be able to help me to solve it. I only have a few minutes so I'll get down to business. You're helping the police invest-igate the case of a Miss Henrietta Lewinton who was found in the boot of a car a couple of days ago. I have an interest in Miss Lewinton.'

'In what way?'

'She works for me, she's one of my girls. Her street name is Candy. I've invested a lot of money in her and so I'm not happy when she just disappears without a word.'

'You own businesses in Luton too?' Mac asked.

'Not in my name you understand but yes. They were some of the first businesses I started and so I'm quite attached to them. So now I have a problem and I don't like problems, they keep me awake at night. If it had just been the one girl you might write that off, these things happen after all. However, Candy isn't the first girl to go missing.'

'How many?'

'Including Candy, three from me, and a further three from my competitors.'

'That's six girls in all. What makes you think they're linked?'

Mr. C waved for the waiter again.

'Please bring me a pen and some paper.'

The waiter returned in less than a minute.

'Here Mr. Maguire, the pen and paper are for you. Please write down what I say.'

41

He then rattled off names, dates and other information. Mac was hard put to keep up. When he'd finished Mr. C took the sheet of paper and checked it.

'That's quite correct Mr. Maguire,' he said.

He returned the paper to Mac who had the strange feeling that he was back at school and had just earned a gold star.

'By the way I'd be grateful if you didn't tell the police where this came from. They don't know I have interests in Luton and I'd like to keep it that way. So now you can see what the problem is. My girls are getting scared and wondering if they will be the next to disappear and that is definitely not good for business. Besides which there is someone out there who seemingly thinks he can get the better of me and, as you know, that just drives me crazy.'

'Which girls were yours?' Mac asked.

Mr. C pointed at Hetty's name and those of two other girls.

'I take it that you've looked into this yourself?' Mac said trying to remember if anyone had been found hanging from a lamp post recently.

'Of course, but we found nothing.'

'So why do you think that I can help?'

'Mr. Maguire we have been at swords drawn, as it were, for many years but you have been a most worthy opponent. I have a great admiration for your powers of investigation and so, with you on board, I am very hopeful of a result. I unfortunately have some bigger fish to fry.'

At this point the waiters returned with their food. They were both silent and appreciative as they ate.

When they'd finished Mr. C said, 'Well Mr. Maguire can you help? After all, you're not a policeman any more, you're for hire. Please name your price.'

'If the information you've given me is correct then I'll be trying with all my might to ensure that whoever is behind this is stopped but I won't be doing it for you, I'll be doing it for Miss Lewinton and her mother and the mothers of all the other girls who've been killed. However, there is something I want.'

Mr. C leant forward, he seemed interested for the first time that evening.

'What might that be?'

'I'll do my best to find who's kidnapping these girls but I want you to leave Henrietta Lewinton and her mother alone. I want you and your people to never come near her again.'

Mr. C gave this a few second's thought.

'Done, Mr. Maguire, and so we have a bargain. She's probably damaged goods anyway from what I hear. Please, write down this number.'

Mac did as he was ordered.

'If you need any information from my side just call this number at any time. Goodbye Mr. Maguire.'

The audience was over. Mr. C wiped his lips with a napkin, got up and walked straight towards the door. One of the musclemen went out first while another stood in the doorway. A few seconds later they were all gone.

Mac sat looking down at the sheet of paper until he remembered that Tim was waiting for him in the pub. On his way out Jaydev, the owner of the restaurant, accompanied him to the door.

'Was everything alright this evening, Mr. Maguire?'

'Yes, as always. Tell me does Mr. C come here often?'

'Not often,' Jaydev said. He looked uncomfortable and obviously wanted to change the subject. 'We haven't seen you here for a while and how is your good lady wife?'

Mac was stopped in his tracks. He didn't know what to reply and so he just said, 'She died, I'm afraid.'

A look of embarrassed shock appeared on Jaydev's face.

'I am so sorry Mr. Maguire, I didn't know.'

He held the door open for Mac.

Then, putting his hand on Mac's shoulder, he said, 'How do you Irish say it...yes, I am so sorry for your troubles, Mr. Maguire, so sorry.'

Mac was touched.

'Thank you, thank you.'

'Please come again and I'll do you something really special.'

Mac promised that he would.

He stood outside on the pavement unmoving, a sudden sadness threatening to engulf him like a big wave. He somehow managed to withstand the force of the emotion and made himself think about the case and the new information that he'd just gained. He slowly walked the two hundred yards to the pub turning over what he'd learned in his mind.

The information that Mr. C had given him had totally changed the whole tenor of the case. By the time he reached the front door of the pub his back was grumbling again but he was so deep in thought he hardly noticed it. It was quite full inside and he had to look hard for Tim who had luckily managed to get a table in the far corner.

'God, you've been gone nearly forty-five minutes. I was beginning to get a bit worried,' Tim said.

'I'll tell you all about it but first I need to call someone. In the meantime, as I don't want to die of dehydration...'

'I'll get them in,' Tim said with a smile and disappeared.

Mac got his mobile out and called Tommy. He agreed to meet them in the pub as soon as he could.

When Tim returned with the drinks, he could see that Mac was deep in thought.

'So, what happened? I can see from your face that something serious went down.'

'Tommy Nugent, the young detective I told you about, is coming to meet us in about an hour. Do you mind if we wait until then? Did you get yourself something to eat?'

'Not yet, I was waiting for you. It's Pie Night tonight and the smell has been driving me mad.'

'Go ahead and order then. I had something to eat in the restaurant.'

They happily filled in the time until Tommy arrived by talking about the seemingly unstoppable demise of their favourite football club. They had nearly sorted out the defence to their satisfaction when Mac saw Tommy's head appear above the crowd. He waved and Tommy came over.

'I wasn't expecting to see you quite this soon,' Tommy said.

'Sit down. This is my friend Tim Teagan, Tim this is Detective Constable Tommy Nugent.'

They shook hands.

'What are you having Tommy?' Tim asked as he stood up.

'Just a coke please, I'm driving.'

'Okay,' Tim said turning to Mac. 'Now don't start until I get back.'

Tommy looked questioningly at Tim as he made his way to the bar.

'Start? I take it you've found something new then, something that couldn't wait until tomorrow.'

Mac nodded. He pulled the sheet of paper out of his pocket and passed it to Tommy.

'Read this while we're waiting for Tim and then pass it to him when he gets back.'

Tommy's expression changed to a sombre one as he read what Mac had written down.

'Bloody hell,' was all Tommy said when he reached the end.

He glanced up at Mac and then read it again before Tim arrived with the drinks. Once Tim had placed the drinks on the table Tommy passed the sheet to him. They both stayed silent while Tim read the sheet.

'Good God!' Tim said. 'That's really spooky, it's just like you were saying earlier.'

He handed the sheet back to Mac.

'How sure are you that this information is correct?' Tommy asked.

'I can't tell you the source but I'm one hundred percent sure it's right. Do you think we should go back to the station after this drink?' Mac suggested.

'Yes, in fact I'd even go so far as getting DI Carter to join us as well. I just hope he isn't still asleep though,' Tommy said.

Back at the station Mac had just finished writing on the white board and Tommy was still banging away at his computer when DI Carter turned up. He looked tired but much improved having changed his clothes and shaved. He still looked very grumpy however.

'Nugent, if you're going to call me away from my wife and the TV at eight in the evening then this had better be bloody good. What have you got?'

'Dan, you've met Mac this is Tim…er…'

'Tim Teagan,' Tim volunteered.

'Yes, Tim is Mac's friend,' Tommy explained.

DI Carter shook Tim's hand and then turned back to Tommy.

'Okay you've got ten minutes and then I'm going back to see what happens at the end of Midsomer Murders.'

Three faces looked at him with puzzlement.

'The wife likes it, okay?' DI Carter said somewhat defensively.

'We got some new information this evening or rather Mac did,' Tommy said. 'He's written it down on the white board. Mac?'

Dan Carter looked at the white board.

Mandy Stokes 21 – found dead on Fri 23 Aug
Barbara Mason 20 – disappears Thurs 22 Aug - body found Sun 14 Sept
Angela Moran 21 – disappears Sat 13 Sept – body found Mon 13th Oct
Annie McTavish 18 – disappears Sun 12th Oct – body found Sun 16th Nov
Kayla James 19 – disappears Fri 14th Nov – body found Sun 7th Dec
Hetty Lewinson 22 – disappears Sat 6th Dec – found in car boot Mon 5th Jan

'This is a list of six women, six girls really. The oldest is Henrietta Lewinton and she's only twenty-two. They all worked in Luton as prostitutes and they all disappeared without trace for a period of some weeks. During that time there was no sign of them in the Luton area. All of the girls left everything behind them, passports, money, clothes and, in one case, a sizable quantity of drugs. Their friends and colleagues said they gave no indication that they were planning on leaving. Five of these girls were found in various car parks and alleys around the red-light district, all dead through an apparent drug overdose. Syringes containing a high dose of heroin were found next to all five girls. We can only conjecture that Henrietta Lewinton would have joined them if it hadn't been for a chance collision.'

DI Carter examined the board carefully.

'Yes, the dates link them, don't they?'

'They're at least very suggestive,' Mac said. 'The first girl, Mandy Stokes, is found dead on the morning of the twenty third of August last year and the second girl, Barbara Mason, disappears without warning on the evening of the twenty second. Then Barbara's body is found in an alleyway on the morning of thirteenth of September, while the evening before girl number three Angela Moran disappears and so on. The dates match too exactly to be entirely coincidental.'

'What about Annie McTavish?' Dan asked pointing to the board. 'She wasn't found until two days after Kayla James disappeared.'

'Yes, we noticed that. Tommy?'

'We have a forensics report that states that Annie had been dead for at least two days when she was found,' Tommy said.

'So, she was lying there dead for two days and no-one noticed?' DI Carter asked.

'Perhaps they noticed and just ignored her,' Mac said.

DI Carter nodded glumly then he took off his jacket and placed it on the back of his chair. Mac knew from his body language he wasn't going to make the end of Midsomer Murders.

'So, you think he dumps one girl's body and then kidnaps another one?'

Mac nodded.

'Where did you get all this from?' DI Carter asked.

'I'm afraid that I can't say but I trust the source one hundred percent,' Mac replied.

DI Carter gave this some thought before saying, 'Fair enough. So, what do you think is going on here?'

'The pathologist earlier this morning came up with quite a chilling idea. He thought that Hetty Lewinton might have been used as some sort of human guinea pig. I think it's possible that the other girls could have been used in that way too. Let's assume that he's right and let's also assume that whatever is going on takes some weeks to complete. Prostitutes are an obvious and easy target. They are willing to go into secluded places alone and, when they do go missing, it's unlikely that the police will be told about it. Let's be honest, even when we are informed, we're not likely to do much about it anyway, are we?'

DI Carter looked like he was about to protest for a moment but he ended up just nodding in grim resignation.

'Now, assuming that Henrietta Lewinton is a typical case, the one thing we do know is that our man is likely to have access to some seriously powerful drugs, drugs that can cause a severe coma as well as large amounts of heroin,' Mac continued. 'We know our man used a stolen car with fake plates so it wouldn't matter if the car was spotted. All he'd need to do is drive around the red-light district looking for a suitable victim, some-one young it would seem from what we know. Once he's got her in the car, he'd take her somewhere secluded. The girl would expect this anyway and she wouldn't be particularly frightened. Then, perhaps while she's in the act, it would be easy to inject her with something that would sedate her or knock her out, perhaps even the hibernation drug itself. All he needs to do then is wrap her up in a blanket and put her in the boot and drive to wherever.'

'It's all too easy, isn't it?' DI Carter commented. 'What about returning them?'

'Just as easy,' Mac said. 'She's already in a coma, so all he has to do is take her out of the boot and place her sitting up in a dark corner of a car park or alleyway and inject a lethal dose of drugs. He then leaves the syringe next to the body and drives off to look for the next victim. She'll be found the next morning, known prostitute, overdose, open and shut case.'

DI Carter flinched as he remembered he'd used the same words to Mac earlier that day.

'Okay, so what else do we know?'

'I've been looking at what we've got on the five dead girls,' Tommy said. 'Unfortunately, there's not much there. All of are down as dying from a heroin overdose.

The analysis showed that the overdose was massive and, in the opinion of the pathologist, they were all injected with uncut heroin.'

'It sometimes happens,' DI Carter commented. 'Drugs get stolen and then it's assumed that it's already been cut so it goes straight onto the street.'

'Outside of the girls here we've had no fatal incidents in the last three years related to uncut heroin,' Tommy replied. 'Not only that but we haven't had a prostitute die on the street from drugs for over a year and then, in less than a six-month period, we get five.'

'It looks like all the facts are stacking up,' DI Carter said as he returned to scrutinise the white board.

'Not only that,' Mac said, 'but my source says that two of the girls, the second one Barbara Mason and the fifth one Kayla James, weren't even users. Apart from the occasional spliff they never touched drugs.'

'Okay, I don't need any more convincing,' DI Carter said. 'Tommy, get back home now, I'll want you back here at eight o'clock sharp. DCS Maguire, do you think that you might be up to helping us out for a few days?'

Mac was more than pleasantly surprised by the offer.

'Of course, I'd be more than glad to.'

DI Carter was still staring at the white board when they left the room.

Tommy was good enough to drive them both back to Letchworth. On the way to the car Mac noticed that Tim was quiet.

'What's up?'

'I notice that he didn't ask me to help out,' Tim said, looking quite put out.

'Tim, you're a furniture restorer.'

'Yes, I know but some of those desks in there are in a tragic state. They could do with some real TLC.'

Mac laughed out loud as he realised that Tim was pulling his leg.

50

'Back to the Magnets for a few more?'

'You bet,' Tim replied. 'And don't forget that, although we've sorted our defence out, our attack is a bloody shambles too!'

Chapter Six

Mac awoke slowly the next morning and went through his usual routine. He stayed horizontal until he was fully awake and the weird lucid dreams, caused by the painkillers he took, had scuttled away out of his head. His pain level didn't feel too bad but that meant little at this point. He'd only know how severe it might be after he stood up and tried to walk a few steps.

He gingerly sat up and checked again, still not too bad. He then took the plunge and hauled himself erect. If the pain was going to hit him it would hit him now. Mac had identified at least six flavours of pain and was grateful that only two of the lesser types were present when he stood up. He knew that this was probably as good as it was going to get. He walked to the bathroom and blessedly the pain stayed bearable. He smiled at himself into the mirror as he shaved. Even if it was only temporary, he was on a case again and doing some proper police work.

It was still only six fifteen but Mac was determined to get there early. It had been his habit over the years to be the first in the office each morning. He'd always liked having a little space of time to reflect about what the day ahead might bring. He made coffee and filled a travel mug. He'd get breakfast at the station. It had been far too long since he'd had a police canteen sausage and egg sandwich.

The traffic was thankfully not too bad and he was back in the incident room just before seven. He sat and looked at the white board letting his mind meander around the facts of the case. He was disturbed some twenty minutes later by Tommy's arrival.

'You're here already? Couldn't wait to get back in harness I bet,' Tommy said.

Mac smiled. It was only the truth after all.

'Yes, something like that.'

'Have you had any new thoughts since yesterday?' Tommy asked.

'No, not really but we do have some leads we can chase up.'

'Like what?'

'I'll tell you everything if you let me know where the canteen is. I could murder a sausage and egg sandwich.'

'My favourite too, I'll be back in a minute.'

Tommy returned ten minutes later with a tray on which were two sandwiches in paper bags and two cups of tea.

'Tommy you're a life saver,' Mac said as he gratefully accepted a sandwich.

While they were eating Tommy asked, 'What leads do we have then?'

'Okay, off the top of my head, we have dates and names. If it is one man kidnapping all these girls it's quite likely that he might have staked them out first. If that's the case then someone might have seen him. We need to question everyone they knew and, if we can connect anyone with even two of the girls, then we might be onto something. We can also look at where the car was stolen from and see where other cars were stolen from around the dates the girls disappeared. It might be that he's stealing cars from an area he's familiar with, perhaps he lives or works there or perhaps it's near where he delivers the girls. Perhaps he favours a particular type of car. The car Henrietta Lewinton was found in was a BMW, perhaps that's what he likes to drive, perhaps that's what he's familiar with. Also, the cars he steals have to be big enough to get a body in the boot so I suppose that narrows it down a bit. Have we any CCTV footage from the area the girls were abducted from or traffic cameras? A long shot perhaps but it might we well worth having a look around the dates the girls disappeared.'

Mac took a big bite from his sandwich.

'And why Luton?' he continued. 'I know with serial killers there's a thing that most of them have about knowing their area of operations well, it's like a comfort zone for them. Is that why he keeps abducting girls from Luton? Perhaps he is or has been one of their clients and, if that's the case, he'd certainly know the drill. If so, it's highly likely he lives here or he's lived here in the past. He'd also know where to drive the girls so he wouldn't be overseen. Then there's probably the most important lead, the hibernation drug itself. I'd guess that the medical research field is quite small so someone might know something about who developed it. That's what I'm going to volunteer to do today.'

'Bloody hell, and that's all off the top of your head?' Tommy said looking impressed. 'So how are you planning on investigating this hibernation drug?'

'We'll need to talk to Dr. Tereshkova at the hospital first and see if there's anything new. Then we can try my neurologist who works at the Royal Free Hospital in London. I'd guess that a hibernation drug must primarily affect the brain so, with any luck, he or one of his colleagues might know about such a thing. I'm also going to see my daughter Bridget who's a doctor at the same hospital. She's a paediatrician but they have a big medical research centre there and she knows some of the researchers. I think it might be well worth a try.'

'That sounds like a plan to me,' Tommy said.

They were interrupted by the arrival of a smiling DI Carter.

'Good morning DCS Maguire, here nice and early I see.'

'Please, I'm no longer a DCS, just call me Mac.'

'Okay, just call me Dan.'

They shook hands firmly.

'Mac's just been telling me his thoughts on what we might do next,' Tommy volunteered.

'Oh really? Would you mind telling me?'

'Of course not.'

Mac went through the leads again as he saw it.

Dan was quiet for a while.

'I must admit I'd thought of most of those. I was going to get the team to start interviewing the girls in the area and I've got a real whizz kid on the computer who I'm hoping might be able to spot any patterns related to the car thefts and look at any CCTV we might have. I must admit that I hadn't really considered the possibility of a hibernation drug though. How would you go about investigating that?'

'We'll try the hospital first, see if they've identified the drug yet. If not then I know a neurologist at the Royal Free who might be able to tell us something and my daughter's a doctor there too. Although she's a paediatrician she also knows some of the medical researchers and I'm hoping she'll know who would be best to talk to. As I was saying to Tommy it's probably a relatively small field so someone must have heard something about such a drug.'

'Right, as you two know what you're doing today, you might as well get on with it. Tommy use one of the unmarked police cars then come back here afterwards and let me know if you've found anything. Mac, would you mind if I have a few words with Tommy before he goes?'

'No problem, I'll start walking towards the car park.'

When Mac had gone Dan looked seriously at Tommy and said, 'You're going to be his minder while he's with us. I had a chat with an old friend at the Met last night and he told me all about Mac. He's a really good copper and we could do with him on board but he has a chronic pain problem, a really bad one, that's why he was forced to retire.'

'He told me about it yesterday. It must be crap being in pain all the time like that.'

'Good, he obviously trusts you if he told you that already. Anyway, just make sure that he doesn't do anything too strenuous and if he looks like he's suffering get him straight home,' Dan ordered.

'I will and thanks Dan. I must admit I'm really looking forward to working with him, he was such a great investigator. Do you mind me asking, is that why you're so keen to keep him on the team?'

'Yes partly. He is brilliant and I've got a feeling that we're going to need some brilliance from someone to crack this one and I really want it cracked.'

'Only partly?' Tommy asked.

Dan cleared his throat.

'Well, last night I could see how happy he was to be back working again, to be involved. That might be me in a few years, who knows?'

'I understand sir and I'll do my best to look after him. I'll see you later.'

Tommy had always thought Dan Carter was a bit of the gruff, uncaring sort but he was beginning to see that there might be another side to him.

As they drove out of the car park Mac asked, 'If I was a betting man, I'd guess Dan just told you all about why I had to leave the force and that he's asked you to look after me.'

Tommy smiled and shook his head.

'I won't ask how you guessed that but yes. He knows about your condition and he wants to make sure you don't overdo it. So officially I'm your minder.'

'That's okay with me but there is something you'll need if you're going to drive me to the hospital.'

'What's that?'

'These.'

Mac produced his blue badge and time card.

'At least we can park somewhere that isn't miles away from the hospital entrance,' Mac said.

'But we can park virtually anywhere when we're on duty.'

'Believe me the nearest spaces are disabled and, as it's not an emergency, I think we'd be better off using the badge. Or would you prefer to see your picture in the papers?'

Tommy could see the headline, 'Lazy Police Nab Disabled Parking Space' and underneath a picture of a woman in a wheelchair who missed her appointment because she couldn't park her car. He nodded and took the badge.

Mac got his phone out and called his daughter. She was having breakfast and promised she'd meet him at the hospital. She also volunteered to speak to Dr. Wilkins for him.

At the hospital Dr. Tereshkova told them that there had been little change in Henrietta's condition.

'She's still unresponsive but she's warming up slowly. The dialysis seems to have reduced the substance in her system a little but we've no idea what a safe level of the substance might be. That's if there is one of course.'

'So, you've no idea yet of where the substance might have come from or how it works?' Mac asked.

The doctor shook her head.

'We've got the facilities here to identify and treat most types of drugs and poisons but not something this exotic.'

'Who might know about something this 'exotic'?'

She thought for a moment.

'Of course, it could be some natural substance we haven't come across before but I think that's less likely than it being man-made. It looks like it has a very complex structure so I don't think that it's something that was cooked up in someone's kitchen. I think you need to talk to someone who's directly involved in medical research. If this is a manufactured drug then it must have been developed somewhere.'

Tommy glanced over and he could see that Mac was really pleased that the consultant had endorsed his plan of action.

Mac went to Section D and looked in through the glass panel before they left. Janet Lewinton was still sitting by her daughter's bedside. She had a book open and appeared to be reading to Hetty. Again, he decided not to intrude.

He quite enjoyed the drive into London which was unexpected. It had been some time since he'd been in the passenger seat of a car and he'd almost forgotten how nice it could be to just sit back, relax and watch the world go by. Tommy found them a disabled parking space close to the main entrance of the Royal Free for which Mac was grateful. His phone went off as he got out of the car. It was a text and it read 'At main entrance now x B.'

Mac smiled. His daughter always put an 'X' on her texts to him. He grinned from ear to ear when he caught sight of her in the hospital lobby. She was very like her mother and Mac had thought her the most beautiful creature in the world. She wore a white doctor's coat over a loose sky-blue blouse and dark blue trousers. Her auburn hair was held back in a bun, for safety reasons she always said. She liked having long hair but her little patients just saw it as something to swing on. Her eyes were of a strange colour, a sort of blue-green, which Mac found enchanting.

He gave her a big hug and then introduced Tommy. Mac could see that Tommy probably wouldn't make a good poker player as his face all too clearly showed his pleasure at meeting his daughter.

'I've arranged for you to see Dr. Wilkins before he starts seeing his outpatients so we only have about ten minutes or so,' Bridget said. 'I'm sorry dad, I meant to call you yesterday but I was so tired when I got home that I fell asleep on the sofa. But there was me worried that you might be sitting around with nothing to do and you've got a case already. Tell me about it.'

It took most of the ten minutes to give her a sketch of what had happened and in retelling yesterday's events Mac realised what a strange tale it was. At the end she took them both up in the lift one floor then down a maze of corridors into one of the outpatient clinics.

She tapped at a door and a voice said, 'Come in.'

Bridget went inside. A few seconds later she opened the door for Mac and Tommy.

'Dad, text me when you're finished and I'll see if I can make some time for us to have a coffee together.'

Dr. Wilkins was sitting behind a desk piled with folders. He stood up and shook hands with Mac and Tommy and gestured for them to take a seat. The neurologist, who he knew must be at least in his early forties if not older, looked so young too. He sighed again. Everyone was looking younger lately, a sure sign of old age his mother used to say.

'Dr. Wilkins, this is my colleague Detective Constable Nugent,' Mac said.

'Yes, your daughter said you were working with the police on something. How can I help?'

Mac told him about Henrietta Lewinton's condition.

'I've certainly never heard of anything quite like that before. It sounds like it might be some sort of catatonia or coma, there's even a rare sort of migraine which can render a person paralysed for a while, but none of them would affect the vital signs in the way you describe. I'll ask around my team if you like.'

'I'd be grateful if you could,' Mac said. 'Whatever that girl has been given might hold the key not just to her case but the suspected murder of five other girls.'

'By the way which consultant is the girl under?'

'Dr. Ludmilla Tereshkova,' Mac answered.

'Lilla? I know her quite well. I'll give her a ring and see what she's found so far. It certainly sounds like an interesting case.'

Tommy passed a card over.

'Thanks doctor, please call me on this number if you do hear anything.'

'I will. Detective Nugent, would you mind if I have a quick word with Mr. Maguire alone before you go?'

'Of course,' Tommy said.

He left them to it.

'So how have you been?' the doctor asked. 'I know we have an appointment in a couple of weeks but as you're here.'

Mac gave it some thought.

'I'm not too bad at the moment if I'm honest. My daughter and my best friend were convinced that I needed to be doing something constructive, you know to take my mind off the pain, and they were so right. I'm really surprised that I've found the energy to do anything at all. Before I started working on this case all I wanted to do was just sleep all day but yesterday I put in a full shift.'

'Pain is a strange thing alright. Tell me how do you envisage your pain?'

'It's like water,' Mac replied without hesitation. 'Every moment of every day is like trying to wade through water, the pain makes it harder to do every-thing. I feel like I'm constantly putting up a barrier of leaky sandbags while the waves are crashing on the other side and sometimes the waves are just too big, they smash the barrier down and I start drowning.'

'That's not a bad analogy. When people ask me about pain, I always say 'It depends'. How much pain you feel depends on the resources you can muster to fight against it. Some life events, such as bereavement, can remove most of those resources making the pain levels experienced feel much higher. How has the pain medication worked out so far?'

'I wouldn't be able to do anything without it. Thanks again for suggesting the patches,' Mac said with some gratitude.

'I'm glad you're back at work. I think that you might be one of those people for whom work is the best pain killer. Okay, I'll let you get on and I'll see you in a couple of weeks.'

'Thank you, doctor,' Mac said.

As he was making for the door the doctor said, 'Oh, about your hibernation drug, you might also want to have a word with Sammy Newell. He leads a team of researchers here. If this is some sort of novel drug Sammy will be the one who knows. He keeps himself abreast of all the latest research that's going on in that area.'

Sammy Newell, yes that was his name, Mac thought. He thanked the doctor again and joined Tommy outside.

'Oh well, at least it's got the ball rolling,' Tommy said.

'Yes. I'll just text Bridget.'

He told her that he was finished with Dr. Wilkins and asked if Sammy Newell was around. She replied and asked him to meet her in the hospital restaurant on the lower ground floor in half an hour.

As they made their way there, Mac said, 'I was trying to think of the name of one of the medical researchers who works here, he was someone that Bridget used to go out with. Thankfully the doctor gave it to me without me having to ask. I believe he's the person you go to here if you want to find out what's the latest in the world of medical research. We definitely need to have a word with him.'

Tommy bought them both coffees which they sipped in silence while they waited.

'She used to go out with this researcher?' Tommy eventually said, stressing the word 'used'.

'How old are you Tommy?'

'Twenty-six.'

Mac sighed again. Tommy looked so much younger.

'So, let me guess. You joined the force at eighteen, did your two years on probation, five years on the beat and then you made detective.'

'Have you been reading my record?' Tommy asked with some suspicion.

'No, that was more or less the same route I took except in my day you only had to do three years on the beat so I was a little younger when I made detective. I was already married by then.'

'So how did your daughter become a doctor?'

'It's what she always wanted to do. I bought her first toy doctor's kit when she was five, the first of many. She used to love watching all of the hospital dramas on TV and she was already reading medical textbooks from the library when she was only eleven. And she did it. Six years at university, two years in training and then she chose paediatrics as her speciality.'

'That would make her...'

'Twenty-six, the same age as you Tommy. Do you have designs on my daughter?' Mac asked pointedly.

Tommy's face reddened.

'Designs? No, I've only just met her and, to be honest, I'm not even sure what that means. She just looks different to anyone I've ever met before, that's all.'

Mac remembered the first he laid eyes on Nora. He'd known straight away that she was the one.

'Let's not talk about this again,' Mac said. 'I'm certainly not going to help you with my daughter...'

Tommy's face fell when Mac said this.

'...but I won't hinder you either. Just keep me out of it. However, there is one thing you should know.'

'What's that?' Tommy asked.

'Bridget's very like her mother in one way, she has a fearful temper, but it disappears as fast as it comes and she never holds a grudge.'

Tommy nodded and simply said, 'Okay.'

When Bridget arrived, Tommy stood up and pulled out a chair for her. She gave Mac a quick questioning glance. Mac replied by rolling his eyes heavenward which made Bridget smile. She thanked Tommy and gave him an appraising look.

'Have you found out anything yet?' she asked.

'No but Dr. Wilkin's going to ask his team, so I'm hoping that one of them might know something. He did mention Sammy Newell's name however. He said if anyone knew he probably would.'

'I tried ringing him just now but unfortunately I've found out that he's on holiday. However, I've arranged for you to see one of his colleagues, Dr. Olsen. I'm sorry dad but I've really got to go. It's my own outpatient clinic soon but Kerry Olsen isn't too hard to find. He's on the fourth floor, turn right out of the lift and it's the first door on the left. Just ask for him there, he knows you're coming. Bye dad,' she said giving him a big hug. 'It's so good to see you back at work, you look so much more like your old self.'

Then, turning to Tommy, she said, 'It's been a pleasure to meet you Detective Nugent.'

'Just in case you think of something,' Tommy said as he stood up and slipped a card into her hand. 'It's got my mobile on there too, you know just in case...you think of something,' he said ending quite lamely.

Mac watched her as she walked away and waited to see what she'd do. As she neared the door, she turned and looked back and she wasn't looking back at him.

Well Tommy, Mac thought, you might just be in with a chance after all.

They followed her instructions and found themselves in a large room filled wall to wall with oversize electronic gizmos and the smell of the seaside. There were a couple of computers but, as for the rest, Mac couldn't even hazard a guess as to their function. A young man with a three-day beard wearing flip-flops and bright blue shorts underneath a white lab coat came over to them.

'Can I help?' he asked in an antipodean accent giving them both a friendly smile.

Mac assumed that he was some sort of lab technician.

'We're looking for Dr. Olson. If you could just tell us where he works?'

'You're looking at him. You must be Mr. Maguire,' he said holding out his hand.

Mac shook his hand and, feeling somewhat foolish, introduced Tommy.

'Your daughter told me something about what you're working on. Some sort of hibernation drug that can slow your vital signs down to near enough nothing. I've never heard of anything like that before. A couple of years ago some researchers found a way to induce hibernation in squirrels and they've found out a fair bit about how bears maintain muscle mass and so on during hibernation but we're nowhere near applying this to humans as far as I know.'

'If such a drug existed what would it be used for?' Tommy asked.

'Well, you see hibernation in a lot of science fiction films, don't you? I believe it would take almost a year to get to Mars, handy if you could pop into hibernation and save on oxygen and food. However, I think the real application would be for people with serious injuries. If we could slow their metabolism down then, instead of a golden hour when intervention is most effective, we might have a golden day or even longer. We could save a hell of a lot more people.'

'So, if you had such a drug why wouldn't you manufacture it?' Mac asked. 'It sounds as though it might make you a lot of money.'

'Absolutely, if such a thing existed every hospital in the world would be buying it. I've no idea why, unless there were some serious side effects of course.'

'Like Thalidomide you mean?'

'Exactly, but most people don't know that Thalidomide is still in use for some types of cancer and auto-immune diseases, we just don't give it to pregnant women anymore. However, some drugs in development have such serious side effects that they could never be used in any circumstances.'

'Is there anything else you can tell us?' Mac asked hopefully.

'Sorry, but unfortunately we're all specialists these days,' he said waving at the gleaming machinery, 'all except Sammy that is. He keeps up with anything and everything to do with the nervous system. He says that we're all tree huggers and, while we may know a lot about a particular tree, we forget about the forest surrounding it. In his work he's across papers from all over the world, looking for patterns in other people's research and, when he spots something, he pulls it all together in one big study. It's really valuable stuff. While Sammy's away I'll ask around though.'

Tommy gave him one of his cards.

'If you hear anything please let us know.'

'Where is Sammy anyway, isn't he contactable?' Mac asked.

'Unfortunately, no he's not. He's gone white water rafting in the US. I did the same thing last year, in fact I recommended it to Sammy figuring that he could do with some time away from his beloved computer. See it's more than the rafting, its two weeks without any modern technology, trekking across the desert and camping out. It's really good fun but there's strictly no technology allowed. They even make you leave your phone at the base camp.'

'Isn't it a bit cold in January?' Tommy asked.

'No way, the average is over twenty Celsius during the day at this time of the year, during the summer it's over forty. It's the best time of the year if you ask me, especially for you Poms who aren't used to the heat. Anyway, he probably won't be contactable for a while but I'll leave a text on his mobile so he'll know when he picks his phone up.'

Holding the card up he said to Tommy, 'Shall I give him this number?'

'Yes please and tell him to ring me on my mobile number any time, day or night,' Tommy replied.

As they waited for the lift Tommy said, 'Bloody hell, I thought he was the lab technician.'

Mac started laughing.

'You did too, didn't you?' Tommy said, joining in the laughter.

'It's a good lesson, never assume unless you have to. Unfortunately, I think we'll have to be doing a lot of that in this case unless we get some hard evidence.'

Mac looked at his watch as they walked towards the car. He was surprised to find it was gone one o'clock.

'Where to now?' Tommy asked.

'That sandwich seems a long time ago now, how about some lunch? I might know a place but first I need to see if someone's free to meet us.'

Mac rang a number and all Tommy heard was, 'Yes, it's has been a long time' and 'Okay, two thirty in the usual place.'

'So where are we going?'

'To New Scotland Yard or at least a pub nearby. We're going to meet an old friend of mine who's something or other in the National Crime Agency. It used to be called the Serious Organised Crime Agency which worked for me. I just don't know why they feel they have to keep changing things. Anyway, I was just wondering if there were any new recreational drugs hitting the streets and, if there are, they'll be the ones who'll know.'

Mac directed Tommy to an old pub called the 'Two Coachmen' and they were lucky enough to find a disabled space immediately opposite the pub. Inside the pub was old fashioned and inviting with studded leather chairs and dark wood.

'The fish and chips are really good here,' Mac said as he led Tommy towards a little alcove. 'Good we've got just under an hour before my friend arrives, let's order.'

They both enjoyed their meals and the waitress had just taken their plates away when Mac spotted a familiar figure.

'God, Katherine it's so good to see you,' Mac said with a big smile.

A smartly dressed grey haired woman in her fifties gave Mac a hug.

'It's been far too long Mac, I did try and ring several times,' she said in a soft Scottish accent.

'I know, I'm sorry but I've been in a strange place these last six months. Let me introduce you to my colleague, Detective Constable Tommy Nugent.'

She shook hands with Tommy and sat down opposite him.

'Tommy, this is Katherine Rattray who is...what exactly are you now?'

'I'm now the Deputy Director of the Organised Crime Command.'

Tommy was clearly impressed.

Mac smiled, 'It's nice to see you're doing so well. Would you like a drink?'

'No thanks, I'm afraid I've only got ten minutes, there are several men in suits twiddling their thumbs and waiting for me to turn up for a meeting. How can I help?'

Mac explained the basic facts around the Henrietta Lewinton case.

'Have you heard of anything new on the streets that might cause such symptoms?'

She shook her head.

'No, most drugs are supposed to give you energy, make you feel more awake or hornier, not put you to sleep. However, I'll ask around and, if anything comes up, I'll let you know. If you do find that there's something new out there make sure you keep me in the loop.'

She glanced over at Tommy.

'Anyway, how come you're still working with CID, I thought you'd retired?'

'I have retired, I'm just helping them out and they've been kind enough to let me.'

She looked at her watch.

'I have to go but take care of yourself, Mac.' She gave him a card. 'Ring me when you have an evening free, I'd love to catch up, and bring Bridget too. You'll definitely do that now?'

'I will,' Mac promised.

They hugged again and Katherine left.

'You know some high up people,' Tommy said 'but I suppose you were one yourself not long ago.'

'Yes, not too long ago. Anyway, I think we've done all we can for the moment.'

As they walked back towards the car Tommy's phone rang.

He listened for a few seconds and then said, 'We'll be right there.' He then turned to Mac and said, 'That was Dan Carter, he needs us back in Luton. It looks like we might have a lead.'

Chapter Seven

It was just after four o'clock when they arrived back in Luton after being caught in traffic. Even with the sirens going they'd made slow progress. Dan was standing in front of the white board when Mac and Tommy entered the incident room.

'Just in time, I was about to start.'

Mac and Tommy found a seat while Dan continued.

'Team, we've got a new member who's joining us for a while. Mac Maguire, who used to be a Detective Chief Superintendent and head of the Met's Murder Squad, has volunteered to help us with this one. Mac, let me introduce the team.'

He waved towards a young man with black rimmed spectacles, stubbled cheeks and hair standing straight up.

'This is Martin and, if you need anything from the databases or off the internet, then Martin's your man.'

Martin managed to tear his gaze away from his laptop for a split second and give Mac the most imperceptible of nods.

'This is Detective Sergeant Adil Thakkar.'

A short but very powerful looking and stocky man in his thirties leant over and shook Mac's hand firmly.

'And this is Detective Constable Mary Sullivan.'

A tall attractive woman in her late thirties with platted blonde hair waved at him.

'...and finally Detective Constable Buddy Singh.'

A very young man with a dark blue turban smiled broadly at him from the far end of the room.

'Okay, I think that we might finally have a lead,' Dan said. 'Adil tell us what you've found.'

The sergeant stood up, notebook in hand, and took Dan's place at the white board.

'We've been trying to track down any friends of the girls who might be able to substantiate the facts on the whiteboard here and hopefully add to them. So far everything we've found out checks with the facts and dates you can see on the board. Mary looked for any known associates of the first girl who went missing, Mandy Stokes, Buddy took Barbara Mason and I took Angela Moran. We've found something, or rather someone, who might link Mandy and Angela. They were both users, especially Angela, who her friend said would take anything she could get her hands on. Anyway, not long before she disappeared one of her clients offered her something as a sort of tip. They were white pills, her client said they were something new and she was stupid enough to take them.'

He consulted his notebook.

'Her friend said she was hyperactive for two to three days, taking all the clients she could and seemingly enjoying the sex. The only problem was that she then crashed and slept for nearly three days straight. Her friend said that when she first found her, she thought that she was dead. She tried to wake her several times but couldn't. Angela finally came around but was groggy for quite a time. She described the man to her friend as being in his thirties or early forties, balding and having an American accent. Mary.'

Mary Sullivan stood up and took over.

'While talking to one of Mandy Stokes' friends she also mentioned an American man who'd been one of her clients. She remembered Mandy being furious about being offered some white pills by him which she threw away. She thought he was trying to fob her off with aspirin or something. This friend of Mandy's, she calls herself Divine but her real name is Elizabeth Eversley, said that Mandy had told her she'd seen this

71

American again. She spotted him walking down Church Street talking to two young men who she said looked as if they were students. One of them called him 'Professor'. Mandy said that, although he dressed younger, he must have been around forty and that he was losing his hair at the front. She also said that he'd been circumcised.'

Mary sat down and Dan Carter took over again.

'Okay, we've contacted the university and they've got several staff members from North America, two Canadians and three Americans. Two of them are women which leaves us three. They've sent me the photos from their staff IDs and out of the three only one is balding. His name is Asher Grinberg, a professor working at the Business School. Martin's checked with our US colleagues and the professor has some previous for drugs but only minor stuff from when he was a teenager. If these pills he's giving out like Smarties are the hibernation drug, or have contributed in some way to Henrietta Lewinton's condition, then we may have just have cracked the case. If not then we need to know what he's pushing and, if it is a class A drug or something hazardous, we need to get him and his pills off the streets. I've been given the green light to go ahead with a raid on Mr. Grinberg's flat, however, Martin's discovered that he'll be attending a university theatre production this evening so I suggest that we delay any action until early tomorrow morning.'

Dan looked at the expressions on his team's faces. They all looked more than up for it.

'Adil, arrange for the Support Unit to meet us here at four thirty and I'll brief them. Everyone else I'll need you here at four for your briefing so I'd suggest that, unless there's something urgent you need to do, it might be best to get home and get some sleep. See you all tomorrow.'

Dan went straight over to Mac.

'That doesn't include you of course Mac.'

'I'd still like to be here for the briefings if that's okay?'

Mac knew that his condition meant that his raiding days were over but he was still surprised that it irked him so much.

'Of course. Did you find anything of interest today?'

Mac shook his head.

'Nothing definite but we've got some top medical people asking around so you never know.'

'What do you think of the lead?' Dan asked.

'It looks like it could be a good one, I especially liked what you said about 'contributing' to Henrietta's condition. It's always possible that she took two or three things that perhaps by themselves might not have been so harmful but, when taken together, might have sent her into that weird coma. What are your thoughts on Mr. Grinberg? Do you think he's our driver?'

'I'm not sure if stealing cars is on the Business School curriculum so probably not but what if he gave Henrietta something that caused or contributed towards her condition? Perhaps her pimp found her, thought she was dead and was trying to dump the body.'

Mac nodded. He had to concede there was an outside chance that he might be right.

'And what about the other five girls?'

'That's where any theory involving the professor probably falls down,' Dan replied. 'He may have been peddling something but it wasn't heroin and as all the girls died from massive heroin overdoses then, no, I don't fancy him for that. Could it be that Henrietta's case and the other five girls aren't linked after all? Anyway, even if we don't fancy him as a serial killer, as he was such a good customer of at least two of the girls then he might know something. Who knows?'

'It's well worth a shot. So, while you're away breaking down the professor's door would it be okay if I started reviewing everything we've got so far?' Mac asked.

'That's a good idea. I'll get Adil to round up all the paperwork and I'll arrange for Martin to give you access to the databases, although I have to admit that I've usually found it quicker to just ask him rather than to try and find anything myself.'

As it was still only five o'clock Mac decided to see how Hetty was getting on before he headed home. Janet was still sitting by the side of the bed, holding her daughter's hand. There had been little change in her condition but her mother was still being as positive as she could.

'They're still in the dark about what's caused it but she's alive, Mr. Maguire, which is more than I could have hoped for when I saw her on that slab last Monday. While there's life, there's hope, isn't there?' Janet said.

Mac could only agree.

'Where are you staying?' he asked.

'I'm staying in a hotel, it's only a short walk from here and I've booked it for two weeks just in case. Not that I've been there much.'

'We're working hard to find out what it was that put Hetty in this coma. If we can track the drug down it might help the doctors to find a cure.'

'Even more hope then,' she said, trying to smile.

He couldn't think of anything else to say. She promised to phone Mac if there was any change.

After leaving the hospital Mac rang Tim. They had a bite to eat and a few drinks in the Magnets as Mac described the events of the day.

Tim thought his friend was looking more and more like his old self but he kept that thought to himself for now.

Even though his team was playing in a local derby that night Mac left the pub early and was tucked up in bed by eight thirty.

For once he had no trouble falling asleep.

Chapter Eight

Thursday 8th January

Mac beat the alarm clock by five minutes. He turned it off and lay there for a moment allowing a strange dream about climbing a giant tree while attempting to phone a call centre about a faulty cooker, exit stage left. It was five to three and, once he'd shaken the remnants of the dream off, he felt wide awake and ready for the day ahead.

He stood up gingerly, checked his pain levels, and said a little prayer of thanks that it was still within limits. He changed his patch and made coffee. While it was brewing, he checked the football results on his tablet. He wasn't surprised to find that his team had lost, a goal scored in the eighty-ninth minute.

He poured coffee into his travel mug and drove out through the dark, empty streets to Luton Police Station. Although he wasn't taking any actual part in the raid, he still felt a sense of excitement. He thought back over previous raids that he'd been involved in, many of which had been brilliant successes. Mac and his team had always tried to cover every angle and they felt that time spent planning would be handsomely repaid by limiting the number of surprises that were likely to crop up. Regardless of that a few still turned out to be absolute disasters being more like something from a comedy sketch than serious police work. Mac made a mental note to share some of them with Tommy.

He walked into the room at ten to four and the whole team was already there. A jug of coffee and paper cups were on a side table and he helped himself. Tommy came over and poured himself a cup.

'How many raids have you been part of so far?' Mac asked.

'Just the one as a detective, a suspected burglar,' Tommy replied, 'but I was in the Support Unit for a few months and I must have done seven or eight with them. It's different as a detective though, isn't it? I mean our work starts when the Support Unit's finishes. I used to be quite envious of the detectives as they'd get to investigate and discover the whole story. It was like only being shown the first page in a book and then having it slammed shut, if you know what I mean.'

'Yes, yes I do. There's something very satisfying about following an investigation all the way through to the end.'

Dan called them all to order.

'The Support Unit will be here in about fifteen minutes. Martin have you got all we need in terms of photos and maps of Professor Grinberg's flat?'

Martin nodded without turning his head and put his hand on a stack of printed pages.

'Good,' Dan continued. 'Our job is really simple. We just stand by and watch the Support Unit gain entry and then we arrest anyone on the premises. Tommy and Buddy, I want you to wait at the scene and work with the Forensics Team should they need help. They'll be on site at five thirty to conduct a search and we'll lend them a hand should they need it. Make sure that you both take a fresh set of coveralls. I want you to stay until forensics are finished, no matter how long it takes, and I want to know within the second if they find anything. While the search is underway the rest of us will make our way back to the station where we'll start interrogating any suspects. Any questions?'

'How many suspects do we think there might be and what are we using to take them back to the station?' Mary asked.

'We think it's highly likely it will be just the one, unless he has someone staying overnight. Just in case he's had a party we've got a van that can take up to eight and a couple of the Support Unit team will drive the suspects back to the station. Anything else? No? Okay, make sure you've got everything you need and we'll assemble in the car park in twenty minutes. The canteen is open for coffee and Danishes so if you haven't had anything to eat yet this may be your last chance for a while.'

Mac walked with Tommy to the canteen. The coffee was from a machine and the Danish pastries were on plates wrapped in cling film, probably put there the night before Mac thought. None the less they both went down very well.

'Mac, how many raids have you done?' Tommy asked.

Adil, Buddy and Mary came nearer.

'I honestly don't know but it must be in the hundreds. Funnily enough I was just thinking about it on the way here. You know it doesn't matter how hard you plan, how much thought you give to the different scenarios or how good your team is, it can still turn out to be a bloody fiasco.'

'Tell me about one,' Tommy asked as he bit into a vanilla crown.

The rest of the team came even closer.

'Okay, it must have been about fifteen years ago now. The suspect was a doctor, a GP in Ruislip who we suspected of helping along two of his older patients. A bit like Shipman I suppose but thankfully nowhere near on the same scale. Anyway, we'd disinterred two old ladies and found very high levels of diamorphine in them and, as the doctor had been generously mentioned in both of their wills, it seemed like we had a good case.

We set up a raid on his house for early in the morning, just like this one, in the hope that we could find a secret stash of diamorphine and other incriminating evidence. I had someone stake out the house for the whole of the day before. They discretely asked all the neighbours and only the doctor appeared to be in residence. So, we broke down the door and the doctor himself gave us no resistance but we were unaware that his mother had been visiting him. She must have been at least seventy and hadn't left the house since she'd arrived so not even the neighbours were aware that she'd been staying with her son. So, there were we thinking 'job done' when this old lady flew out of her bedroom with a metal topped walking stick lashing out at everyone around her and her dog biting anything that moved.'

Mac stopped to pick up another Danish and also to create a bit of suspense.

'We finally disarmed her and locked the dog in another room but by then three of our team had been injured. One had severe concussion, one had his nose broken and one was bleeding profusely from a bite wound on his inner thigh. The doctors said if the dog had bitten a few inches to the right he might have been singing soprano for the rest of his life. The funny thing is that the very next raid we carried out was on a notoriously violent gang leader and, on that raid, there were also injuries. Two of our team got splinters in their hands from a damaged bannister. That's the thing about raids, even with the best of plans, you can never be quite sure how they'll turn out.'

The team all smiled.

'Thanks for that Mac,' Adil said. 'Come on team, time to go.'

Mac got back to the incident room just in time to see the Support Unit leave. Dan gave him an excited smile as he walked out behind them. In his heart Mac would have given anything to be with them. As it was all he could do was to walk back into the silent incident room. Martin was there but he still felt alone.

Adil had left him a pile of files to go through so Mac got to work.

He first read everything the police had on each of the six girls. They all had records but Angela Moran's was the most impressive. She'd been charged with soliciting and drug use no less than sixteen times over the past three years. For most of these offences she was only cautioned but the year before she'd been sent to jail. She'd gotten nine months and had served five. She'd been caught injecting heroin while sitting on a bench in an indoor shopping mall and the magistrate hadn't taken kindly to that. She'd been caught on CCTV so it was pretty much an open and shut case.

He looked at a picture of her. Even slumped dead in the corner of a car park he could see that she'd been very pretty. He wondered what sort of life these girls had before going on the street. He looked again at Angela Moran's file. No sign of a father, her mother was an alcoholic and she'd ended up in care at the age of nine. For some reason the name of the children's home seemed familiar.

'Martin can you do me a favour?'

'Sure,' Martin replied without looking up.

'The Bradeley Grange Children's Home, can you see if you can find anything.'

Martin's fingers flew over the keys.

'It used to be in Shepherds Bush, London. Closed down four years ago after several of the staff were jailed for child abuse. It had been going on for years according to this news article.'

'Thanks, Martin,' Mac said.

Mac felt quite sad picturing a little nine year old girl, all alone and being regularly abused. He could understand why Angela ended up as a prostitute, she needed the drugs to help her forget and to get the drugs she needed money. But what about Henrietta? What had made her go down the same road as Angela?

Mac opened her folder.

Just two cautions for soliciting. The first one was while she was still at university, the second just a month ago. There was nothing in the folder that would explain why a well-off university girl would choose to hang around on street corners selling herself to anyone with enough money. Was it just the drugs? Mac wondered why some people seemingly couldn't live without them while most of us had little or no problem in leaving them alone. He remembered interviewing a user once and he'd asked him that exact question.

He'd just shrugged his shoulders.

'There's this big gaping hole, just here,' he'd replied, putting his hand on his heart. 'Nothing in the world will fill it, not even drugs. They just help me forget it's there for a while.'

Mac wondered if her father dying when she was so young had left Hetty with a similarly gaping hole that she just couldn't cope with.

He looked through the other papers. The latest forensic reports on the car and Hetty's clothing were a complete dud as Mac had predicted. All the prints and DNA they found in the car either belonged to Hetty or to the family who owned it, the dress was new and only had Hetty's DNA on it. There were also some maps which showed where the girls had lived and where they'd usually worked. They were all in more or less the same area but that would be expected given their line of work. There were also some analyses around drug use in the area but nothing leapt out at him.

He suddenly realised that his back was getting stiff so he stood up and stretched. He felt as though he'd been struck by lightning as a blinding bolt of white-hot pain shot down his left leg. It made him gasp but, thankfully, it only lasted a split second. He looked over at Martin who was still glued to his computer screen. Mac was grateful that he hadn't noticed anything. He gingerly sat down again.

'Sciatica is it?' Martin asked without looking over.

'What?' Mac replied in some surprise.

'That pain just now.'

Mac looked over again at Martin. There was obviously more going on underneath the straight-up hair that he'd given credit for.

'Yes, it was sciatica. How did you know?'

Martin turned and looked at Mac.

'My dad's had it for years. He used to be a policeman too but, unfortunately for him, he got involved in a crowd disturbance at a local football match and got trampled on. His back was no good after that and some days he can hardly walk.'

'How is he now?' Mac asked, finding himself more than a little interested in hearing the answer.

'He's still in pain but still going and, you won't believe this, he still goes to all the football matches.'

'Good for him!' Mac exclaimed with some emotion. 'How come you don't get to go out with the rest of the team?'

'I'm not into the rough stuff. I'm a Forensic Computer Specialist and my crime scene is in here somewhere,' he replied pointing to his laptop. 'I'm helping out Dan's team, it's a pilot to see if computer specialists can improve team performance but I'm also working on two other cases at the same time, one's a computer fraud and the other a suspected theft of data from a company by an ex-employee.'

'So, they keep you busy then. Do you mind me asking, how old are you?'

'I'm twenty-three.'

'How did you get into forensic computing or whatever you call it?'

Martin laughed.

'I've always loved computers. I had my first proper computer when I was five and started writing code before I was nine. I really got into it but I was basically on the other side until I was seventeen. I was a hacker, mostly kid's stuff though. A few years back I was seriously considering joining this group, they were hacking corporations, US defence systems, really big stuff, challenging stuff. Then some of them got very publicly arrested and that made me think again. My dad persuaded me to go to university instead and here I am.'

'And how do you like it?' Mac asked.

'It can be fun sometimes especially when I get to pit my wits against people like myself, a much tougher challenge than big industry or even defence. I'm hoping to work at the Met some day, I'm thinking of joining CEOPS.'

'Child protection?'

'Yes, even though it's all online, that would be real detective work tracking down the people who peddle child porn.'

'I wish you luck with that.'

'Thanks.'

'What about this case though? Dan said you were looking at the crime statistics and CCTV,' Mac asked.

'I've found nothing as yet. We've got six possible instances of car crime in six months, not enough to show up as a pattern in the stats, and CCTV was a non-starter really. We only cover a few routes with number plate recognition and, unfortunately, he didn't use any of those. If we knew the time and direction that he left Luton around those dates then it might be worth going through all the videos but it would probably take days. It's something that we still might have to consider if we get stuck but, even then, I'm not sure what it would really tell us. What we need is something unusual. There were over four thousand car crimes last year, so six more doesn't make that much difference.'

'Yes, I can see your problem. It would have to be something unusual to show up. The fact that five prostitutes were found dead in Luton town centre was unusual though, wasn't it?' Mac asked.

'Yes, but data analysis broadly consists of two things, the data and the analysis. The data may be out there but unless someone's actually looking at that particular data set, or it forms some sort of regular report, then it won't get picked up.'

'You know, I thought with all this technology...'

Martin smiled.

'That's what a lot of people think but the big problem is that computers are still very stupid and, for all the effort that's gone into it, they still don't know what things mean. They're working on it but, for now at least, any analysis is still more or less reliant on us humans.'

'I wish I knew more about it but I'm a bit long in the tooth I suppose.'

Mary Sullivan's head poked around the door.

'We're back. Dan wondered if you wanted to help him interview the professor.'

'You bet!' Mac replied enthusiastically. 'How did the raid go?' he asked as they walked towards the interview room.

'No problems. There was just the professor and a student in the house and they both came quietly.'

'He was sleeping with one of his students?'

Mary nodded.

'I wonder what her mother will make of that?' Mac asked.

'His mother you mean, it was a male student.'

'Oh.'

Mary stopped outside the door, 'Dan's in here. Adil and I are interviewing the student down the hall.' Seeing Mac's excited face, she added, 'Have fun, I'll see you later.'

Mary gave him a little smile and left him to it.

Dan nodded at Mac as he entered the room and gestured at the empty chair next to him. On the opposite side of the table sat a balding man in his forties. He was wearing a thin pullover over a tee shirt. His face was pale and covered with a light sheen of sweat. He couldn't seem to keep still for a second. He drummed his fingers noisily on the table and his arms and legs seemed to have a life of their own.

Next to the balding man sat a man in a crumpled suit who was reading from a file. Mac guessed that he was the duty solicitor. Unlike his client he was very still, the only movement he made was when he turned a page.

Dan pressed the button on the recorder.

'Officers present are DI Carter and ex-DCS Maguire acting as a consultant. Also present are the duty lawyer, Mr. Ken Fawley and the interviewee. Can you please state your name and address for the record?' Dan asked.

The professor gave his details in a low shaking voice.

Dan read him his rights and then asked, 'Professor Grinberg, have you any idea why you're here this morning?'

'None whatsoever,' the professor stated.

Mac looked at him closely. He was absolutely certain that the professor had something to hide.

'How long have you been resident in the UK?'

'Just over three years.'

'Professor, in that time have you ever used a prostitute?'

'No never, why would I?'

'Do you recall the names Mandy Stokes or Angela Moran?' Dan asked. 'You might know them better as

Randy and Angel, those were the names that they used on the street.'

'No, I don't know anyone with those names.'

'We have statements that you gave both of the women named some substance in the form of white pills. Is that correct?'

'Is that what this is about?' the professor asked.

Mac thought that he looked even more uncomfortable.

'Please answer the question,' Dan insisted.

'No, I never gave anyone any pills. You've obviously mistaken me for someone else.'

'Do you have any such pills on your premises or in your possession elsewhere?'

'No, apart from some paracetamol, I suppose.'

The professor kept his eyes on the table and Dan had to turn his head to the side to make eye contact.

'Are you sure you don't want to reconsider your answer? We're searching your premises right now and my team will miss nothing.'

The professor said nothing for what seemed an eternity. Eventually he answered in a voice so quiet it was almost inaudible.

'No.'

'I'm sorry but we didn't hear your answer,' Dan said firmly. 'Please repeat what you said.'

'No!' the professor almost shouted.

'This interview is suspended at five fifty eight,' Dan said as he turned off the recorder.

Mac followed him out of the room.

'What do you think?' Dan asked.

'He looks as guilty as hell to me,' Mac replied.

'I agree. I just thought that I'd let him stew for a while, soften him up a bit. It also gives forensics a bit more time to find something. Fancy a coffee?'

Mac followed him to the canteen. They'd only just sat down when Dan's phone rang. He pulled it out and listened and, as he did, a smile grew on his face.

'Thanks Tommy, that's excellent news.' Dan put his phone away and continued, 'That was Tommy. He said that forensics have found a box containing around two to three hundred little white pills. It was hidden under a loose floorboard, not very original for such an apparently bright person. Oh well, no rush, let's finish our coffees first.'

'Take me through the raid,' Mac asked.

'Sure, there's not a lot to tell to be honest. The Support Unit had the front door down in a couple of seconds. The professor and his friend were still in bed and half asleep when we entered the room. There was no resistance. They dressed when they were told and then we slapped on the handcuffs. And best of all we've now found the pills, God I wish every raid was so easy!'

On their way back Dan interrupted the questioning of the student to tell Adil about the discovery of the pills. A few minutes later Mac was back in his seat in the interview room. The professor was beginning to look very stressed indeed.

Dan turned the recorder on.

'The interview is resumed at six twenty five. Professor Grinberg, I'd like to summarise the answers you've given so far if that's okay?'

The professor had a whispered conversation with his lawyer and then nodded warily.

'Please say yes or no,' Dan said.

'Yes.'

'Okay, I asked you if you recalled the names Mandy Stokes or Angela Moran, also known as Randy and Angel and your response was negative. I also asked if you were in possession of any white pills and you said that, apart from paracetamol, you were not. Is this summary correct?'

'Yes,' the professor said with some hesitation.

From his expression Mac could see that the professor was starting to smell a rat.

'So, if I told you that we found a box containing two to three hundred white pills under a loose floorboard in the room in your flat that you use as an office, would that come as a surprise?'

The professor covered his face with his hands and didn't answer for the better part of a minute. Dan stayed silent.

When he removed his hands Mac could see a look of resignation on the professor's face.

'No, it wouldn't be a surprise.'

'I take it that these pills aren't paracetamol? We will of course be analysing them,' Dan said.

The professor's former agitation had left him. His lawyer whispered something in his ear but the professor shook his head.

His body was quite still as he said, 'They're Crystal Meth.'

Now it was Dan's turn to look surprised.

'Crystal Meth? We don't see a lot of that in Luton.'

'I brought them over from the States the last time I was there. I'm not an addict you understand but they help me get through things.'

'So, can I ask you once again. Have you ever met Mandy Stokes or Angela Moran, also known as Randy and Angel?'

The professor nodded.

'Yes, I went to both of them several times.'

'What about Barbara Mason, also known as Babs, Annie McTavish also known as Tanya and Kayla James also known as Kayla?'

The professor looked really puzzled.

'No, I don't know any of those names.'

Mac believed him and apparently so did Dan.

The professor's lawyer piped up, 'Can you tell us what this is really about? I'm getting the feeling that my client isn't the real focus of your investigation.'

'No, I'm afraid that I can't at this moment,' Dan said. 'Thank you for your cooperation Professor Grinberg. You have admitted possession of a Class A drug. You will be kept in custody until formal charges are prepared. I'll now let you have a word with your lawyer. Interview suspended at six thirty five.'

Dan stopped the recorder and Mac followed him out of the room. Outside in the hallway Dan punched the air.

'That's how I like them, short and sweet!'

'Crystal Meth? That's a bit of a surprise though,' Mac said.

'We've only had the one case of someone found with Crystal Meth to my knowledge, an American passing through the airport a few years back. Unfortunately, its use is growing though. They busted a drugs factory up North a few months ago and found over twenty kilos of the stuff, apparently worth well over a million on the street. Another factory was recently found in London. It won't be long before it hits the streets for real and then that'll be yet another problem for us, as if we haven't got enough.'

'It was a result today though,' Mac said, trying to be positive.

Dan smiled broadly.

'Yes, we should celebrate our little victories when we get them. The only problem is that it doesn't help us much with the Lewinton case and the death of all the other girls does it? I mean Crystal Meth, it's not our hibernation drug, is it?'

'It's a step forward though, a suspect crossed off the list.'

'So, we need to think of some other way of cracking this case. Any ideas?'

Mac shook his head.

'Not at the moment but I'm sure something will turn up.'

'I certainly hope so,' Dan said. 'There's something quite chilling and distasteful about this case. The thought that young girls could be kidnapped, held for weeks and disposed of like unwanted dogs. I mean this is Luton for God's sake!'

'I know exactly what you mean. I think that this might be one of those cases that you have to keep chipping away at but I'm sure we'll get there in the end.'

Mac sincerely hoped he was right.

Chapter Nine

They only had to wait a few minutes for Adil and Mary to join them.

'Anything?' Dan asked.

'No, not really,' Adil replied. 'He admitted that he and the professor had smoked cannabis a few times but he said he didn't know anything about any Crystal Meth. I believed him.'

Mary nodded her agreement.

'Okay we appear to be back at square one again. We may not get Tommy and Buddy back for a few hours so I think we should crack on. We still have two girls to follow up on, Annie McTavish and Kayla James. I suggest that Adil and I take Annie and that Mary and Mac take Kayla. We'll meet up here no later than four when we'll debrief and call it a day. I suggest the first thing you do is to get some breakfast, it's going to be a long day.'

Mary took Kayla's file and Mac followed her out to the car park.

'Is there any reason in particular he paired us up?' Mac asked as they walked out.

Mary looked at him and gave him a little smile.

'Yes, I asked him to. I'm up for my sergeant's exams soon and I was just curious to see how you worked. I suppose I'm hoping that something might rub off.'

Mac smiled too as he thought back to when he'd taken his sergeant's exams.

'It took me two goes.'

'Really?' she said in surprise. 'Yet you were so good at what you did.'

'Exams have nothing to do with police work. They're just another hurdle you have to jump over, a bloody barrier might be nearer the truth. Some of the best coppers I ever worked with never made sergeant,' Mac stated.

'I know but you have to make that jump if you want to get anywhere in the force and I want to get as far up the ladder as I can. Anyway, I just thought it would be nice to work with someone with your experience.'

'Okay, where do we go first?' Mac asked.

'There's a pub down the road that does a more than acceptable Full English. I'm always starving after a raid for some reason.'

'Now that sounds like an excellent first step,' Mac replied with a smile.

As they ate Mac asked Mary what the plan of action for the day was.

'Unfortunately, we don't have any information on who might be associated with Kayla James. She'd only been on the streets for a couple of months before she disappeared and she only had the one caution for soliciting. We do know that Kayla James' pimp is a sleaze who calls himself Jay Dee, real name Jaydev Dhaliwal. He runs a string of girls in High Town. It's strictly small time but we suspect that there's some-one bigger behind the operation although we have absolutely no idea who that might be. We need to see if we can somehow get some information out of Jay Dee about the other girls he's running so we can interview them too. Hopefully one of them might know something that might be of use. If, as is all too likely, he tells us nothing then we'll have to start back tracking, see if we can contact family members, school friends and so on.'

'Where was she from, was she local?' Mac asked.

'No, she was from Watford. I sincerely hope Mr. Jay Dee talks or we'll be in for what will probably be a wild goose chase for the rest of the day.'

Mac said nothing but he had a feeling that Mary might be surprised about how cooperative Mr. Jay Dee was going to be.

They drove past the rail station and into a Victorian area of the town that had seen better times. The car pulled up outside a scruffy terraced house in front of which a Porsche four by four with black tinted windows was parked. As they climbed out Mary noticed Mac looking at the car.

'Might as well have a neon sign outside saying pimp lives here,' she said.

She knocked loudly on the door and kept knocking until a dishevelled young man dressed only in a T shirt and shorts opened the door.

'Police, Mr. Dhaliwal,' Mary said as she flashed her warrant card.

'I can't be dealing with this right now. I've only just gone to bed, can't you come back later?' he replied testily.

'Just a few questions, that's all, then you can get back to your beauty sleep,' she said.

'Okay, let's get it over with then.'

He led them down a dingy hallway into the living room. There was an accumulation of empty beer cans and pizza boxes strewn around the room.

'Had a party, have we?' Mary commented.

'No, it's the maid's day off, isn't it? Come on, ask your stupid questions so I can tell you to go fuck yourselves and then get some sleep.'

'We're investigating the death of Kayla James and we'd like to interview any friends she may have had and any other girls she worked with.'

'I've never heard of anyone called Kayla James. Now go fuck yourselves, I'm going back to bed.'

'Mary, would you mind leaving me and Mr. Dhaliwal here alone for two minutes?' Mac asked.

Mary gave him a surprised look.

'Are you sure?'

'Yes, please just wait in the hall, it won't take long.'

When Mary had left the room, Mac gave Mr. Dhaliwal a measured look.

'What you looking at me for old man? Didn't know they let cripples in the police, must be getting desperate, ain't they?'

Mac still said nothing.

'That's it, I'm off to bed. Let yourself out, if you can walk as far as the door that is.'

'I'd stay if I were you and I'd also answer all of the nice lady's questions. By the way I'm not a policeman, I'm a private detective.'

'Detective? I thought they were only in films and stuff. So, what if I don't answer any questions? What are you going to do about it?'

'Me? Absolutely nothing,' Mac replied, 'but I know a man who might. In fact, if he knew that you were wilfully obstructing my investigation, I'd say that he'd definitely do something about it.'

'A man? You've got me all scared now,' Jay Dee replied. 'Who is he, the boogie man? Tell this man to fuck off, I ain't scared of no-one.'

'Then you're more stupid than you look.'

Mac stood up.

'Okay, I'll pass your message on to Mr. C and I'll also let him know that I can't find out why someone is abducting his girls because a certain Mr. Dhaliwal won't cooperate. Best of luck, you're really going to need it.'

Mac went to leave but a hand drew him back.

Jay Dee's face had turned a couple of shades whiter.

'You know him?'

'Of course, we go back a long way. I know that Kayla was one of his girls and he wants to know what happened to her.'

'Can I make a quick call?'

'Please do that and tell your boss my name's Mac Maguire. I'm sure Mr. C will have mentioned me.'

Mac joined Mary in the hallway.

'What the hell is going on?' she asked in a low voice.

'Let's just say we need Mr. Dhaliwal's cooperation so I mentioned the fact that we have a mutual acquaintance. He's just checking something out.'

Mary gave him a puzzled look but she didn't say anything. They stood in silence until Mac heard his name being called out from the living room.

Jay Dee was licking his lips as he walked in.

'Mr. Maguire I'm so sorry. Please get the lady back in, I'll tell her anything that she wants to know.'

'You'll do it politely too. Oh, and don't mention Mr. C's name to the police, he doesn't want his role in this advertised.'

'You won't say anything to him about me, will you?' Jay Dee implored.

Mac could see real fear in his eyes.

'Not if you tell the nice lady everything she needs to know. And another thing, when we go, I want you to ring around everyone whose address you're about to give us and tell them to cooperate too.'

Mac opened the door and called Mary back in.

'Ask what you like,' Mac said.

She gave Mac a puzzled look before asking, 'Mr. Dhaliwal we need the names and addresses of all the girls who work for you and any other acquaintances of Kayla James that you know of.'

'No problem.'

He then reeled off a string of names and addresses which Mary wrote down in her notebook.

'Is there anything you can tell me about the night Kayla disappeared?'

'It was just a normal shift. I didn't even know she'd gone until the night after.'

'Who knew Kayla best?'

Jay Dee gave it some thought.

'Probably Chanelle, they shared a flat together.'

'That's it for now, you can get back to bed. We may need to return to ask more questions, is that alright?'

'Fine, great, anytime you like,' he replied with a smile that wasn't a smile.

Outside Mary stood on the pavement and looked at Mac with wonder.

'Just how the hell did you do that? One minute he won't tell us what day of the week it is and then the next he's giving us the phone book.'

'I just convinced him that it was in his own interest to cooperate,' Mac said with a shrug.

'His own interest?'

'Well, let's put it this way, I let Mr. Dhaliwal know that someone way up the food chain wants this case solved. He checked and found out that I was right.'

'I'll bet you can't tell me who though?' Mary asked.

'You're absolutely right there.'

'I was expecting to be surprised by you but I find I'm still surprised. Okay at least now we have something to go at. Let's see...' she said as she opened her note-book. 'Yes, let's try Chanelle Burdon first. She was Kayla's flat mate and she's also just around the corner.'

A few minutes later Mary was knocking on the door of another scruffy terraced house but this time she didn't have to knock twice. A pretty young girl with tired eyes wearing a pink dressing gown opened the door. She beckoned them to come inside. The house was the exact opposite of the one they'd come from being recently decorated and fairly tidy.

'Jay rang and said you were coming,' Chanelle said. 'I was surprised at him helping the police though, perhaps he did feel something for Kayla after all.'

'If that's what you want to think,' Mary said. 'What can you tell us about Kayla, especially around the time she disappeared?'

'Me and Kayla started doing this at the same time so we kind of hung around together and became friends. She wasn't hard, like a lot of the girls you meet, she'd had proper jobs before but could never keep them for long. I suppose she wasn't too bright but she was really fun loving, so she'd either get the sack for making mistakes or for mucking around, or usually both from what she told me. Then her dad threw her out. He was getting remarried and needed the room, he said. So poor Kay was on her own, no money, no job and nowhere to sleep.'

'So how did she end up here?' Mary asked.

'She had a friend in Luton so she came here and, when she found out that Kay had no money, this friend introduced her to Jay. Some friend she was! Anyway, as she saw it, she didn't have any choice. She said that she was only going to do it for a year or two until she could save enough money to go back to Jamaica. She had some aunts there and she thought that they might be able get her some work, real work I mean not this. Worst comes to worst, she always said, at least the sun will be shining.'

'Do you remember anything about the night she disappeared or anything unusual leading up to it?' Mary asked.

'I've thought about it again and again but no, nothing out of the ordinary happened that night as far as I can remember.'

'When was the last time you saw her?'

'It was the fourteenth of November. I'll never forget that date. It was about nine o'clock and we were on our usual corner. Well, this big Jag pulls up and it was Kayla's turn but, as I was a bit behind, she let me take it. I've wondered ever since if it was that kindness that killed her. If she'd have taken the Jag, as she should have done, then she might still be alive.'

Chanelle gave Mary a sad look.

'So, she was still standing on the corner when you left?' Mary asked.

'Yeah but, when I got back, she'd gone. I didn't know at the time that she was gone for good.'

'Was anyone else with her when you left?' Mac asked.

Chanelle gave it some thought.

'Yes of course, Denise was there when I got back. I remember her saying that she'd been stuck there for a while. Maybe she saw Kay.'

Mary looked in her notebook.

'That's Denise Maybrook?'

Chanelle nodded.

'Right stirring cow she is though, I try to have nothing to do with her.'

'Is there anything else you can think of that might help us to find who did this to Kayla?' Mary asked.

'I'm sorry no. I'm glad that you're looking into Kayla's death though, I tried reporting it myself but got nowhere. A policeman laughed at me when I reported her missing, hardly a priority for you people, is it? Then, when they found her, I went and told them that Kay wasn't a user, that someone had done that to her, but they wouldn't believe me.'

She wiped away a tear as she said this.

'Are you scared? Are the girls out there scared right now?' Mac asked.

Chanelle hugged herself and nodded again.

'Some of them are so high or so stupid they don't care but I feel it. I feel like I've been marked out for something, like there's something terrible out there waiting for me,' she said bleakly.

'So why carry on?' Mary asked.

Chanelle shrugged her shoulders.

'I've got nowhere else to go.'

Mac was curious.

98

'You've told us how Kayla got into the business but what about yourself?'

'Just bad luck, Mr. Policeman, bad luck.'

Outside on the pavement Mary turned to Mac and said, 'There but for the grace of God...I felt so sorry for her Mac.'

'I know, some people never seem to get any luck in life but right now the best way we can help her is to find whoever killed Kayla.'

'You're right there. Come on then, Denise Maybrook is next.'

After a short drive they found themselves outside yet another scruffy terraced house. A blowsy blond woman in her early thirties only partially covered by a worn dressing gown opened the door. Mac could only think that she must look better with make-up on.

She looked at them through bleary eyes. Mary flashed her warrant card. The woman nodded at them to follow her inside. Inside it was dingy and smelt ripe, as though something was decomposing somewhere. Denise didn't seem to notice.

'Jay rang. He actually ordered me to tell you everything I knew. Bloody world's coming to an end, isn't it? Anyway, I'm knackered, can we get this over with as quickly as possible?' she asked as she lit a cigarette.

'I want to ask you about the night Kayla James disappeared. I believe that you might have seen who she went away with,' Mac said.

'Yeah, I remember that night, another one gone. Never got on with Kayla though, too much mouth, never stopped talking that girl. I knew Babs though, I got on with her alright, bloody shame that was.'

'Do you mean Barbara Mason, the second girl who disappeared?' Mac asked.

'Yeah, oh well she's probably better off out of it. Anyway, when I came on that night there was just

Kayla there so we just said hello and that's it. As I say we don't get on. I was only there ten, fifteen minutes and this car pulled up, nice car it was, and Kayla bends down to speak to the driver. Then she gets in and off they go. She never came back that night as far as I know.'

'Denise, please this is very important, think again. Anything at all you can remember, no matter how small, might be important. Can you remember the make of the car, colour, anything?' Mac asked.

Denise took a drag on her cigarette while she gave it some thought.

'It was dark coloured, I think it was blue but under the street lights it's hard to tell.'

'Was there just the one person in the car?'

'Yes, just the driver, there was no-one in the back as far as I could see.'

'I don't suppose you got a look at the number plates?' Mary asked hopefully.

'You're kidding, I'm keeping me eyes skinned looking for customers not looking at bloody number plates.'

Mary gave her a card.

'Please call me any time, night or day, if you think of anything else.'

As Denise led them to the door she said, 'Pity that bitch Brenda didn't get that bloke, perhaps he'd have done her in instead.'

Mac stopped and turned to face her.

'Tell me,' he ordered.

'Well that Brenda and her gang have a spot down the road but she keeps moving up the road trying to steal our customers.'

'How?'

'Well, sometimes the punters are a little bit shy and they'll park a bit down the road a bit and just look for a while. When they pluck up the courage, they'll drive over but sometimes they just drive away. It's happened a few times because that mad cow has come down the road and tapped on their window and frightened them off. I've had words with her about it. Anyway, that night, the man in the car, he'd been parked across the road watching us ever since I came on and then I see that Brenda sneaking up on him. She must have spoken to the driver as her head disappeared for a minute. I was getting ready to go over and pull her hair out when the car drove over and Kayla got in. I shouted at Brenda to go back to her own end of the road which she did do but not before she stuck two fingers up at me. I'd love to swing for that cow, I really would.'

'Do you know her full name?' Mary asked.

Denise shrugged.

'I just know her as Brenda but she's on her corner of the road most nights. You can't miss her, big blonde bitch.'

Mary wrote down the address, then, giving her a card, said, 'Thanks Denise, now don't forget, if you think of anything else call me.'

As she started up the car Mary said, 'We might be on to something here Mac, the only problem is we'll have to wait until tonight before we can speak to her.'

'Not necessarily. Can you hold on for a moment?'

Mac got out of the car and rang the number that Mr. C had given him.

A man with an Asian voice answered.

'How can I help you Mr. Maguire?'

Mac gave him Brenda's name and the address of the street corner that she usually operated from.

'I'll call you back in a few minutes.'

The line went dead.

Mary got out and looked at Mac suspiciously.

'What's going on, Mac?'

'I'm just waiting for some information.'

101

A few minutes later his phone rang. Mac listened and then spoke to Mary.

'Her name is Brenda Smith, have you got your notebook handy?'

Mary pulled out her notebook and Mac gave her an address not far from High Town Road. Mac ended the call and got back into the car.

'That's the second time,' Mary said. 'Was that the 'someone up the food chain' again? Bloody handy person to know if you ask me!'

'Believe me you wouldn't really want to know this person but yes, in this case it is handy. For once our aims are the same, we both want the person who's killing these girls to be caught.'

Brenda lived above a newsagent's shop. Mary banged on the door for several minutes until they heard a voice on the other side.

'Alright, alright! If you're not knocking on my door to tell me I've won the lottery then fuck off!'

'It's the police, Brenda. We just want to ask some questions.'

The door opened a fraction and Mary showed her warrant card. The door opened wider. A tall blonde woman in her thirties with a Yorkshire accent and a very ample bosom showed them in. She was wearing a purple dressing gown and slippers that made her look as if she was wearing two full sized dogs for shoes. She led them into a living room that, while being tidy enough, just had too many primary colours.

'What have I done now?' Brenda asked as she lit a cigarette.

'Nothing,' Mary replied. 'We're looking into the death of Kayla James and I believe that you may have spoken to the man she was last seen with. He was parked over the road from Kayla's pitch and Denise Maybrook saw you speak to him. Do you remember?'

'I don't get on with that Denise, she's a bitch but Kayla wasn't too bad, she liked a laugh anyway. Shame her dying like that. I remember one of the girls the day after telling me that Kayla had disappeared. I must admit it scared me, I'd heard of girls disappearing but, as I didn't know any of them, I wasn't too worried. Kayla going though was getting was a bit close to home for me. Let's think.'

She took a drag from her cigarette and then looked at it.

'Yes, that's it, I remember now. I'd ran out of fags and I was going to the shop when I spotted this car, a BMW it was. I could see the driver was watching Kayla but I thought 'What can I lose?' and tapped on his window.'

'What happened next?'

'He wound the window down and said, 'Fuck off, I don't need an old slag like you'. Nice eh?'

'Did he have an accent?' Mary asked.

'Yes, I saw a film recently, a good one it was too with loads of explosions and stuff. Anyway, the baddie was from the Russian mafia and this guy spoke a bit like him.'

'Did you get a good look at him?'

'Yes, I suppose so. He was in his mid-twenties, slightly chubby face and I remember he had a moustache. We don't see many men looking for our services with moustaches nowadays, gay thing, isn't it?'

'What happened then?'

'I asked him if he had a cigarette and he threw a packet at me and then wound up the window. He drove off and stopped over the road and then I saw Kayla getting in. I picked up the packet but there was only one cigarette left. I smoked it, even though it tasted strange, not like English cigarettes.'

'What made you think the cigarette wasn't English?' Mac asked.

'Well, the packet looked different and the writing wasn't in English. I don't read so well but even I could see that.'

'What were they called?' Mac asked.

Brenda shrugged her shoulders.

'I'm not sure but I think they were called Soapy something. Sorry but that's all I remember.'

Mary stood up.

'Okay Brenda, get dressed please. We need you to come with us to the station.'

'No way, love. The only place I'm going now is back to my bed. You can see yourselves out.'

Mary got out her notebook and showed her a page.

'That's the address of your pitch, isn't it, Brenda? By the way this here is my boss DCS Maguire. What do you say boss, could you spare me for a week or so? I wouldn't mind doing nights for a change as I really want to keep my friend Brenda here company for a while. Of course, I'd have to warn off anyone who tried to ask for her services, perhaps arrest a couple of them for kerb crawling, what do you say?'

Mac played along.

'It's a bit slow at the moment so take two weeks if you like.'

Brenda got the message.

'I'll just get changed then,' she said with a conciliatory smile.

Chapter Ten

Dan and Adil were waiting for them when they got back to the station. Mary had parked Brenda in an interview room and stationed a uniform outside in case she had any second thoughts.

Mary told Dan and Adil what they'd discovered. When Mary made some comments about 'Mac's wonderful powers of persuasion' and how helpful Jay Dee had turned out to be, Dan looked questioningly at Mac but didn't explore it any further.

'It seems as if you two have really gotten onto something,' Dan commented. 'The police artist will be here in a few minutes. Mary can you keep Brenda company until he arrives and then drop her back home afterwards?'

Mary gave Mac a rueful smile.

'Sure boss. Did you find anything?' she asked.

'We spoke to Annie's pimp first which was a total waste of time. However, as young as she was, Annie had been on the streets for over five years so we had the names of some of the girls who worked with her on file. The only possibly relevant information we got was from a girl called Karin Ivanovic who was a friend of Annie's and, apparently, the last one to see her alive. She saw Annie get into a car that night, a BMW, and, while it was unfortunate that she didn't get a look at the driver or remember the number plate, she did hear Annie say something. Adil, what were her exact words?'

Adil got his notebook out.

'She said, Oh, I haven't seen you for a while.'

'She knew her killer then!' Mac exclaimed.

'It would appear so.'

A uniform poked his head around the door.

'Sir, the police artist is here.'

'See you later,' Mary said.

As she left the room Tommy and Buddy came in. Dan went through everything again for their benefit. While he did so Mac went over to Martin who was quietly tapping away as usual.

'Martin, do you have a minute?'

'Just lining up all the databases I'll need if the artist comes up with something recognisable. What do you need?'

'The girl who's helping us also said our man gave her a cigarette pack, it was foreign and all she could remember was that the name was 'Soapy' or something similar. Any chance you could have a look?'

'Sure,' Martin said. Mac went to walk away. 'Might as well wait, this shouldn't take long.'

Martin opened Google and started inserting key words. Mac was amazed not just the speed he input them but the logic behind the words he used. In a few seconds images of cigarette packs filled the screen, all called Sopianae.

'They're Hungarian,' Martin explained.

'Can you print that page off for me?' Mac asked.

'Done,' Martin said as he went back to his databases.

Mac picked up the print off and took it over to Dan who was just finishing off.

'Martin reckons this could be the brand of cigarette that our man gave Brenda. They're from Hungary.'

'Hungary? I suppose that would explain the accent and perhaps even the moustache but why might an Eastern European be involved?'

'Well, they've have been known to be heavily involved in prostitution so maybe he's trying to muscle in and start a war between the rival factions running the girls?' Adil suggested.

'Anything's possible I suppose,' Dan said. 'If that is the case then he's bound to be on record somewhere. If we can get a good enough likeness then, with some luck, we might just be able to identify him. I'll take this to Mary, we'll see if Brenda recognises the cigarette pack.'

Dan looked at his watch, it had just gone one o'clock.

'The artist may take a while so I suggest we grab a coffee and a bite to eat. We'll meet back here in half an hour.'

Tommy accompanied Mac to the canteen.

'That's strange that she knew him. You said that he might have been a client, that he might have lived here.'

Mac shrugged.

'Good guess that's all.'

Tommy's expression showed that he didn't agree.

'Your source, he must be pretty powerful to scare that pimp so much.'

'Please don't ask about him. Although I promised I wouldn't mention his name, if I'm honest, the main reason I'm not going to reveal his identity is for everyone's protection. Believe me when I say that you do not want to be on this person's radar.'

Tommy could see from Mac's face that he was deadly serious. He just nodded and decided that he'd never bring the subject up again.

'Anyway, it's fish and chips today Mac. Maybe not as fancy as they did in that pub but perhaps I can treat you this time.'

'You just said the magic words, lead on,' Mac said.

He suddenly felt ravenously hungry again and, fancy or not, he enjoyed his meal every bit as much as he had the day before.

'So, what do you think our mysterious Hungarian was doing here?' Tommy asked.

'I've no idea.'

'Do you think it's possible that Adil was right, that he might be from some Hungarian mafia or something?'

'As Dan said anything's possible but, if I'm honest, no I don't,' Mac replied. 'I've seen take-overs before and they usually involve a show of overwhelming force of some kind not one man skulking around kidnapping girls. Anyway, he's taken girls from at least two separate organisations when it would probably have been more logical to pick them off one at a time. For me though, the real clincher is that I know who he'd be up against and, if my source thought there was the slightest chance that someone was trying to muscle in on one of his businesses, there'd be a high body count by now believe me. No there's something else going on here but I'm damned if I know what it is.'

'Hungary?' Tommy stood up as he asked himself a question. 'What do I know about Hungary? Budapest is the capital and they eat goulash, that's about it.'

As they walked back down the corridor Mac added, 'They invented the biro, Liszt was born there, they had a great football team once and they tried to throw the Russians out in the fifties and unfortunately failed. That's all I know.'

'More than me anyway,' Tommy said with a smile.

Mac suddenly stopped walking and stood as still as a statue.

'Mac, are you alright? It's not the pain again is it?' Tommy asked with some concern.

After a few seconds Mac came back to life again.

He shook his head and said, 'No, it's not the pain, it was what you just said.'

Tommy looked confused.

'About the goulash, it's given me an idea.'

When they returned to the incident room Mac had a word with Martin who, a few seconds afterwards, wrote something on a sheet of paper and gave it to Mac.

'What is it Mac?' Tommy asked, still in the dark about the significance of his goulash remark.

'It's the address of a food shop.'

'They have a Hungarian food shop in Luton?'

'Not just Hungarian, they stock food from all over Eastern Europe. It might be worth showing them our man's picture, if he did live in the area there's a good chance that he might have visited them at some time.'

'That's brilliant. And you got that from me talking about goulash?' Tommy asked.

'Yes, and something else too, something I remembered. My mother was from Ireland and, when you mentioned goulash, I thought of a shop that she used to take me to when I was young. It was over a mile there and a mile back from where we lived but we happily walked that far because the shop stocked Irish food. Sometimes she only bought a pack of biscuits if that was all she had the money for. Food from home is special, isn't it? Even now, when I manage to get my hands on some proper Irish sausages, it instantly brings back memories of when I was five or six, of relatives arriving from Ireland on the night boat and knocking on our door early on a Saturday morning. They always brought loads of sausages, white pudding and corned beef. My mother would do us all a big fry up and it was wonderful, like a party. It isn't just the food, it's the memories and everything else that comes with it.'

Tommy was about to say something but he was interrupted by Mary's arrival.

'We've got it as good as we can. The artist is sending it over to Martin. Brenda also identified the cigarette packet.'

Martin gave the thumbs up.

'How many do you want me to print off?' Martin asked.

'Do me twenty for now,' Dan replied. 'Make sure you send copies to Interpol and the Hungarian police.'

'Will do, I've also got the databases lined up, I'll see if I can get a match.'

Dan went over to the printer and started distributing the picture to the team. Mac examined the portrait. Not a bad one as these things go, he thought. As Brenda said he had a moustache and was slightly chubby faced but it wasn't a thuggish face as Mac might have expected. It was an ordinary face, Mac thought, but not one lacking in intelligence. He went over and had a few words with Dan.

He was smiling as he returned to Tommy.

'Okay we're on. I need you to drive me here.'

He handed Tommy the paper with the address on.

'I know where this is, it's only around the corner. We could walk there is five minutes...' he looked at Mac and quickly said, 'I'll get the car and meet you in front.'

Tommy had been right about how close the shop was to the station. Two minutes later, in a busy narrow street full of retail businesses, they pulled up outside the 'Europeast' food shop. Its sign was emblazoned with various flags and it stated that it stocked 'Quality Food from Eastern Europe'.

A bell rang as Tommy opened the door. Inside it was dark and there was a strange mixture of aromas made up of cooked meats, cheese and spices. Mac found it enticing. The shop was mostly shelving up to the ceiling packed with packets and cans of all shapes and sizes and, from a quick glance, he had little or no idea what most of them contained.

At the back of the shop a man in his early forties stood behind a deli counter.

'Can I help?' he asked in an Eastern European accent.

His hands rested on top of a long glass fridge that acted as a counter. Underneath the man's hands Mac could see on the cold shelf below trays full of sliced

110

meats and cheeses, sausages, joints of meat and other things that he couldn't identify. It all looked very inviting.

Tommy showed the man his warrant card.

'Are you the owner of this shop?'

'Yes, my name is Meszaros Bela.'

'Well Mr. Bela...'

'Sorry, forgive me I should have said it the other way around, I keep forgetting, I've not been here too long. It's Bela Meszaros.'

Tommy looked a little flustered.

'Okay Mr. Meszaros, we're looking for this man,' he said as he showed the shop owner the picture.

He looked at it intently and then shook his head.

'No, I'm afraid he doesn't look familiar.'

'You say you've not been here long,' Mac said. 'Who owned the shop before you?'

'My uncle, he ran the shop here for over twenty years but he got a little too old for it and so I took over.'

'I must say your English is very good, where are you from?'

'From Hungary.'

'So, you'll have heard of Sopianae cigarettes?' Mac asked.

Mr. Meszaros smiled.

'Of course, Sopianae is the old Roman name of the place I was born, Pecs. I've heard of the brand but I don't smoke myself.'

Mac was curious.

'What did you do before you bought the shop?'

The man gave Mac a sheepish smile.

'I was a professor at a university in Budapest.'

It was an answer that Mac hadn't been expecting.

'A professor? What did you teach?'

'Philosophy.'

'And you're happy to work as a shop keeper?'

'Believe me it pays much better and it's far less troubling, all that deep thinking can make you a little mad, plus I like living in the UK.'

'Your uncle, has he gone back to Hungary?'

'No, he's...' Mr. Meszaros pointed upwards.

'Dead?'

'No, upstairs. He came with the shop, it was the only way I could have afforded it on my salary but I don't mind, he's a good man and here in the UK I can afford to rent a whole house just for me and my wife.'

'Can we have a word with your uncle?' Mac asked.

'Sure, I'll go and get him.'

A few minutes later Mr. Meszaros returned with a white-haired man in his late sixties.

He introduced him, 'This is my uncle, Mr. Jozsef Molnar.'

'Mr. Molnar?' Mac asked hoping he'd gotten the name the right way around.

The nephew smiled and nodded.

'We're from the police and we're looking for this man. Can you help us?'

Mr. Molnar put his glasses on and examined the picture. A finger went up in the air and his face had an excited expression.

'Yes, I remember him. He used to come in here for, now what was it? Yes, he always bought the hot paprika and salami. He'd sometimes get other things but always the paprika and salami. Nice boy, intelligent boy.'

A look of sudden concern came over the old man's face.

'He's not done anything wrong has he?'

'No, it's just a routine enquiry. We just need to exclude him from our investigation,' Mac lied. 'When did you last see him?'

The old man thought for a while.

'It must be more than two years ago now. He used to come in here every couple of weeks or so and then one day he told me that he was going home.'

'He went back to Hungary?' Mac asked.

'Yes, back to Budapest. I knew straight away he was from Budapest, he had a tattoo on his arm.'

He thought again for a moment.

'Yes, the left arm.'

He smiled a conspiratorial smile at Mac and nodded towards his nephew.

'The young ones, they think I'm losing my marbles but see what a good memory I've got.'

'How did you know he was from Budapest just by a tattoo?' Tommy asked.

'He was an MTK fan see, he had it tattooed on his arm.'

Mr. Meszaros explained, 'MTK is a football club based in Budapest.'

'Yes, yes,' the old man said, 'but me I don't like MTK, I'm a Pecsi supporter. Anyway, even if he was an MTK fan it was nice to talk about football with him.'

Tommy wrote it all down in his notebook.

'Do you know his name?' Mac asked.

'Yes of course, I wouldn't talk football to people whose names I didn't know.'

'What was it?'

'What was what?' the old man asked.

'His name?' Mac asked.

The old man's face creased with effort.

Eventually he shrugged his shoulders and said, 'I don't know, I've forgotten.'

He looked sheepishly up at his nephew.

'Is there anything else that you can tell us about him?' Tommy asked.

'No, we only talked about football.'

'Do you know if he drove to get here?' Mac asked somewhat desperately.

113

'Now why would he drive when he only lived down the road?' the old man said.

Mac and Tommy looked at each other in excitement.

'Where?' they asked in unison.

'In a flat over the kebab house about three or four hundred yards down the road. You can't miss it, Spiros the idiot and his big red sign.'

'Spiros?' Mac asked.

'Spiros Andreou, he owns the kebab shop and he's an idiot,' the old man said a dismissive gesture.

Mr. Meszaros accompanied them to the door.

'Don't mind my uncle. He and Spiros are good friends really, they've known each other for years. He's only mad because he got beaten by him at dominoes for the third time in a row last week.'

'If you or your uncle think of anything else,' Tommy said as he gave Mr. Meszaros his card, 'please ring me at any time.'

'It looks like your idea might be getting us somewhere,' Tommy said excitedly as he started the car up.

'We'll see,' Mac replied. 'Just remember that we haven't even got a name as yet.' He glanced down the road. 'I think I see what the old man meant. I can see a red sign from here.'

A few seconds later Tommy pulled up outside 'Spiros Kebabs and Fish and Chips'.

'Yes, that sign is very red indeed,' Tommy agreed.

A 'Closed' sign was hanging on the door but they could see that there was a man inside who was busy cleaning the work surfaces down. Tommy rapped on the door and the man came towards them expansively waving his hands to indicate that the shop was closed.

Mac looked at him closely. He was dark skinned with black hair greying at the sides and a neatly trimmed white beard. His age was hard to pin down and Mac thought that he could have been anything from forty to sixty.

Tommy pressed his warrant card to the window. The man unlocked the door and just as expansively waved at them to come in.

'Are you Spiros Andreou?' Tommy asked.

'Yes, that's me.'

'The flat above the shop, do you own it?'

'Yes, but I hope there's no trouble with the girls who are renting it. They seem such nice girls.'

'No, we're interested in this man,' Tommy said as he showed Spiros the likeness.

'Yes, this is Matyas, he used to rent the flat upstairs but I haven't seen him for at least a couple of years. What's he done?'

'Nothing as far as we know. Have you got a rental agreement or any document with his full name and perhaps his address in Hungary?'

'Yes, I suppose I must have but, as I have quite a few properties, I don't handle the paperwork myself. You'll need to see my son George, he's a solicitor and he handles all my business paperwork.'

He wrote down an address and gave it to Tommy.

'What was Matyas like?' Mac asked.

'He was quiet, always paid his rent and was one of the few who left the flat better than he found it.'

'A good tenant then?'

'One of the best I've had.'

'Was he working while he was here?' Mac asked.

'He was an educated man, you could tell that, but his English wasn't so good when he first came so he was limited in what he could do. He was working hard, too hard in my opinion, for one of those cleaning companies and they were paying him peanuts. So, I got him a job with my son, he owns a taxi business.'

'Is this George again?' Tommy asked.

'No, no, no, it's my son Stelios who owns the taxi business.'

He went behind the counter and came back with a business card for 'Stelly's Taxis.'

'How long did he work on the taxis?' Mac asked.

'Around six months or so, then he got a job in the University. As I said he was educated so I suppose that his English got good enough so he could get a proper job.'

'Have you any idea where he worked in the university?'

Spiros shrugged his shoulders.

'He didn't talk about his job much but I think it was something to do with biology but I can't be sure.'

'What did he talk about?' Mac asked remembering what Mr. Molnar had said.

'Football mostly. He knew so much about football that I told him he could have been a one-man quiz team. He was from Hungary but we'd talk about the Premier League or Barcelona and Real. We also used to talk about Greek and Cypriot football, he even knew all about my home team, AEK Larnaca. Then I'd occasionally see him at the football when I took my two younger sons to the game.'

'Was that Luton Town?' Mac asked.

'Yes, not exactly Barcelona maybe, but it's still football.'

'Do you know why he went back home?'

'He said his contract at the university had finished and that his English was good enough now.'

'Good enough for what?'

'He said that there were lots of American and UK companies moving into Hungary and that they'd all need translators. I think he was happy to be going home.'

'Did he have any particular friends that you know of?' Mac asked.

'No, I think he kept himself to himself most of the time, although he did go out for a beer with one of my sons a few times.'

'Was that George, Stelios or one of the two younger ones?' Tommy asked.

'No, no, the younger ones are only ten and twelve, it was my son Dimitrios that he went drinking with. Dimitrios is a teacher now but he was a student when Matyas worked at the university.'

'Does he still live locally?' Mac asked.

'Not too far away, he teaches in Letchworth, at the St. Hilda's School and he has a flat not far from the school.'

Again, he wrote down an address and gave it to Tommy.

'Is there anything else you can tell us?' Tommy asked.

'Don't you think I've said enough?' Spiros said with a wide smile.

'Thank you very much, Mr. Andreou,' Mac said as he and Tommy made to leave.

As Spiros held the door open for him Mac asked, 'By the way how many sons have you got?'

'Just the eight,' Spiros replied, a proud smile covering his face.

Back in the car Tommy said, 'He's some character, isn't he?'

'He certainly is. He's one of the few people I've met who might just fit into my friend Tim's favourite category.'

'What's that?'

'People you wouldn't mind being locked in a pub with.'

Tommy laughed out loud.

'Anyway, he's given us more than enough to get on with. So, let's see, we've got a solicitor, a taxi owner and a teacher to see.'

'Are the first two fairly local?' Mac asked.

'Yes, not too far,' Tommy replied as he looked at his watch. It was just coming up to three o'clock. 'Dan wanted us back around four and I must admit I'm starting to feel a bit tired myself. How about you?'

Mac was quite surprised to be able to say, 'I'm not too bad actually. Why don't we try the first two now and, if you give me his address, I can have a word with the teacher on my way home? The school isn't far from where I live.'

'Well, that's fine with me as it saves me a long trip to Letchworth and back. Right the solicitor's the nearest, let's start there.'

They drove out of the narrow streets and onto the wide ring road. Five minutes later they pulled up outside a large multi-storied office block just off one of the main traffic islands.

'This must be it then,' Tommy said pointing to a sign which said 'Spiros House'.

'When he said he had properties I thought he meant two or three more flats,' Mac said in some surprise.

George Andreou Solicitors were on the ground floor, in fact they had all the ground floor.

'And here was me thinking that it would be a pokey back street operation,' Tommy said.

'Assumptions can be so wrong. From all we've heard so far, our man is hard working, polite and pays his way. He's not exactly what we were expecting is he?'

A young blonde receptionist asked how she could help.

Tommy showed her his warrant card.

'We'd like to have a few words with Mr. George Andreou. Is he free?'

She had a look at her screen.

'He's in conference right now but he'll be free in fifteen minutes. Is that alright?'

'Yes, yes that's fine we'll wait over there,' Tommy said pointing to a seating area containing a sofa and two easy chairs.

'What questions do you think we should be asking George Andreou?' Tommy asked as they sat down.

'We'll need copies of all the documents he has related to this Matyas. Once we get a full name then we'll be really getting somewhere. Unless they knew each other socially that will probably be it.'

A meticulously groomed man in his early forties, wearing a dark tailored suit and shoes you could see your face in approached them. He looked at them with some apprehension.

'You're the police? Is everyone okay, it's not my family or anything?' he asked.

'No, no, it's nothing like that Mr. Andreou,' Tommy said as he rose to shake hands. 'Do you have an office we can use?'

He led them to a small room behind the reception area.

'I'm sorry, we don't have the police call here often, I thought it must be something...anyway how can I help?'

Tommy showed the solicitor the likeness.

'This man, Matyas, used to be a tenant of your father's. We'd like to know as much about him as possible. Did you ever meet Matyas yourself?'

The solicitor shook his head.

'No, it's been quite a few years since I visited the kebab house, I don't know why my father doesn't sell it and put his feet up, he certainly doesn't need the money.'

'Would it be possible for us to have copies of any rental agreements that Matyas signed, anything with an address or a signature on?' Mac asked.

'Certainly, so long as it's okay with dad. You won't mind if I give him a ring?'

'No, please go ahead.'

The solicitor left the office. He returned a few minutes later.

'Well, it's okay with dad and so it's okay with me. I've arranged for someone to locate and copy the documents. They should be with you in five or six minutes. He mentioned that you might want to speak to Stelios too. I just thought I should warn you that he won't be out of bed until nine or so as he normally does the night shift. Now, if you don't mind, I've got another meeting to go to.'

'No that's fine, thank you,' Tommy said.

Mac quickly interjected, 'Sorry, before you go, I was just wondering what type of solicitors you were, seeing as you don't have the police calling that often?'

'We're business and commercial solicitors, so we're mostly involved in contract work, commercial litigation, property management and so on.'

'It pays well,' Mac commented.

When the solicitor smiled, he looked more like his father.

'It certainly does. I'll see you later gentlemen.'

Tommy checked in with Dan while they waited.

'They're still meeting at four which doesn't give us much time really. If it's still okay for you to take the teacher then I'll get a few hours in bed and see if I can catch up with the taxi driver around nine or ten. What do you think?'

'That sounds like a plan to me.'

The receptionist came in a few minutes later and handed over a large manila envelope. In the car Tommy excitedly opened up the envelope.

'There it is,' he said triumphantly handing a document to Mac.

A name was printed alongside a signature 'Matyas Toth-Kiss'.

Tommy's phone went off and after listening for a while he said, 'Yes we'll drop by now on our way back to the station if that's okay.'

Turning to Mac he continued, 'That was Mr. Meszaros, he said that his uncle's remembered something.'

The enticing aroma assailed Mac once again as they entered the shop. Mr. Meszaros and his uncle were standing behind the counter just where they'd left them.

'Hello again,' Tommy said cheerfully. 'Mr. Molnar your nephew said that you remembered something?'

'Yes, yes. I've still got some marbles maybe?' he said turning his nephew. 'Anyway, his name. I remembered that he never told me his family name but I remembered his first name,' he said triumphantly.

'We know that already,' Tommy said. 'In fact, your friend Mr. Andreou has given us documents with Matyas' full name on.'

The old man gave a dismissive wave of his hand.

'Matyas? That's what the Greek knew him as but I thought we were talking about Sandor?'

'Sandor?' Tommy took out the likeness again and gave it to the old man. 'You knew this man as Sandor?'

'Yes, because that was his name.'

'How can you be so sure?' Mac asked.

'The first time he came into the shop he was looking at all the cans over there on the shelves and he was talking on his phone which was quite loud. I could hear every word, he was talking about a football game the day before between MTK and Honved, a local derby as you say it, and the man he was speaking to called him Sandor. When he'd finished his call, I apologised for listening but I asked him about the game and that's how we got started talking about football. I told him my favourite uncle was called Sandor and that was what I called him every time we met.'

'What did you make of Spiros calling his tenant Matyas while he knew him as Sandor?'

'I asked Sandor about that once and he said that his first name was Matyas but he didn't like the name and

121

so all his friends called him Sandor which he took for his middle name. That's why he said he liked me calling him Sandor, because we were friends.'

Very plausible it all sounded too, Mac thought. He was obviously playing up to the old man by implying he was his friend while Spiros was not.

'Is there anything else you've remembered?' Tommy asked.

The old man shook his head.

'Just the name but I thought that it might be important,' he said looking a little crestfallen.

'Thank you, Mr. Molnar. I think that you may very well be right. In fact, I think it might be the most important thing we've found out today.'

The old man's face beamed as Mac said the words.

He turned to his nephew and said, 'See Bela, if you have any marbles they're going to be from my side of the family. An old man but such marbles I've still got.'

'That was very nice of you,' Tommy said as they made their way out onto the street.

'I meant every word of it,' Mac said seriously.

Once they'd seated themselves in the car Mac pulled out the rental agreement again.

'Have another look at that name.'

Tommy did.

'Matyas Toth-Kiss. What am I supposed to be seeing?'

Tommy looked again.

'Oh my God, the initials! Why didn't we see that right away?'

'Yes MTK, a bit of a coincidence him having exactly the same initials as his favourite football club, isn't it?'

Chapter Eleven

Mac started riffling through the other documents as Tommy drove them back to the station.

'Are you looking for anything in particular?' Tommy asked.

'Yes, sometimes landlords photocopy passports as proof of identity but I can't see anything like that in here. Perhaps they didn't bother as he was from the EU.'

Mac continued reading through the documents.

'They've made a note of his passport number though, that may prove useful, and here's his address in Hungary.'

Mac went silent and appeared deep in thought. He looked at the clock on the dashboard, it was three forty five.

'Tommy, can you drive me back to the shop again?'

'Again? What for?'

'I have one more question to ask.'

The bell rang as they opened the door and Mr. Meszaros looked up in some surprise.

'I'm sorry but I have one more question,' Mac said.

'I'll go and get my uncle,' Mr. Meszaros replied.

'No, the question is for you. You worked at a university in Budapest and I was just wondering if you'd heard anything about how young people could get fake passports or identification papers so they could travel abroad?'

Mr. Meszaros looked a little uncomfortable.

'I never knew anything for certain but there were lots of rumours.'

'Rumours?'

'Well, perhaps more than rumours. For instance, a few years ago there was a student in my university who was desperate to get to England once he'd graduated. He wanted to learn English so that he could get a better job at home but his big dream was to work in the US in Silicon Valley for one of those big tech firms. His only problem was that he wasn't Hungarian, he was from Ukraine and, as it's outside the EU, you need a visa, a sponsor and so on. Even then you might get refused. So, he decided to cut some corners.'

'He got a fake passport?' Tommy suggested.

'No, he got a real one but he used a false identity to get it. He simply went to a graveyard and picked the name of someone who died very young who would be around his age. He then got a copy of the birth certificate and applied for a passport in that name. So now he has a Hungarian passport he can travel to England with no problems. With a passport he can work here, open a bank account, get a mortgage, anything.'

'It's all too simple isn't it?' Mac replied. 'So, in your opinion it wouldn't be too hard for someone in Hungary to get false documents.'

'No, not hard at all.'

'Thanks very much,' Mac said as he made for the door. He stopped after a few feet and turned. 'By the way what happened to the Ukrainian, do you know?'

'He's still here, he's married and doing very well. He has his own IT company and I've heard that he now employs well over seventy people.'

'Good, it looks like the UK got the best of that deal then,' Mac said with a smile.

Tommy waited until Mac had gotten himself back in the passenger seat before asking, 'Now before I start the car are you sure that you won't need to go back again for anything else?'

'Wasn't it a question worth asking though?'

Tommy started the car.

'It certainly was. I've heard of that passport scam somewhere before. Wasn't it in an old film or something?' Tommy asked as he drove off.

'Yes, but it was in a book first, The Day of the Jackal. Even here in the UK, while they say that they check for this type of scam, I'd bet you'd still get away with it more often than not. Anyway, that wasn't the central point.'

'What was the central point?' Tommy asked.

'That someone doesn't necessarily have to have criminal intentions to apply for a false passport, they might just be cutting corners like our Ukrainian friend. Anyway, so far our man is coming out as being squeaky clean, so squeaky clean I'm beginning to wonder if he even is our man.'

'But if he wasn't from Hungary why did he have MTK tattooed on his arm?'

'Perhaps he'd lived in Budapest for a few years and was a genuine fan and perhaps he felt that the tattoo made him that little more Hungarian or both, who knows? Anyway, if he was using a fake passport we'll know soon enough when we get Martin to run this passport number by the Hungarian authorities and he'll hopefully get them to check their death records too.'

They were the last to get back to the incident room. Mary yawned and it set off a chain reaction of yawns in the team. They all looked like they were ready for bed.

Dan went to the white board and addressed the team.

'Okay, so what have we found out since lunchtime? Martin?'

'Nothing yet,' Martin replied without moving his eyes from the screen.

'Keep trying. Mary?'

'As you suggested I got back in contact with the police artist and he's supplied us with another portrait.'

She handed the new likeness out to the rest of the team.

'That moustache was bothering me if I'm honest,' Dan explained. 'It made me wonder if the reason he'd grown it was so he could shave it off if he had to.'

Mac took a good look at the new likeness. Without the moustache Sandor, or whoever he was, looked even more ordinary and even more unthuggish.

'Adil and Buddy?' Dan prompted.

Buddy spoke for them both.

'We've taken both versions of the portrait to the Immigration people at the airport as you suggested. They've put it on their watch system. They said they'd let us know if they find anything.'

'Okay Mac and Tommy?'

Tommy nodded for Mac to speak.

'We questioned the owner of an East European food shop in the town. Fortunately, the owner of the shop knew our man, he even knew where he lived, and through that we found more information. We know that our man lived in Luton for nearly two years and left to go back to Hungary around two years ago. He had a passport in the name of Matyas Toth-Kiss but we suspect that it may be a false identity and that his real name is Sandor something or other. He worked as a taxi driver for six months and then at the University for nearly a year as some sort of technical assistant. Tommy's going to interview the owner of the taxi firm later this evening and I'm seeing some-one who knew our man when he worked at the university. He's also very knowledgeable about football, that's it really.'

The team all looked blankly at Mac.

'And you found this out in just over two hours?' Dan exclaimed.

Mac and Tommy both nodded. Dan looked impressed.

'What makes you think he's using a false passport?' Adil asked.

'The initials of the name on the passport are the same as his favourite football team plus, when he was on the phone, the owner of the food shop heard someone call him Sandor,' Tommy explained.

'So, does that make it more likely that our man is a criminal if he's using a false passport?' Dan asked.

'We spoke to someone who told us that might not necessarily be the case,' Mac replied. 'Apparently students from outside the EU have been known to apply for false passports while studying in an EU country. This saves them having to jump through all the hoops with visas and so on when they want to travel within the EU.'

'Mac, Tommy, great work!' Dan said. 'This really gives us something to go on. What's in the envelope by the way?'

'Sorry, I was nearly forgetting,' Mac replied. 'These are copies of the documents relating to our man's rental of a flat. They've recorded the passport number and there might be other information in here, I haven't gone through it all yet.'

'Even better, can you pass those over to Martin?'

Dan turned and raised his voice slightly.

'Martin can you go through these and follow up on anything you find? See if you can contact the Hungarian authorities and get a copy of the passport photo too.'

Mac took the envelope over to Martin who gratefully received it. He quickly scanned through the documents.

'Some proper data to go on at last, thanks Mac,' he said.

'Okay, it's been a long day so let's all go home and get some rest,' Dan advised. 'That includes you too Martin unless there's something earth shattering in that envelope. Everyone back here at seven thirty tomorrow morning and we'll see where we're up to.'

The team were shuffling towards the door when Dan called Mac's name.

'I've got something to give you before you go,' Dan said as he produced a warrant card with Mac's photo on.

Mac was nearly speechless.

'How did you do that? Are you even allowed to do that?'

'Absolutely you're a civilian employee now, acting as a consultant to Bedfordshire Police. I got the photo from a friend of mine in the Met, in fact it's from your last warrant card. I didn't know your first name was Dennis though.'

'Always was, my family still call me Denny.'

'So how did you end up being called Mac then?'

'Now that's a long story. Thanks, Dan, really thank you.'

For some reason that even Mac couldn't fully understand having the card really meant something to him.

'I just need to know where to pay your salary into.'

'It's called COPS, Dan.'

'The Care of Police Survivors charity, that's fine with me. You've done really great so far, just make sure you don't take on too much.'

Martin had stayed behind.

'Just thought I'd check a few things before I left. I had a quick look at the tenancy documents and this is the address in Budapest where Matyas said he lived.'

Mac and Dan took a look at Martin's screen, it showed a large Lidl supermarket.

'You're sure that's the address?' Dan asked.

'Yes, I've checked it twice. There's a large car park on one side of the supermarket and a green space on the other. The nearest residential properties are quite a way off and they have numbers that are nowhere near the one Matyas gave.'

'Okay, so at least we know that he's not been honest about the information he gave to your kebab shop owner. Home now Martin,' Dan ordered.

As he drove back to Letchworth Mac felt quite buoyant until he realised that he'd forgotten to call his friend. He took the first chance he could to pull over and ring Tim. They arranged to meet at six in the Magnets. Before he set off again, he glanced again at Dimitrios Andreou's address. All he needed was the number, he knew the road he lived in well. Back in Letchworth, Mac drove past the school where Dimitrios worked. It was a large private school for girls and it had a really good reputation.

Mac pulled up outside a house that was just a stone's throw from the school. The house would have been a very big one except for the fact that it had now been split up into flats. Mac rang the bell for number four. He could hear someone pounding down the stairs just before the door opened to reveal an exceptionally good-looking young man with a huge smile on his face. The smile dropped the second he saw Mac.

'I'm sorry but I was expecting someone else. Oh, you must be the policeman my dad spoke to earlier, please come in.'

Mac struggled up the stairs, his back was starting to play up a bit now. Dimitrios showed him into a minimally but beautifully furnished room.

'Please sit down, Mr...?'

Mac got out his brand-new warrant card and showed it to Dimitrios.

'So how can I help you Mr. Maguire?'

'I believe you knew this man?'

Mac produced the likeness and gave it to the young man.

'Sure, that's Matyas, he used to live above dad's kebab shop.'

'Tell me what you can about him.'

'He was a quiet guy, okay to have a drink with, or so I thought. He certainly knew his football and he'd talk about it whether I wanted to or not.'

'What did he do at the university?'

'He worked in one of the research biomed labs, setting up equipment and helping out. He told me they even let him supervise some of the smaller experiments.'

'Biomed? Is that medical research?' Mac asked.

'Absolutely, Matyas had a biomedical degree and from what I heard he certainly knew his stuff.'

Mac felt as if he was just beginning to see a glimmer of light at the end of the tunnel.

'Do you know the name of anyone he worked for?'

Dimitrios had to think for a moment.

'There was a professor he worked with, what was her name? It was the same as the football manager...yes, that's it, Professor Ferguson.'

From his expression Mac could see that the name had brought back some troubling memories.

'Is there anything else you can tell me about Matyas?'

Dimitrios shifted uncomfortably in his seat.

'There is something, isn't there?' Mac prompted.

'It was the way he sometimes used to talk about women when he'd had more than a few drinks. He called them 'kurvak', which at first I took as referring to their shapes, but he said it with such disdain that eventually I went and looked it up. In Hungarian it means 'whores' which is not so nice. I eventually figured out that he actually disliked women for some reason. He was a really nice guy generally but when he'd had a few...'

'What do you mean by dislike? Was he a misogynist or do you mean he was gay?'

130

Dimitrios pulled a face.

'Well, he absolutely wasn't gay if that's what you mean. We generally get on really well with women even if we don't like them in that way.'

The penny then dropped with Mac as to why such an obviously good-looking young man might get a job teaching packs of teenaged girls.

Dimitrios continued, 'Yes, I'd say describing Matyas as a misogynist might be just about right but it only ever surfaced when he was pretty drunk. I don't know, I found it puzzling and not a little scary to be honest. On the one hand he had a need of women, for instance he talked sometimes about using prostitutes.'

'And on the other hand?'

'Dislike is probably too mild a word, I'd say he really hated them too.'

'Hated them? What made you think that?' Mac asked.

'Well the last time I had a drink with him he'd had a few before we met up and he was quite drunk by the end of the night. He'd had some sort of run-in with this Professor Ferguson and he kept going on about her. Then he said he was going to go home soon but, before he did, he was going to teach her a lesson. He was going to show her what a real man was. I just thought it was the drink talking but the more I thought about it, I mean he didn't actually say he wanted to rape her, but he was sort of implying it. I never drank with him again after that.'

'What did you do?'

'Even though he was drunk there was real male-volence in his voice when he said it. So, the next day I went and had a quiet word with the professor and I got the feeling that it wasn't a total shock to her. I heard later that Matyas had been accused by one of the female technicians of 'inappropriate behaviour' I think they called it. I'm not sure what he was supposed to have done but his contract got cancelled and thankfully he went home.'

'He's back again,' Mac stated.

'Good God!' Dimitrios exclaimed. 'I wonder if the professor knows? I can't explain it but I always thought that Matyas wasn't the type to forgive and forget somehow. I think he might be one of those people who like to nurse their grudges.'

'I know what you mean. He's probably been in the country for a while now but it's best not to take any chances.'

Mac got out his phone and called Dan.

'Perhaps he's not so squeaky clean after all,' Dan said after Mac had gone through his conversation with Dimitrios. 'I'll check and see if she's in the area. If she is then I'll get a uniform to her straight away. He can tell her that Matyas is on the loose and to take no chances. Then we'll get her in tomorrow and see what she knows.'

Mac rang off and turned back to Dimitrios.

'Is there anything else you can tell me?'

'Sorry, nothing comes to mind.'

'Thanks, if anything does would you ring Luton Police and ask for DI Dan Carter or leave a message? By the way, if you don't mind me asking, who were you expecting?'

The smile returned to his face.

'My boyfriend Max. He's been working in Germany for the last two weeks, I thought he'd come back early.'

Mac was curious.

'If you don't mind me asking how does being gay go down in your family? Please just tell me go away if you don't want to answer that.'

'No, that's okay. Well, my mother guessed years ago, before I even knew myself, I think, and my other brothers weren't all that surprised when I finally came out to them. However, I must admit that I was genuinely worried about telling my dad. He likes to play the macho self-reliant Greek patriarch and I genuinely wasn't certain how he'd take it. Well, after I graduated, we all got together and I told him. I was so worried because for a few seconds he didn't say anything at all. Eventually, he said, 'I want more grandkids so you other seven will just have to work harder.' Then my Dad's face lit up and he said, 'I was reading about it just the other day, an article about a gay couple adopting a kid. When you meet the right man, you can adopt me some grandkids, so that's alright.' We had a bit of a party after that. I've introduced him to Max and they seem to get on really well, they're both football mad. He's really something is my dad.'

'He certainly is,' Mac agreed.

Once outside he called Eileen, his favourite taxi driver, to meet him at his house. He parked his car and climbed into the waiting taxi. A nice chat later he was comfortably seated in the Magnets explaining what had transpired to his friend Tim.

'So, you've still got it,' Tim stated with a smile.

Mac was puzzled.

'Got what?'

'The old Mac magic,' Tim teased.

'I just got lucky,' Mac said a little defensively.

'It's just that you tended to get lucky a hell of a lot when you were in the force. It's nice to know it hasn't deserted you then.'

'Let's not talk about it. For me it's like trying to analyse a joke, you can do it but the joke isn't funny afterwards. Anyway, it's your round.'

While Tim was at the bar Mac became aware of how tired he was and how much he needed to lie down. The pain in his back was getting worse, just one more drink, he promised himself and then it was bed for him.

As Tim made his way back with the drinks Mac's mobile started ringing. It was Dan Carter.

'Mac, I need you back here as soon as possible. Are you up to it?'

'Of course,' he lied. 'I'll order a taxi straight away. What's happened?'

'Don't bother with the taxi. I take it you're in the Three Magnets pub?'

'Yes, how did you know that?'

'Tommy said you might be there. If you go outside now you should find a police car waiting for you.'

Tim came back and put the two drinks on the table.

'I'm sorry Tim but I'm afraid I've got to go. I'll ring you later and explain.'

On his way to the door he asked Dan, 'What's happened?'

'I sent a uniform over to Professor Ferguson as we discussed. He found her dead. She's been murdered Mac, quite brutally murdered.'

Chapter Twelve

Outside the Magnets a police car with its blue lights flashing pulled up. Mac opened the passenger door.

'Taxi for Maguire?'

'Yes sir,' the young policeman said with a smile. 'You're for Luton Police Station, is that correct sir?'

'Yes, and as fast as you like.'

'Fast I can do sir.'

With the sirens on and the blue light flashing they made it to Luton in far less than half the time that Mac could have done it in. Although they were going at a terrific speed Mac felt totally safe, the driver had obviously been very well trained.

Outside the station Mac got out and said, 'That was great. If you ever do become a taxi driver please let me know.'

'Will do, sir,' the young policeman promised with a straight face.

The rest of the team were already there and Mac arrived just in time to catch the end of Dan's briefing.

'Okay just to go over it quickly again, Adil will be in charge on the ground at the professor's house until I get there and he'll organise the door to door inter-views with the neighbouring houses. We know at least one neighbour saw something so there's a chance that others did too. Buddy's still got some new coveralls handy so he'll shadow the forensics team. Mac and myself are going to interview the professor's boss and see what we can find out from him. We'll join you at the professor's house as soon as we can. Okay let's go.'

Dan waved at Mac to follow him.

'The forensics people might be a while,' Dan said as they walked to the car park, 'I just thought that we might as well be doing something productive while they're at it. We're going to see a Professor MacFarlane, apparently, he was Professor Ferguson's boss and the head of the Life Sciences department. Tommy said that you've met him before.'

'God yes, he's the pathologist who was going to do the autopsy on Henrietta Lewinton. It all seems a long time ago now.'

With everything that had been going on Mac had nearly forgotten about Janet and Hetty Lewinton. He made a mental note to pop into the hospital as soon as he could.

'I take it that you've spoken to Tommy?' Mac asked.

'Yes, he said that he was going to see the taxi driver who employed Matyas for a while. I said that he might as well carry on, see what he could find out.'

Mac looked over at Dan and said, 'You know I'm just wondering if there was another reason why you needed me here.'

Dan glanced quickly at Mac and smiled.

'You don't miss much do you? Martin's done a quick search and Professor Ferguson was a well-known and seemingly quite well liked academic. She's published quite a few papers and Martin says that she's cited in lot more which means that her work is taken very seriously.'

'And...' Mac prompted.

Dan grimaced.

'And the Chief Constable has a bee in his bonnet about the university and how important it is to his patch. I had to ring him as soon as I heard in case the press found out and he warned me that I had to be on my best game...'

...or else you'd get your arse kicked,' Mac finished for Dan.

'Spot on. So, I asked you along for two, quite selfish, reasons. The first being your undoubted talents as an investigator, which we'll need now more than ever, and the other the undoubted wealth of experience you must have had in dealing with the idiots upstairs. If this case drags on a bit, I don't want to have to spend valuable time keeping the Chief 'in the loop' as he puts it. I just want him kept happy and well out of my way while I get some work done. So, any ideas?'

Mac gave this some thought.

'Yes, had the same problem myself once. Eventually I had one of my team who was good on computers put together what we called an 'Investigation Dashboard'. It looked really pretty with graphs and the like. We used to update it daily, mostly useless stuff, and send it to our boss by email. It kept him out of our hair for most of the time and gave him the illusion that he was fully informed without him having to bother to shift his arse from his armchair. It kept us both happy.'

'Now that sounds like a bloody good idea,' Dan said enthusiastically. 'I'll get Martin to put one together.'

'Tell me what you know about Professor Ferguson's murder.'

'Well, I asked for a uniform to go to her house straight after you called me. He found her next-door neighbour waiting outside. He was quite impressed with our performance as he'd only rang the police thirty seconds earlier. The neighbour said that he'd seen someone leaving the professor's property over the back fence and he assumed that it must have been a burglar. He'd tried knocking on the front door but, when he couldn't get an answer, he'd called us. The uniform climbed over the side gate, which was locked, and got inside the same way the intruder did, through the French doors at the back. The intruder had smashed a single piece of glass and unlocked the door from the inside. Once inside the uniform had a quick look around and found the professor in her study. She was lying on her back on her desk and she was naked from the waist down. Her face had been severely beaten on the left-hand side only and her throat was cut.'

'So, there'd be quite a lot of blood I should imagine,' Mac observed.

'Yes, that's what the uniform said in between throwing up his dinner.'

'And you think that it's our man Sandor or Matyas or whatever he's called?'

'I think that he should be our starting point until we find out differently.'

Mac shook his head.

'Amazing isn't it? Five young girls die and one's vegetating in a hospital and, except for chance, no-one would have lifted a finger. One professor dies and everyone's jumping up and down. One life shouldn't be worth more than another but we all know it is. What a world we live in.'

Mac looked out of the window and, noticing they were in the countryside, asked where they were going.

'A village called Toddington. There are some really nice houses there but, unfortunately, they have really nice prices too. I occasionally find some time to take the wife out for a drive and she really likes Toddington. I always tell her we'll seriously start looking for a house there when I'm Chief Constable. There'll be no bloody chance of that if we don't solve this case though.'

They pulled up outside a very large house just off the high street. Mac had to admit it looked impressive but he still wouldn't have swapped it for his prefab.

The professor opened the door himself. The last time Mac had seen him he'd been in his element, confident and in control. Now he looked shaken and quite a few years older.

After Dan had introduced himself and Mac, the professor led them into a large comfortable lounge and offered them coffee. They both accepted. After bringing in the coffee, the professor poured himself a large scotch and sat down.

'I still can't believe it, Fiona dead and in such a way. Believe me, there are plenty of people working at the university who, if you told me that they'd been found murdered, I wouldn't have been in the least surprised but Fiona, well, I just can't see anyone wishing her harm.'

'Why is that?' Dan asked.

'Generosity of spirit I'd say. She was generous in sharing her work with others. She had no ego either, she'd often let the research students get sole credit for a piece of work even though she might have contributed greatly to it. She was generous with her time too, a great researcher and a great teacher.'

'Did she have any enemies that you know of?' Dan asked. 'You say she was well regarded at the university but what about her private life?'

The professor shook his head.

'She had no enemies I was aware of, apart from a jealous few I suppose, but there was definitely no-one who'd want to see her dead. Her private life was as uncomplicated as she was. She divorced three or four years ago and seemed to be quite happy leading the single life.'

'What's the ex-husband like?' Mac asked.

'Oh, I know you people always like to put close family in the frame first but, while I must admit that you might be right more often than not, you'd be way of the mark in Fiona's case. Her husband John and she split up well before the divorce. It wasn't acrimonious and John had been living with his new partner for some time before that. In fact, Fiona has been to dinner at John's quite a few times to my knowledge.'

'We've got his name as John Ferguson. From what you've said I take it that's correct?' Dan asked.

139

'Yes, he works at the university too, in Journalism and Communications. I know that Fiona thought about changing her name after the divorce but with all the papers she'd published it would have been confusing so she just kept it as it was.'

'We'd also like information on all her former students and colleagues. How could we access that?'

'I can show you some of it from here if you like, apart from her emails and of course her private area. I don't have access to those or to information on colleagues for whom I'm not a line manager.'

'Who do we need to speak to in order to get full access to that information?' Dan asked.

'I'll check now if you like,' the professor said.

He went over to his laptop which was on a large dining table the rest of which was covered by stacks of folders and documents. It only took him a few minutes to find what he needed before he picked up the phone.

'Hello, is that the IT Help Desk? My name is Professor MacFarlane, Head of Life Sciences. I urgently need to let the police remotely access a colleague's work area on the system including all her emails and her private area.'

He listened for a while.

'No, she won't be able to give permission as she's been murdered, that's why the police need access. They may also need to access the records of people who worked with her.'

He listened for a while longer then turned to Dan.

'They'll need a formal Data Request Form from you and they also want to ring the police station direct for security's sake. Who should they ask for?'

'Tell them to call Luton Police Station and ask for Martin Selby, he's my computer expert. He can supply them with any formal requests that they might need,' Dan replied.

Once the professor had finished on the phone Dan asked, 'Is there anything else you can tell us that might help?'

The professor slowly shook his head.

'I'm sorry nothing comes to mind but, if I'm honest, I'm not thinking very straight at the moment. It's strange to think that, after seeing all those anonymous dead bodies, that someone you know well will end up on the same slab.'

Dan gave him his card.

'If you do think of anything else, please call me.'

'I will,' the professor promised. 'Are you going to see John now?'

'Yes, he's next on the list,' Dan replied.

'Poor man, he just lost his mother a few months ago. Fiona was at the funeral of course, she got on tremendously well with her mother-in-law. I'm glad he's got Gerry, he's going to need someone when he hears the news.'

'Who's Gerry?' Dan asked.

'John's partner Geraldine, she works in the university too, a student councillor or something along those lines. Do you need his address?'

'No thanks, we've already got it,' Dan replied.

'Okay but break it to him gently if you can. Even thought they were divorced I know that he still had a lot of regard for Fiona.'

Dan promised that he would. Dan and Mac made their way outside.

'Right we're off to Barton-Le-Clay, which isn't too far away,' Dan said as they got into the car. 'Yet another nice and very expensive little village. They must pay these university people a bloody lot more than they pay us, that's for certain.'

Dan glanced over at Mac and he could that he was deep in thought. He left him to his thoughts for five or six minutes but eventually he had to say something.

'Mac, what are you thinking about?'

Mac's head snapped around as though he was surprised.

'I'm sorry, I was miles away.'

He rubbed his face with his hands.

'Bit tired too I should think,' Dan said. 'I'm sorry for dragging you out tonight, perhaps I should have left you in the pub.'

'Oh no, I wouldn't have missed a minute of this investigation for anything. Anyway, you asked me what I was thinking about. I was trying to figure out why our man might have delayed his revenge on the professor for so long.'

'That's a good question. Did you come up with any answers?'

'Possibly. If Sandor/Matyas is our man then, when Dimitrios knew him, he hadn't yet killed. He seemingly had the hatred but it's a hard line to cross, taking another human being's life. Had something happened to him when he went back home? Did he carry out any murders there? His MO was pretty slick so I'm wondering if he'd had practice. Once you cross that line and carry out your first murder, the second is usually easier. We think he may have killed at least five times and he would have made it six except for chance. So, now he's a fully-fledged serial killer, why would he wait until now to kill the professor? He's got to have been in the country at least six months or more, so why now?'

'Any ideas?' Dan asked, totally absorbed in Mac's suppositions.

'I think it's because he's going home or at least leaving the country. He's left her until last because he knew it would cause a big investigation. I'll bet that he's planned how he's going to leave the country and, as he's had at least a couple of hours start by now, he might even have already left.'

'I'll get Martin to send another alert out to all airports and ports.'

Dan pulled over. He got out of the car and made his call as he walked up and down in front of the car. Mac wondered why people had to walk as they talked. Dan got back in and they got on their way.

'The university people have already contacted Martin. He seemed really happy to be getting 'more data' as he put it. Any other thoughts?'

'I'm just thinking about how much of what we 'know' might just be just assumptions. Do we know that this Matyas/Sandor character even killed the girls? We have an idea he might have abducted them but no direct evidence for him killing them. Is there someone else involved and something bigger going on than just a one-man string of serial killings?'

'What makes you think it isn't just him? Most serial killers work by themselves after all,' Dan pointed out.

'True but here's two things that bother me and one just occurred to me while you were phoning Martin.'

Dan turned in his seat and looked at Mac intently.

'Tell me.'

'The first is the hibernation drug. The experts I've spoken to haven't heard of anything like it and the doctor at Luton Hospital said that it wasn't something you could cook up in your kitchen.'

'Doesn't our man have a degree in biomedicine though?' Dan asked.

'Yes, and he worked in a biomed lab for a year but my feeling is that something like this drug is way beyond him. It's got some really top medical people scratching their heads.'

'Okay I'll buy that. And the second?' Dan asked.

'The time the girls went missing for.'

'Well, three or four weeks is a long time but it has been known for women to be kept that long and then murdered.'

'Yes, but it's very unusual, isn't it? Anyway, it's not that, did you notice that three of the girls were missing for around four weeks while for the other two it was only three weeks?'

'Yes, I noticed that but...'

'It's just occurred to me that the two girls who were missing for only three weeks weren't drug users.'

Dan thought about this for a few seconds.

'Yes, I'm wondering why I didn't see that too now you've pointed it out. Do you think he kept the other girls longer to get the drugs out of their systems?'

'It's a good hypothesis. Now, if our man was only keeping the girls for his own gratification it wouldn't matter if they had drugs in their systems. If Professor MacFarlane is right though, and someone is using them as human guinea pigs, that might make a big difference.'

'Christ, you might be right, but it's a bloody chilling thought though,' Dan said. 'Anyway, our best lead, in fact our only lead, is this Hungarian. We can only hope that if we follow him then he'll lead to anyone else who's involved,' Dan said as he started up the car.

'If he isn't halfway across Europe by now,' Mac muttered.

Dan had to stop just a couple of hundred yards down the road as his phone went off.

All Mac heard of the conversation was, 'Yes..... yes.... bloody hell! Where are you? Okay we'll be there as soon as we can.'

Dan turned and with a shocked expression said, 'That was Tommy. There's been another murder.'

Chapter Thirteen

Dan drove back to Luton at speed, sirens howling and blue lights flashing.

'Who's been killed?' Mac asked as he held on to his seat.

'Stelios Andreou, the taxi driver. He was run down just a few minutes ago.'

'There's no chance of it being an accident I suppose?'

'Not according to Tommy but we'll know more in a few minutes.'

They were soon back in the built-up suburbs of Luton. Dan made for the ring road and soon pulled off down a side road that was lined with small industrial units. Mac knew they'd arrived when he saw Tommy on the side of the road waving them down.

A small crowd of people had assembled outside of the building behind Tommy. Mac had witnessed scenes like this many times right after a murder, friends and bystanders just milling around aimlessly because they don't know what else to do. On the other side of the road an ambulance was parked and its back doors were open. Inside a body lay covered by a red blanket. The paramedics weren't attempting resuscitation.

As Mac got out of the car a lightning bolt of pain went down his left leg.

Not now, he said to himself, please not now!

Luckily, once the sudden pain had dissipated a little, he found he could still walk but only just.

'What happened?' Dan asked Tommy as he led him away from the crowd.

Mac was pleased that neither of them seemed to have noticed anything. They too had been looking at the body in the ambulance.

'It's bloody unbelievable,' a white faced and shocked Tommy said. 'I was just talking to him outside the taxi office here when one of the operators shouted that he'd got a job. His car's parked over the other side of the street, the black one there, but he never made it. A silver coloured BMW came out of nowhere, no lights and went straight into him.'

'Any chance of it being an accident?' Dan asked.

'Well, the BWM stopped after hitting him then backed up and ran over him again and once again as he went forward. No, I don't think it was an accident.'

'Me neither,' Dan conceded. 'Did you get the plate?'

'Sorry, I couldn't. The light isn't that great around here but even so I should have gotten something. It was like the plates were covered with mud or something.'

'But you managed to have a word with this Stelios before...'

Dan was interrupted by a car screeching to a halt behind the ambulance. The driver left his door open, lights on and the engine running and made straight for the ambulance. It was Spiros Andreou and he still had his white apron on. Mac figured that he must have come straight from the kebab shop. He seemed to be having an argument with the paramedics, so Mac crossed the street.

He flashed his warrant card at the paramedic who was stopping Spiros from getting into the ambulance.

'He's the father,' Mac said. 'Let him see his son.'

Spiros followed the paramedic inside and he pulled the edge of the blanket down so that he could see the face. Spiros looked and motioned for the paramedic to put the blanket back. He turned and gave Mac a look so bleak that it chilled his bones. He suddenly wanted to ring Bridget to hear the sound of her voice and to make sure that she was safe and sound.

'We're going now,' the paramedic said to Spiros. 'Do you want to stay?'

'He's my son,' was all Spiros said.

The paramedic folded up the step and closed the back doors and they drove off. They drove slowly, no lights flashing. Mac turned Spiros' car engine and the lights off and locked it up. Then he rejoined Dan and Tommy.

'Was that his father?' Dan asked.

Mac nodded slowly. He handed the car keys over to Dan.

'Can you get one of the uniforms to drop them back to the family?'

Dan nodded solemnly and pocketed the keys.

'I still can't quite believe it,' Tommy said, still looking quite shaken. 'It just happened so quickly. Should I have done something? I thought about trying to follow the car but I had to see if Stelios was all right first and...'

Dan interrupted, 'Tommy, I know we're trained to always act, to respond in lots of different ways, but sometimes there's just absolutely nothing you can do.'

Tommy was thoughtful for a few moments.

'I pretty sure it's our man who did this.'

'Tell me,' Dan ordered.

'Stelios told me what happened while Matyas was working here. I think it would be fair to say that he didn't leave on good terms. He said that when he first took Matyas on he seemed really grateful for the work, he was always on time and never missed a shift. Then, about six months after he'd started, Stelios asked Matyas to help him out with some 'special' jobs, in other words ferrying around prostitutes for a local pimp. The driver who normally did this was in hospital and Stelios thought that Matyas, being so polite, might be okay with the girls. Everything seemed fine for a few weeks but then he started getting complaints from the girls. They were saying that he was rude to them and one said he tried to touch her up. Finally, one of the girls told him that she wouldn't get in a car with Matyas again, she said that he'd tried to rape her. She told Stelios that if he didn't get rid of Matyas she'd tell her pimp. Stelios knew that, if she did say anything, then there was a good chance that both he and Matyas would be joining the other driver in hospital, so he had no choice but to sack him.'

'How did he take it?' Mac asked.

'Stelios saw a different side of Matyas that night. He totally lost it, used just about every swear word in the book and a few he hadn't heard before. He said that Stelios wasn't a real man if he took the word of a whore over his and he swore he'd get even.'

'Did Stelios ever tell his father about this?' Mac asked.

Tommy shook his head.

'He knew his father liked Matyas and, as he was living over the shop, he decided it was best to let sleeping dogs lie. Then Matyas got the job at the university and, from time to time, he'd ask his father about him but everything seemed okay. He said that he thought Matyas was probably all mouth but he was still relieved when he heard that he was going back home to Hungary.'

'Dimitrios!' Mac exclaimed.

'What about Dimitrios?' Dan asked.

'He was the one who warned the professor about Matyas. Can you get a car around to his flat straight away and see if he's okay? It would probably be best if they could give him a ride to his father's house, he should be safe enough there.'

Dan rang and arranged for a car to pick him up.

'Good thinking,' Dan said. 'He's got two tonight, perhaps he's going for the hat-trick.'

He turned back to Tommy.

'Anything else you can tell us?'

'Yes, apparently our man had some unusual skills. Not long after Matyas had started one of the drivers had left his keys in his car and somehow managed to lock the doors. He didn't have a spare and, as the car was a few years old, he thought he'd have trouble getting another key from the dealers. He and Stelios thought the best thing might be to smash the glass on the passenger side and then claim it on the insurance. Of course, the problem with that was the driver wouldn't be able to work until he got the glass replaced. Matyas asked them to wait and a few minutes later he returned with a piece of stiff wire. Stelios said he couldn't see exactly what he did with it but it took him less than ten seconds to get the door open.'

'It all fits, doesn't it? I'd better check in with Adil,' Dan said as he took out his phone and walked a little distance away.

'Are you okay Tommy?' Mac asked.

'Not really. It's not exactly something you see every day is it, someone dying right in front of your eyes? He seemed such a nice man too, I felt so bloody helpless, Mac.'

'I know the feeling well. The only way we can help Stelios now is to catch Matyas and anyone else who's involved with him. It might help his father a little too.'

Dan returned, 'I've asked Adil if he could handle everything at the professor's house. He's sending the team home now and he's going to debrief us tomorrow morning at nine thirty so we'll all need our beauty sleep tonight. Unfortunately, before we can get to bed, we'll need to interview that lot over there,' he said gesturing towards the small crowd still waiting in front of the taxi office. 'There'll be a couple of uniforms coming to help us but it will have to be all hands to the pumps. Will you be okay to help us for a couple of hours Mac?'

'Of course,' Mac lied.

His back was getting more painful by the minute but he couldn't refuse.

'Are you looking for anything special?' Mac asked.

'I don't expect they'll be able to add any more about what's happened tonight but they may know something about this Matyas and a few more clues definitely wouldn't hurt.'

A police car pulled up and two uniformed officers stepped out. Dan used them to make sure no-one left until they'd been questioned and to get their names, addresses and contact details. Altogether there were twenty-two people so Dan took eight and Mac and Tommy seven each.

In between the second and third interviews Mac went into a little kitchen area to get a glass of water as he needed to take some pills. Through the window he could see the Road Traffic Accident team in their fluorescent jackets, flashes flickering as they photographed and measured the tyre marks. Like a photograph he once again saw the anguish on Spiros' face in his mind and he made himself a promise.

It took over two hours to finish the interviews and towards the end Mac was flagging. He was only just about managing to keep the pain at bay.

As they drove back to the station Dan said, 'Did you ask anyone to come in and make a statement?'

Tommy answered first.

'No, three of the drivers I spoke to had only started recently and didn't know Matyas and the other four couldn't add anything new. None of them actually witnessed the murder as they were all out on jobs.'

'I just asked the one,' Mac replied. 'He was having a smoke outside and saw the BMW run Stelios over. He couldn't add anything new about Matyas and neither could any of the others. It looks as if he didn't make many friends. 'He kept himself to himself' one of them said. Did you find anything?'

Dan shook his head.

'No, I drew a total blank too. It seems most of the drivers were out on jobs, they only came back to the office when they heard about Stelios on their radios. The operators couldn't see anything from where they sit and none of them had anything to add about our man. He was very nice and polite, one of the operators said. She obviously hadn't heard about his wandering hands.'

'Our man obviously has a real problem with women,' Mac said. 'It was also interesting what Stelios said about our man being able to break into a car so easily. He must have learned how to do that when he was in Hungary, perhaps he has a record there for car theft or joy riding?'

'Good thinking,' Dan said. 'I'll get Martin to check it out tomorrow.'

He looked at the clock on the dashboard.

'God, it's nearly one, it's been a long day. Are you still okay Mac?'

Mac nodded. He couldn't speak because another bolt of pain ran down his left leg, if he opened his mouth Dan would know.

Dan dropped Mac and Tommy off at the car park. Mac leaned against a car and waited until Dan had driven off.

Then, with an effort, he said, 'Tommy, I've got a problem. I won't be able to drive, in fact, I don't think I'll be able to walk more than a yard or two.'

Tommy looked concerned.

'Why didn't you tell Dan?' Before Mac could answer he added, 'You're afraid he'll take you off the case, aren't you?'

Mac nodded.

'Okay wait here,' Tommy ordered.

A few minutes later he returned with an office chair that was on wheels.

'Your taxi,' Tommy quipped.

Mac gingerly sat down and Tommy slowly pushed him up the ramp into the station. He could feel every little jolt along the way and he only just about managed to keep from making a sound.

He rolled Mac along a corridor and stopped outside of a door.

'Your room is ready.'

He opened the door and wheeled Mac inside.

The room was a medical recovery room. It had a desk and a couple of chairs, a big first aid kit and a defibrillator. However, Mac wasn't interested in any of these, he was looking lovingly at the narrow bed that was pushed up against the far wall.

'Will this do?' Tommy asked.

'You're a genius Tommy.'

Tommy pulled back the bed sheets and helped him up out of the chair into a sitting position on the bed. He removed Mac's shoes and jacket so he could lie down and then covered him with the sheets. Mac couldn't help letting out a loud grunt a few seconds later.

'Don't worry,' Mac said, 'when I lie down it always gets a little worse for a few minutes but it will ease off soon enough.'

'Is there anything you can take for the pain?' Tommy asked.

'Yes, here,' Mac said as he took out his wallet and pulled out a small flat plastic pack. 'Can you cut the top off with a pair of scissors, just where the little arrow is?'

Tommy did as he was ordered and returned the opened pack to Mac. He took out a small, clear rectangle of plastic. He undid the top three buttons of his shirt and removed another small plastic square from his right shoulder blade. He stuck it to the outside of the pack. He then carefully removed the two clear plastic wings that protected the gluey surface of the patch and stuck it on his left shoulder blade. He gently patted down the surface of the patch with his finger.

'Do you do that so it will stick better?' Tommy asked.

'No, it sticks fine, you can shower and even swim with these things on,' Mac replied. 'I'm trying to warm it up a bit, the drug in the patch is released by body heat.'

'Why didn't you leave the old one on as well as the pain's so bad?' Tommy asked.

'It would definitely help with the pain but, believe me, tomorrow I'd be going around calling everyone 'man' and saying 'peace, love, dope'. I need to keep my brain as sharp as I can, so hopefully the new patch and a bit of rest will do the trick.'

'And if it doesn't?'

Tommy asked.

'If it doesn't someone might be calling an ambulance for me tomorrow.'

Tommy searched Mac's jacket and found his phone. He placed it within reaching distance.

'Call me if you're in trouble. It doesn't matter what time it is.'

'I'll be okay Tommy, a bit of rest is all I need,' Mac replied.'

He said a little prayer that he might be right.

Chapter Fourteen

Friday 9th January

Mac had to wait until the pain eased off a little before he finally fell asleep. For a while he slept in fits and starts, the pain only punctuated by weird lucid dreams. At some point in the night he must have dropped off properly because the next thing he knew he was being gently shaken.

'Mac, are you alright?' Tommy asked in a low voice.

Mac rubbed his eyes.

'I'll let you know in a minute.'

He got himself into a sitting position and then, very gingerly stood up and took a few steps. He gave Tommy a wide smile.

'It isn't great but it's a hell of a lot better than it was.'

'I've got you a little present,' Tommy said as he handed him a supermarket carrier bag.

Mac looked inside. He saw a pair of shorts, a pair of socks, a shirt and a pack of disposable razors. He looked up at Tommy with some surprise.

'You got these for me?'

'Well they're not for me,' Tommy replied with a smile. 'They're a bit on the big side. Come on I'll show you where the shower room is and then we can get a sausage and egg sandwich in the canteen.'

Mac found that he was really touched by Tommy's thoughtfulness. The warm water on his back felt really good and, with new underwear, socks and a shirt on he felt like he could face the world again.

As they made their way to the canteen Mac asked, 'What time is it Tommy?'

'It's only eight. I thought it might be best to come in a bit earlier, before the rest of the team shows up, to give you a bit more time.'

'To save me from being seen you mean. Thanks Tommy.'

'You really want to carry on with this case, don't you?'

'I do. Even with the pain this is the most alive I've felt in quite a while but, if I'm being honest, the real driver for me now is Spiros Andreou.'

'What do you mean?'

'I saw his face after he'd looked at his son's body. I can't explain it but for a brief moment I could feel his pain and believe it was worse than anything I've ever experienced. I've promised myself that I'm going to help catch the bastard who killed his son.'

'Fair enough,' Tommy said as he held the door open for Mac.

The smell of frying food hit him and he was suddenly ravenous.

'Sausage and egg sandwich anyone?' Tommy asked.

'They smell so good that I might have two,' Mac said with a grin.

It was eight forty five when they returned to the incident room. It was empty except for Martin who was busy tapping away at his laptop.

Mac asked Martin if he'd managed to have a look at the data from the university yet.

'There's nothing much there I'm afraid. It mentions Matyas but all it said was that the contract was terminated by mutual agreement.'

Martin shrugged his shoulders.

Dan arrived just after nine and seemed surprised to see Mac.

'God, you put me to shame. Here you are ready to work and I haven't even had breakfast yet. I bet you've been here for a while, haven't you?'

'Yes, quite a while,' Mac replied as he gave Tommy a conspiratorial grin.

While Dan was away getting his breakfast, the rest of the team started drifting in. Mary was the last to arrive, she looked tired. She pulled out a little mirror and started applying make-up as Dan returned with a half-eaten sandwich in his hand.

'Okay team,' Dan said as he stood at the whiteboard. 'Adil, can you take us through what you found last night?'

Adil stood up as Dan moved to the side and took a bite from his sandwich.

'Unfortunately, there's not that much to tell. We interviewed the professor's neighbour who saw our man climbing over the back fence but, apart from the fact he wore dark clothes and possibly a balaclava, there was nothing else he could add. The door to doors also proved a waste of time, so we're hoping that the autopsy results and the forensics report might provide us with something. We should get them later this morning.'

'Did forensics find anything obvious last night that might be of use?' Dan asked.

Buddy piped up.

'They did say that it looked like the professor had been sexually assaulted but they couldn't find any obvious signs of semen so they reckoned that her assailant probably wore a condom. They're still hopeful that there might still be some trace evidence though. They also found a good shoe print in some soft soil near the back fence.'

'Okay so we'll just have to wait for the reports,' Dan said. 'Adil, can you carry on with the professor? As you, Buddy and Mary have already started probably best if you carry on while Tommy, Mac and myself, will carry on with the taxi driver.'

'Sure, no problem,' Adil replied, looking quite made up to be given such responsibility in a major murder case.

'So, what's your next step?' Dan asked.

'We've still got some door to doors to finish. At least two of her nearby neighbours weren't in last night and I want to make sure that we've covered everyone. Who knows if they might have seen something earlier? I'd also like to expand the door to doors. There's an entry way on the other side of the fence where our man climbed over. There are just the two exits, both coming out into residential areas. Someone might have seen him come out that way and, if he drove, he must have parked his car somewhere in that area so I think that's worth a shot. Once we've done that we'll go to the university and question her colleagues and students.'

'It sounds like that should keep you busy for the rest of the day. We'll go back to the taxi office just in case there's anyone we missed. Then we'll need to interview Stelios Andreou's family. They might be able to tell us a bit more about this Matyas.'

Dan turned to Martin.

'Martin can you read all the forensics and RTA reports as they come in and give Adil and myself a ring if there's anything we need to know. Also, it turns out our man is more than competent at breaking into cars, so check with the Hungarian police to see if he has any previous form. If he has a record it might help us to confirm his true identity. Oh, and don't forget about the passport photo as well.'

'No problems, I'll give Maria a call,' Martin replied.

'Who's Maria?'

'She's a police officer in Budapest, she's been helping me out,' Martin replied with a grin.

'Young and good looking too I'd bet.'

'I thank God for Skype video calls daily,' Martin replied with a cheeky grin that confirmed Dan's speculations.

'Okay team, stay in contact then get back here no later than five for a debrief, unless you've got a hot lead of course. The Chief is organising a press conference for six so even if you are following something up make sure that Martin is fully aware of what you've been up to.'

Dan drove Tommy and Mac to the taxi office.

'Tommy, would you mind if I drop you off here for the day? I'd like you to hang around and speak to every driver who comes on shift. Someone has to know something that will help.'

'Sure, no problem,' Tommy replied.

'Ring me if you find anything, otherwise I'll hopefully pick you up before five.'

Dan glanced over at Mac as they drove towards the Andreou's house.

'I'm really not looking forward to this.'

'Me neither,' Mac said with a frown.

They pulled up outside a large, prosperous looking house in the suburbs. With eight sons Mac supposed it would have to be large. A woman in her late fifties dressed in black opened the door. Her eyes were reddened from crying.

Dan showed her his warrant card and introduced himself and Mac. She introduced herself as Mrs. Andreou.

'We're investigating the murder of your son Stelios. We'd like to talk to your husband and sons about Matyas. I know this isn't a good time...'

'There never will be a good time for this, will there?' she said as she held the door open. 'My husband has gone to work but my sons are all here.'

'Your husband's at work?' Mac said with some surprise.

'He goes to work so he can pretend for a while that everything's normal, that he still has eight sons. This has broken his heart.'

'Was Stelios married?' Dan asked.

'Yes, his wife Sofia is resting upstairs. It has broken her heart too.'

'I'd be grateful if we could see her for a minute.'

Mrs. Andreou nodded and waved at them to follow her. She led them upstairs and then gently knocked at a door before opening it.

'Wait here,' she ordered and went in closing the door behind her.

A few minutes later the door opened.

'She'll see you but please don't be too long. She's looking very tired.'

Dan thanked her and entered the bedroom. Sofia Andreou was lying down in bed and it was her eyes that Mac immediately noticed. They were very dark with deep black rings around them and they had that same look of inconsolable loss that he'd seen in Spiros' face in the ambulance. A woman who looked very like her sat on the other side of the bed and held her hand. She introduced herself as Sofia's younger sister, Lia.

Sofia sat up and said, 'What can I do to help you find this dolofonos?'

Mac didn't know what 'dolofonos' exactly meant but he got the general idea from the venom with which she said it.

'Is there anything you can tell us about your husband and Matyas?' Dan asked.

She shook her head.

'I've thought of little else but Stelly never talked about work much. I noticed that he was upset for a time and I heard from someone else that he'd had a bust up with that malaka Matyas. My husband never let things get him down for long so I was quite surprised at how relieved he was when we heard that Matyas had gone home. It seems he was right to have been so worried after all.'

Dan persisted, 'He told you nothing at all about having to sack Matyas?'

'No, all he liked to talk about was his family and football. We talked a lot about having our own family, we've been trying for a child for years and Stelly's dad is so keen on having more grandkids. And now... and now...'

She couldn't go on and broke down in floods of tears. Dan and Mac quietly made their way to the door. Lia followed them.

'Look after her,' Dan said.

'I will,' Lia replied. 'She'll need lots of looking after, she's pregnant.'

'When did she learn?' Mac asked.

'Just this morning, crazy isn't it? She'd been feeling strange for a few weeks now and it reminded me of how I was when I had my first, so I bought a testing kit. I've never really seen anyone cry and laugh at the same time before.'

'Have you told anyone else yet?' Mac asked.

'No, she wants the doctor to confirm it first, just in case. He's coming over later today.'

'Tell Spiros as soon as you know for sure. If anything could help him at this time that might just be it.'

Lia promised that she would.

Downstairs in the large living room there must have been twenty or more people sitting or standing around. They all went quiet when Dan and Mac walked in.

'Good morning,' Dan said. 'We're from the police team that's investigating Stelios Andreou's murder. We'd like to speak to anyone who ever met the man you knew as Matyas or who has any other information about him. The smallest detail might help us find this man so if you think you can help please hold your hand up.'

Eight hands went up.

'Okay, four each then Mac.' Dan then turned to Mrs. Andreou. 'Do you have a couple of rooms we could use?'

She led them down a corridor and opened the door of a room that was used as an office and another next door that had a pool table and a games console.

'Will these do?' she asked.

'They're perfect,' Dan replied. 'Mrs. Andreou, it would speed things up if you could send another one in when we've finished with the previous interview.'

'Anything to help,' she half turned away and then turned back. 'Mr. Carter, I'm so sorry that I didn't thank you earlier.'

Dan looked a bit mystified.

She continued, 'For sending a car for my Dimitrios, it was so kind of you to think of his safety.'

'Not a problem.'

'I know you'll do your best to catch this…no I can't say his name…this devil who killed my son. Stelios may not have been the cleverest of my sons but he had a good heart. He didn't deserve this.'

'We will Mrs. Andreou, we'll do everything we can.'

She nodded and left them.

'Which one do you want?' Dan asked.

Mac had noticed that there was a large, comfortable looking executive chair behind the desk in the office.

'Mind if I have this one?'

Dan smiled.

'No problem, I can always brush up my pool technique in between interviews.'

Mac made himself comfortable. A few minutes later there was a hesitant knock on the door and Mac felt strangely like he should be saying 'Next patient please'.

The door didn't open so Mac actually had to say, 'Come in please.'

161

A young man of around eighteen came in and sat on the edge of the chair. He looked sorrowfully up at Mac.

'I can see that you're one of Stelios's brothers, you all look so like each other,' Mac prompted.

'My name's Nikos but everyone calls me Nicky,' the young man replied.

'Okay Nicky, what can you tell me about Matyas?'

'Not much really. He was mad about football. He knew everything there was to know about it. We sometimes saw him at the match. I used to go with my dad when I was younger.'

'The match? You mean Luton Town.'

Nicky nodded.

'So, is that what you've come to tell me?' Mac asked.

'No but I'm not even sure it's anything really.'

'As we said even the smallest detail might end up being massively important.'

'Okay, I sometimes work in the shop with Dad, you know Saturday nights and other times when it gets busy. When Matyas lived over the shop he often came in late at night to get a kebab. We used to have a small TV in there and I remember that there was this one time when he got really angry about a news story. I was curious so I went over and had a look. The news story was about the trouble in Ukraine. I often wondered why a Hungarian would get so angry at that but I supposed it was possible he had family there or something like that.'

'Is there anything else you can remember?' Mac asked.

'No, I'm sorry but that's it. It's not much is it?' Nikos said shrugging his shoulders. 'I wish I could help more I really do,' he said with emotion.

'You have helped. What you've just told me could be really important. Thanks Nicky.'

The young man left with the ghost of a smile of his face.

Mac did indeed think that Nicky's information could be important. It might narrow the search down a bit if they knew they were looking for someone from Ukraine who had lived in Hungary rather than a Hungarian national.

The door opened and a short stocky man in his forties came in. He held out his hand to Mac and he shook his hand vigorously.

'My name is Stavros, I'm Stelly's cousin.'

'Full name?' Mac asked.

'Stavros Andreou,' he replied.

'I take it that your father is Spiros' brother?'

'Yes, he's the eldest of the five brothers.'

'Spiros has four brothers?'

'Yes, but only he and my father came to England. The other three stayed in Cyprus and looked after the family farm.'

'So, what can you tell me about Matyas?'

'Not much, if I'm honest, I only bumped into him once or twice in my uncle's shop but one thing I do know is that he really loved BMWs.'

Mac was intrigued.

'How do you know that?'

'Well one of our businesses is the newsagents just down the road from here and I remembered that we used to order some magazines for him when he was living in my uncle's flat. They were just about BMWs and they weren't cheap either. He was a good customer back then as he used to order all the football magazines and papers too.'

'Did he ever order anything else?' Mac asked.

Stavros shook his head.

'No, just magazines about football and BMWs.'

Mac thanked him for his time.

He stopped before opening the door and turned to Mac.

'Who'd have thought?' he concluded mournfully.

163

Dimitrios was the next to walk in and Mac was pleased to see a familiar face.

'Mr. Maguire,' Dimitrios said as he offered his hand, 'I was hoping we might have been meeting again in more pleasant circumstances but...'

He held his hands palms out in an expression of helplessness.

'Have you remembered anything else about Matyas since we last spoke?' Mac asked.

'I've been thinking about nothing else. I'm afraid I've not much to add, just something Stelly said to me a while back. I'm not even sure if it's really relevant.'

'Go on,' Mac prompted.

'My brother said at the time that he thought it was strange reading for a taxi driver. Matyas hadn't told him that he had a university degree.'

'What was it?'

'Matyas had been waiting in the taxi office for a job and he was reading some print-offs from a folder. Stelly had seen the folder before and he was curious as to what Matyas was so interested in. When he got called for a job and left the folder behind Stelios took a look. It was mostly a list of pharmaceutical companies, pages of them, plus some research he'd printed off on a few.'

'Was there anything special about the ones he'd researched?' Mac asked.

'Stelly said he only glanced at the top sheet and that featured an article about a UK company that was setting up a branch in Hungary.'

'When did he tell you about this?'

'Not long after Matyas got the job in the university. I told Stelly that I'd seen him there and what he was doing. He thought that probably explained his interest in the pharmaceutical companies. It looked to both of us like Matyas had been doing some research on possible future employers.'

164

'Thanks, Dimitrios, that's really interesting.'

'I wish I had more for you but...,' he shrugged his shoulders, his face crumpling slightly as he tried to hold back the tears.

'How are the family holding up, your dad?'

'As you can see, we're all here, supporting each other as best we can, but dad...I really fear for him, he loves us all so much. Are you going to see him?'

'Yes, we have to I'm afraid,' Mac replied.

'I know but please go easy on him.'

'We will, don't worry. How about you?'

'I'll be okay, as okay as anyone can be in such a situation. I just thank God that I've got Max's shoulder to cry on. I don't know what I'd do without him.'

He got up and made his way towards the door.

Then he turned and said, 'You'll do your best for our Stelios, won't you Mr. Maguire?'

'I promise that I'll do my best.'

'Thank you, Mr. Maguire,' he said and left.

Mac sat back in the seat and thought how the ripples of an event can affect so many people. For this family it was more of a tsunami than a ripple though.

Another knock on the door.

'Come in.'

Mac was surprised when a black man with dreadlocks down past his shoulders walked in. He sat down and looked sadly at Mac.

'As you may have guessed I'm not one of the family,' he said in a soft Caribbean accent.

'And you are?'

'Jacob Murphy, people call me Jake.'

'And your connection with Stelios?'

'Stelly was my partner in the taxi firm. We've both worked so hard over the past ten years or so, him being the front man and me working in the back office. We were really starting to get somewhere and then this.'

165

Mac was interested.

'Tell me about yourself and how you and Stelly got together.'

'We go back quite a while. Believe it or not I'd been trained as an accountant back in Jamaica but I found work hard to get. These made sure of that,' he said pointing to his dreadlocks.

'You're a Rastafarian?'

'Yes, but unfortunately not everyone in Jamaica at the time was a Bob Marley fan. So, I came to England and guess what? I couldn't get work here either due to this and this,' Jake said pointing to his black skin and the dreadlocks again.

'So, as I didn't want to go home with my tail between my legs, I worked where I could, labouring in factories mostly, before finally becoming a taxi driver. That's where I met Stelly. He was a really happy-go-lucky guy, what I'd guess they'd call a 'people person' these days. I wasn't so good at that but I was good at figures and I'd taken some management courses too. Together we had this dream of owning our own taxi firm and between us we made it happen. We made a good team, Stelly being the front man and me running the back room, a bloody good team.'

Jake's eyes began to fill with tears as he added, 'We were good friends too, the best.'

Mac gave him a moment before asking, 'What can you tell us about Matyas?'

Jake's face hardened at the name.

'Matyas was a very private person. I don't think any of us at the firm could say that we really knew him. The only time he mentioned anything personal to me was when he came into the office one day and asked me about how he could send some money abroad. He said that it was urgent. I asked him if the person he was sending the money to had a bank account but he wasn't sure, so I recommended a local agency that I'd used before. I told him how much they charged and he went away quite happy as far as I could tell.'

'When was this?'

'About a month or so after he started with us.'

Mac wrote down the name and address of the agency.

'Is there anything else you can tell me?'

'I'm sorry no, as I said Matyas was a very private person.'

'Thanks Jake, if you think of anything else...'

Jake looked levelly at Mac.

'I am ashamed to say that I have prayed about this to Jah.'

'Why are you ashamed about a prayer?'

'My prayer was that I might get to meet Matyas before you do.'

Jake stood up and left Mac to himself.

Mac sat there in silence chewing over what he'd heard until he was disturbed by Dan poking his head around the door.

'Finished? Shall we go?' Dan asked.

Mac was more than happy to go. It looked like a few more people had joined the mourners in the living room. They said their goodbyes to Mrs. Andreou and Dan gave her a card in case anyone remembered something.

Outside Mac gratefully breathed in the cold air, trying to wash a familiar sadness away.

'It was a bit oppressive in there, wasn't it?' Dan said as he unlocked the car.

Mac could only nod his head.

They sat in the car and exchanged notes. Mac went first.

'Okay, so what I learned was that Matyas is possibly Ukrainian, that he loved BMWs, that he was actively researching pharmaceutical companies for some reason, possibly for employment opportunities, and that he once needed to send money abroad. I've got the address of the agency he might have used to do that too. You?'

'Only that he loved football and supported MTK, which we knew anyway, but George did say something interesting. There was a family celebration, one of the younger brother's birthdays, and he and Stelios were chatting. It was just after Matyas had been sacked from the taxi company and George was interested in how he'd taken it. Stelios told him what Matyas had said and that he reckoned that it was just talk. George wasn't so sure so he said he had some of his business acquaintances call on Matyas.'

'So, George put the frighteners on him?'

Dan nodded.

'That's what it looks like and it might also be the reason why Matyas didn't do anything sooner.'

'Did you mention the fact that George himself might not be in Matyas' good books?' Mac asked.

'I did but George said he could look after himself and I believed him. Anyway, George also confirmed what Sofia had said about Stelios being relieved when he heard that Matyas had gone back to Hungary.'

'Are we going to the kebab shop now?'

Dan gave Mac a lugubrious look.

'Yes, but I'm not looking forward to it.'

'No, if I'm being honest, neither am I.'

Chapter Fifteen

A short while later Mac once again found himself outside the locked door of the kebab shop and, just as before, he could see Spiros working away inside. He was vigorously scrubbing down the work surfaces. He looked up when Dan knocked the door, thought for a long moment, then went over and unlocked the door.

Dan opened the door and he and Mac walked into the shop. Spiros had already gone back to his scrubbing.

'Mr. Andreou, can we talk for a moment?' Dan asked.

Spiros stopped working for a second, gave Dan a hostile glare, and then carried on working.

'Please Mr. Andreou, we need to talk.'

Spiros stopped and glared at Dan again.

'And where will talking get us? Will it bring my Stelios back? I think not.'

Dan looked at Mac for help.

'Mr. Andreou, this Matyas hasn't only killed Stelios, he's killed others too,' Mac said. 'There are other families out there who have experienced the sorrow you are feeling right now and there will be others in the future too if we don't catch your son's murderer. We need to talk.'

Spiros considered this for some time. Eventually he nodded his head.

Dan indicated that Mac should continue the interview.

'It's Mr. Maguire, isn't it?' Spiros asked.

Mac nodded.

'My Dimitrios told me about you. He looked you up on the internet and he said that you might be the one who could catch Matyas. I don't care about that, catching Matyas won't ease my pain, but now you say he might kill again?' Spiros said as he looked at Mac's face for confirmation. 'Okay, I'll answer your questions if it might save someone else from going through this. What do you want to know?'

'You might know more about Matyas than anyone as he lived upstairs. Just tell us anything you know about him, even the smallest detail could be crucial.'

Spiros thought for a moment.

'Well, you already know about his love of football. He loved my kebabs too, always took hot chilli sauce with them. How I wish I'd put rat poison in the chilli sauce back then.'

He stopped for a moment to gather his thoughts.

'I'm not sure I can add anything else. I worked here and he lived upstairs, I didn't see that much of him really.'

'Please try and think again Mr. Andreou,' Mac pleaded. 'Anything could be important, so matter how small.'

Spiros shook his head.

'I'm sorry, really but I can't. All I can think is that Stelios being dead is my fault, if I hadn't suggested that he take on Matyas then he might be alive now.'

He gave the policemen a despairing look.

Dan glanced at Mac.

'Okay we'll leave a card with you, if you think of anything else contact us straight away,' Dan said.

As they turned and headed for the door Spiros said, 'There was a letter, it was strange as it had the right address but the wrong name.'

'Tell me,' Dan said excitedly as he turned back.

'The postie put it in the shop's letter box by mistake. We're 123A and the flat upstairs is 123B. It had the right address and post code but the name was wrong.'

'Can you remember what the name was?'

Mac found that he was crossing his fingers while Spiros thought.

'Yes, I remember thinking that the first name wasn't that much different to the Greek. The name was Alexander but spelt differently, Oleksandr I think it was. The surname was easy to remember as it was the same as the footballer's, Shevchenko. Yes, that was the name on the letter, Oleksandr Shevchenko.'

'Thank you, Mr. Andreou. You have no idea of how important that name might be,' Mac said.

Before they'd left the shop, Spiros had gone back to his work. Mac glanced back and said a little prayer that he'd never have to feel such pain himself.

'Do you think that might be his real name?' Dan asked excitedly as they walked towards the car.

'It's possible. Oleksandr could certainly be shortened to Sandor, couldn't it?'

Dan eyes widened.

'Yes, bloody hell you could be right there.'

Mr. Molnar tipped his hat to the two policemen as he passed them. Spiros opened the door and the two men hugged each other fiercely. Spiros started crying, his body shaking with the force of his sobs.

Suddenly wanting to be somewhere else Mac looked at his watch, it was just gone two.

'Why don't we check this agency out? Let's see if they recognise the name.'

'Good idea,' Dan replied.

The address turned out to be a newsagent's shop that was no more than five minutes away by car. The shop was crammed with papers, magazines, sweets, packets and cans of food. There was a small freezer and a fridge containing butter and milk. You could also send a parcel, dry clean your clothes and pay for your electricity and gas as well as wire money abroad.

A young slim Asian girl with long black hair stood behind the counter. When Dan asked for the owner she went behind a curtain and returned with an old man with a grey beard and an orange turban.

'I am Mr. Kapoor, how can I help the police?'

Dan showed him his warrant card but Mr. Kapoor waved it away.

'How far back do you keep records on your money transfers?'

Mr. Kapoor smiled.

'You had better ask my daughter Hardit here about that, I'm afraid that I'm no good with computers.'

The young girl said, 'I'm sorry but I can't give you any information about the money transfers we make from the shop.'

'Why is that?' Dan asked.

'We can only input data at this end. We don't have access to any information about our customers.'

'Oh, I see,' Dan said. 'Then who might have that information?'

'Only the head office of the money transfer company in London. There's someone there who I speak to from time to time, when we're having problems with the system. Do you want me to call him?'

'That would be very helpful.'

While Hardit was ringing the number Mac's eyes ran around the shop and fixated themselves upon some sandwiches in a cold cabinet in the far corner. He suddenly realised he was ravenously hungry.

'Joe, this is Hardit from Luton. No, I haven't got a problem but I have the police with me. They'd like to ask you a question.'

She passed the phone over to Dan.

'Joe, this is Detective Inspector Dan Carter here from Bedfordshire police. It's very important that I quickly get some information about a money order that was sent from this office..... No not recently, in fact it could have been well over two years ago.....the name of Shevchenko...Yes please check the name both as sender and recipient. Thanks Joe, can you please send any information to this email address.'

Dan read out Martin's email address. He handed the phone back to Hardit.

'He should have the information within the hour he says,' Dan said.

He turned to see that Mac wasn't there. He was looking intently at something in the far corner of the shop.

'What is it Mac?' Dan asked as he came nearer.

'Sandwiches,' Mac replied.

'Bloody good idea, I'm starving.'

They selected two each and a cold soft drink from another chiller cabinet. Dan insisted on paying and soon after thanking Mr. Kapoor and his daughter they were seated in the car wolfing down their lunch.

After they'd finished Dan commented, 'You sometimes forget that you have a stomach in this job.'

'Too true,' Mac concurred, feeling a sense of comfort that only an empty belly made full can bring.

Dan glanced at his watch.

'It's not even three yet but I fancy going back to the station. I can't wait to see what if the money order company come up with something.'

'Good idea,' Mac said.

He was really wondering if he could slip off to the medical room to spend a little time flat on his back. He was suddenly feeling tired now he'd eaten and the pain was beginning to get worse. Lying down was the only thing that might help that didn't involve heavy-weight drugs and he wanted to keep his mind as clear as possible.

'To be honest I don't want to go home but I could do with a lie down for an hour.'

Dan glanced over at Mac.

'It's my fault keeping you up all night and then I thought you were pushing it a bit being in so early and all. No worries we've got a bed in the medical room back at the station. I'll show you where it is when we get back.'

'Thanks Dan, I really appreciate it.'

Mac was really struggling by the time he reached the medical room. His gait had started rolling from side to side and the tiredness was beginning to overwhelm him. With deep gratitude he slid between the sheets and into the blackness of a deep sleep.

Mac had a strong sense of déjà vu. He was being gently shaken and he could hear Tommy's voice asking him to wake up.

'What, what?' was all he could say.

For a few seconds he had no clear idea of where he was or what time it was. Suddenly it all came back to him.

'Is it time for the briefing?'

'In ten minutes,' Tommy replied. 'You've just enough time for a quick wash.'

When they walked into the incident room Dan came over and asked how he was. His pain was still bad but the tiredness had backed off a little. However, Mac assured Dan he was okay, hoping that, in a couple of hours, he'd be tucked up safely in his own bed.

'Okay team, here's what we've found out today,' Dan said as he wiped a whiteboard clean. 'It's likely that our man may actually be Ukrainian rather than Hungarian.'

He wrote it down on the whiteboard as he said it.

'He appears to be a big fan of BMWs so that might help narrow things down a bit for you Martin. Also, at one point he was actively researching pharmaceutical companies. He seemed to be interested in UK companies who were thinking of opening branches in Hungary and, finally, we think his real name might be Oleksander Shevchenko. Mr. Andreou received a letter addressed to the flat our man was renting with that name on it. Martin is checking the name now with his

174

contact in Hungary. Just so we don't get confused can you all still use the name Matyas to refer to our suspect. We have also just received some information from a money transfer company. Some time ago money was sent to a Mr. Leonid Shevchenko in Budapest by someone who only called themselves 'O'. The money was picked up at a local office so we have no address for the recipient. However, this confirms that the name may be right. The Hungarians have also come up with the passport photo for Matyas Toth-Kiss and here it is.'

Dan stuck an A4 sized photo on the board. It was very like the police artist's portrait and once again Mac was struck by the ordinariness of the face. He could have been anyone, anywhere. Perhaps that was part of their problem.

'They've also confirmed that the real Matyas Toth-Kiss died at the age of three. We've unfortunately not had much from forensics. They've got a good shoe cast and some DNA from underneath the professor's fingernails, however, we have nothing to compare them to at the moment. The RTA report also states that the car that hit Stelios was doing around fifty and only started braking after he'd been run over which was pretty much what Tommy said anyway. Adil, tell us what you found,' Dan said, offering Adil the marker pen as he stood up.

'The investigation took place on two fronts today, talking again to the professor's neighbours and then to her colleagues at the university. We didn't get much from the neighbours. They all agreed that she was a nice, sociable woman but other than that not a lot. One of the residents who lives near the one of the exits from the entryway said that they saw a man in dark clothing get into a BMW and drive off. He noticed the car because no-one owns a BMW in that part of the street. He just thought that it must have been someone visiting. The timing's right but, of course, there's a chance that it might not be our man as there are lots of BMWs around. The university was also something of a blank. We managed to interview the woman who made the complaint about Matyas. Apparently, he'd tried to touch her breasts and, when she told him where to go, he called her a whore and a whole lot more besides. She reported it straight away to Professor Ferguson.'

'Have you arranged for some protection for her? She could be next on his list,' Dan asked.

'I'm not sure that'll be necessary,' Adil replied. 'She's taking some time off work and she's flying home for a while.'

'Where's home?' Dan asked.

'Australia.'

'That should be far enough away I suppose. Make sure she gets some protection in the meantime.'

Dan turned to Martin.

'If Adil gives you the address can you tip off the police in Australia just in case?'

'No problem,' Martin replied.

Adil carried on, 'We also managed to speak to one of the technicians who'd worked with Matyas and he remembered the day he left. He said Matyas never said a single word to anyone, just packed his things and walked out. I asked him if they'd been friends but the technician said that when he came to think of it all they ever talked about was football.'

'Matyas was obviously a bit socially deficient and that's why he being a football buff came in handy. It always gave him something to talk about,' Mac observed.

'Like most bloody men,' Mary muttered.

'What was that?' Dan asked.

'Oh nothing,' Mary replied. She thought quickly. 'By the way the ex-husband turned up while we were at the University.'

'Is that right?' Dan asked Adil.

'Yes, I was just getting to that. We'd nearly finished when he came in. He'd heard that we were interviewing his ex-wife's colleagues and wondered why we hadn't contacted him yet.'

'We were on our way to see him last night when we got the call about Stelios Andreou. What did he say?' Dan asked.

'Not much. He was obviously still in shock. I asked him if he could shed some more light on the situation around Matyas getting his contract cancelled. I wondered if his ex-wife had perhaps confided in him about it but apparently it was all news to him. I asked him where he was last night. I know we have a suspect but you never know. Anyway, he said that he was running a seminar at the University the night before, there were drinks afterwards and he stayed at a hotel in Luton. This was confirmed by some of the people we interviewed and by the hotel staff.'

'Good work team,' Dan said as he looked at his watch. 'Okay I have to go and tell the boss what we've found so far. He's planning on holding a press conference in just over half an hour.'

Mac looked at his watch. It was coming up to twenty to six. The Detective Chief Superintendent was obviously timing the conference so that it would get prime coverage on the live news bulletins.

'Tell him not to mention our man's real name or even that we have a clue about it,' Mac said. 'We're not totally sure of it yet anyway and, if our man hasn't left the country yet, he soon will if he thinks we're getting too close. For all we know he might have a stack of fake passports and with such a forgettable face I'm not sure he'd have that much trouble getting away.'

'Don't worry, I'll make sure that he keeps it generic, you know 'making progress', 'solid leads' and all that,' Dan said before he turned to the rest of the team. 'You all might as well call it a day. We'll meet up again tomorrow at eight and be on time as it's likely to be an eventful day.'

Dan left the room but none of the team made a move to go.

'Coffee anyone?' Mary asked.

They all put their hands up. Buddy volunteered to help her.

'I take it that everyone's staying to see the press conference?' Mac asked Tommy.

'Yeah, might as well. We've all got bits of paper-work to catch up on anyway. So, what do you think so far?'

'It's been a good, solid investigation so far. I think we've found out quite a lot about our man and I wouldn't be surprised if we had him in a few days.'

'A few days? You really think that we might be that close?'

'Once you get a few pieces of information they often snowball quite quickly. We know his name, we think, and we have his photo. We can start doing some serious work now.'

Tommy gave Mac a little smile.

'It would be great to think we could get him off the streets, us, this team.'

Mary and Buddy returned with the refreshments and they all settled down at their desks for a few minutes. Mac was quite happy to sit quietly and let the day's events rattle around his head. At six Adil turned the TV on to the BBC News. A few minutes later the announcer said that they were going to Luton for a breaking news story. Adil turned the sound up and the team gathered around.

The Detective Chief Superintendent stood at the microphone with Dan by his side.

'I know there's been a lot of interest in this case nationally, especially because of the brutal murder of such a well-known and well-liked academic as Professor Fiona Ferguson.'

What about the five girls and the taxi driver? Mac thought. He should at least mention them.

He didn't.

'The investigation has been excellently run by Detective Inspector Dan Carter here,' the DCS said gesturing towards Dan, 'and, although it is early days, Dan and his team have uncovered some vital information about a suspect and have identified the fact that he may also be involved in other crimes. In order to secure his capture as soon as possible I can tell you that he goes under the name of Matyas Kiss-Toth but his real name is likely to be Oleksandr Shevchenko. I have a photograph of the suspect that will shortly be distributed to you all.'

At this point the photo appeared on the screen and all the team groaned. Mac turned away from the screen in disappointment and didn't catch the rest of the conference.

'Going Mac?' Tommy asked.

'Might as well. After that we'll be bloody lucky if we ever see our man again. See you tomorrow.'

Mac rang Tim from the car park and apologised for not being able to make it to the pub. Tim, being the good friend that he was, and knowing how up and down Mac could be with his health problems, took it with a good heart.

Mac was just too tired, in too much pain and more than a little disappointed.

Chapter Sixteen

Saturday 10th January

The alarm went off at six thirty. Mac opened his eyes and felt wide awake. Against all the odds he'd actually had a good night's sleep. He manoeuvred himself into a sitting position and then slowly stood up. He smiled at the absence of any severe pain and said a little prayer of thanks.

He pulled the curtains back and looked out into the garden. It was still dark and rain was spotting the window glass. He showered and shaved and was in a good mood until the memory of the press conference from the evening before came into his head. That still left a sour taste in his mouth.

He went over it in his mind while he made coffee and filled his travel mug. He'd had his run-ins over the years with the 'lot upstairs' as his old boss used to call them and it never failed to amaze him how little knowledge of real police work some of them had.

He wondered how Dan felt about it. No doubt he'd find out soon enough.

He had to drive fairly slowly and keep the wipers on their fastest setting as the rain pelted hard against the windscreen. He wondered which way the investigation would go now. Of course, the cat was out of the bag with regard to their suspect but, trying to look on the bright side, he supposed that it might possibly get them more information to work with.

Mac arrived early in the incident room but he wasn't the first one there. Dan sat staring at the white board, hands clasped behind his head, deep in thought.

'You're in early today. Making sure you beat me to it?' Mac joshed.

It raised a slight smile from Dan.

'I couldn't sleep, things were just going around and around in my mind so I thought I might as well come in. Did you see it yesterday?'

Mac didn't have to ask what. He nodded.

'Bloody disaster wasn't it? Christ you tell them one thing and then they go and say another. There was too much pressure he said, he had to give the press something. I'd have given them, and him, a good kick up the arse if I had my way. Oh well, now it's out there we might at least learn a bit more about our man, who is probably sunning himself on a beach in Timbuktu, if they have any beaches that is.'

'I've been thinking the same,' Mac replied.

'About the beach in Timbuktu?'

Mac smiled, 'No about getting more information. You never know it might all work out for the best after all.'

'We'll see,' Dan said without much conviction. 'Fancy some breakfast?'

'I thought you'd never ask.'

On the way to the canteen they bumped into Tommy who joined them. Mac took a bite from his sausage and egg sandwich and felt immediately better. Police food could be very comforting Mac had found, he supposed it needed to be considering what they did.

'So, what's the plan of action for today?' Mac asked.

'As soon as Martin arrives, we'll see if anything's come in overnight, otherwise, if I'm honest I'm not really sure. We'll see what ideas the team come up with. To be honest as it's a Saturday we might knock off at lunchtime if nothing comes up...'

At that moment Dan's phone rang.

Dan said 'yes' three times and then wrote something down.

He then said, 'We'll be right there.'

Dan ended the call. Mac could see that he was both excited and puzzled.

'It looks like they've found our man.'

'Where?' Mac and Tommy asked in unison.

'They found him in a car on the Ashridge Estate, near Berkhamstead in Hertfordshire. He's dead. Come on,' Dan ordered.

Mac still had half of his sandwich left. He wrapped it in a paper napkin, popped it back into its paper bag and took it with him.

Dan made a call when they returned to the incident room. Martin had just arrived and, when he'd finished on the phone, Dan had a few words with him.

He then turned to Mac and Tommy, 'Let's go, this can't wait.'

'I've let the boss know and I've asked Martin to give me a ring if he hears anything new. I've also asked him to get Adil to find the team something to do while we're away.'

Mac and Tommy followed Dan to the car park.

'Does anyone know anything about Ashridge?' Dan asked as they took the road towards Dunstable.

'Yes,' Mac replied. 'It's an old country estate, a big one too, about five thousand acres if I remember right. It's owned by the National Trust these days and people go there for the forest walks, it's really nice in the summer. Kids like it there too.'

He took his sandwich out of his pocket and gave it a big bite. He suddenly remembered that he used to go there on the odd Sunday with Bridget when the weather was good. It had been one of the few things they did without Nora. Nora stayed at home and worked in the garden and on the Sunday dinner while Mac and Bridget wandered under the leafy canopy of the forest walks that they liked the most. It was something that Bridget had really liked doing until she reached the

182

age of ten or so, when she began to prefer the company of her friends. Mac had been really sad about that.

Looking back, he realised that those walks, holding Bridget's little hand in his while she warbled on about this and that, were amongst some of the happiest moments of his life. What was it Nora had said when Bridget was getting older and more independent?

'We know they need to grow up but isn't it a pity that you can't keep a small version of them as well.'

'It's a big place then, funny I've never heard of it before,' Dan said breaking Mac's reverie.

'Did they say exactly where they found him?' Mac asked.

'Yes, a place called Thunderdell Wood. What a name!'

'He was actually in the wood?'

'No on the road. They said that some walkers noticed the car parked there at around seven this morning. God, you'd think that at this time of the year and in this weather, people would just stay in bed on a Saturday morning. Anyway, the car's engine was running and they saw the driver slumped over the steering wheel but it was the pipe running from the exhaust to the car window that gave the game away.'

'He killed himself?' Tommy exclaimed.

'No-one's saying that yet but, from what they told me, it certainly looks like a possibility.'

Even without seeing the circumstances of Matyas' death Mac had his doubts. He'd pictured Matyas as one of those who would always blame others before themselves and people who think like that are not normally good candidates for self-immolation. However, Mac decided to keep such thoughts to himself for now.

The day was lightening up now that the rain had stopped. Once past Dunstable they were in the countryside and a thin winter sun appeared over the horizon gently lighting up the green fields around them.

They approached Ashridge from a direction that was unfamiliar to Mac but he soon got his bearings once he saw the tall monument down a side road. That was where the visitor centre and main car park were situated.

Dan carried on and then turned left past an ancient chequer-board patterned house and up a narrow road. About four hundred yards further on they saw a silver coloured BMW that was parked on the side of the road. It was cordoned off by yellow tape bearing the message 'Crime scene-do not cross'. Mac noticed that the car was parked in a passing place, leaving plenty of room for other cars to get by.

On the far side of the car an ambulance was parked with its back doors open. Two paramedics were sitting on the step, legs dangling, as they observed the scene. Four uniformed officers were in attendance along with two men in white coveralls. One of them was examining the car for prints while the other was taking photographs from various angles.

'Forensics got here quick,' Dan observed as he parked the car behind the BMW.

A uniformed officer came over and Dan introduced himself, then Mac and Tommy.

'I'm Inspector Rigby. All I can tell you at the moment is that two walkers, Ben and Eleanor Travers-Smythe came across the car at around seven-oh-five this morning. They called 999 straight away and we were on the scene at seven eighteen. We turned off the engine as soon as we arrived and then opened the passenger side door to allow the fumes to dissipate. We were able to ascertain that the driver was dead at seven twenty one. He felt cold to the touch so he'd probably been dead for a quite a while. We shut the door again and called in forensics. I'm afraid that's all I can tell you at the moment.'

'What made you certain that he was the man we were looking for?' Dan asked.

'One of my officers noticed the resemblance. We were certain when we pulled his photo up on our phones. It's him alright.'

'Have you checked the car registration yet?' Mac asked.

The inspector took out his notebook.

'Yes, it's registered to a Mr. Mark Brody whose address is in Stevenage, Hertfordshire. We've checked and it's not yet been reported stolen.'

'It probably soon will be,' Dan said. 'Thanks, Inspector Rigby. I'll just need a quick word with the forensics boys.'

Dan walked over to the car and started talking to one of the men in coveralls.

'Have you had many instances of people doing this before in this particular area?' Mac asked the Inspector.

He shook his head.

'I've been working here for over twenty years and there's been none at all as far as I can remember. It's not something you'd easily forget. I've only come across a couple of cases of suicide by car exhaust fumes in my time and both of those were in their own garages.'

'Isn't it harder to do now most cars have catalytic converters?' Tommy asked.

'In the cases I mentioned both cars were fitted with converters but they still managed to kill themselves. They were both males in their fifties and had drunk the equivalent of a bottle of spirits so they were probably already unconscious even before the carbon monoxide got to work, just takes a little longer I guess.'

Dan came back.

'They'll let us know what they've found when they're finished. Is there anything else you can tell us while we're waiting?'

'Well, the car must have been parked here sometime before eleven last night,' the Inspector said.

Dan looked impressed.

'How can you tell that?'

'It was dry all day yesterday until the rain started around eleven. The road is dry underneath the car.'

'Bloody well noticed,' Dan said, complimenting the Inspector. 'Anything else?'

'He left what looks like a suicide note but it was on the floor on the driver's side so I wasn't able to read it.'

'Was any alcohol found?' Mac asked.

'Not as far as I could see. There might be something in the boot though, we didn't look in there as I thought we'd leave that to forensics. I've had my men comb the woods in the vicinity just in case he threw anything, like an empty bottle perhaps, but we found nothing.'

'What's down the other end of the road?'

'There are just some storage buildings that belong to the golf club. It's a cul-de-sac, the road ends there,' the Inspector replied.

'I remember there being a big house somewhere nearby. What's that used for?' Mac asked.

'Oh, you must mean the Conference Centre,' the Inspector replied. 'Yes, it's no more than ten minutes walk from here. Just walk down the road and turn right down the grass track.'

Mac turned to Dan.

'We'll have to check it out.'

'Let's wait and see what forensics say first,' Dan replied.

They didn't have to wait long. A few minutes later one of the forensics team ambled over.

'Hi, I'm Andy Smith.'

Dan introduced Mac and Tommy. Like most forensics people Andy didn't offer to shake hands.

'Did you find anything we should know about?' Dan asked.

'Well there was a note, not signed, but that probably doesn't mean much in this computer age.'

Andy produced a plastic bag inside which was a single piece of A4 paper.

Dan read the note out loud.

'So many lives I've taken. I've been blind but I see clearly now, I see my sins for what they are and I can no longer live with them. I know I will only kill again, it's in my nature. So just one more death. My own.'

'How bloody convenient,' Dan added with more than a hint of sarcasm.

'I take it that you think he took his own life?' Mac asked.

'That's what it looks like,' Andy replied. 'There were no signs of violence as far as we could see. The prints on the hose and the piece of gaffer tape that was used to seal the window only seem to have one set of prints on them, the victims.'

Mac looked at the hose. It had once belonged to a vacuum cleaner. The nozzle end had been jammed into the exhaust while the other end was held in place by the driver's side window. The hose was very taut.

'What about the hose?' Mac asked.

'Yes, it seems to be a little short for the purpose but I guess he could have gotten in via the passenger door and climbed over into the driver's seat.'

'Did you find any footprints or car tracks?' Dan asked.

Andy shook his head.

'Nothing nearby but then again it had been very dry for quite a few days and it looks like the rain arrived not long after the suicide, or whatever it was, took place. If there had been any prints they would most likely have been washed away.'

'Was there anything in the boot?' Mac asked hopefully.

'No, there was absolutely nothing.'

Mac turned and looked at the car. It just didn't feel right somehow.

'Is it possible that someone could have staged this to look like a suicide?' Mac asked.

'Well yes, that's always that possibility but we've found nothing definite yet to support such a theory. From what I've seen so far, I'd go for suicide, keep it simple and all that.'

'Is it okay if we have a quick look?' Dan asked.

'No problem, just don't touch anything.'

He ambled off again.

'Come on, let's make sure it really is Matyas,' Dan said.

He headed off towards the BMW. The driver's side door had been left open. A man's body lay back in the seat, his eyes shut. He could have been asleep.

Dan looked closely.

'It's definitely Matyas or Oleksandr or whatever his bloody name was.'

Dan turned to see a very sceptical look on Mac's face.

'Somehow I get the impression that you're not all that convinced,' Dan observed.

'There's no evidence to the contrary but I can't shake off the feeling that this has all been staged and that our man here was murdered.'

'Why do think that?' Tommy asked.

Mac shook his head slowly.

'I don't know exactly. Perhaps it's all a bit too neat. If our man was working with someone else the timing wouldn't be a coincidence now would it?'

'You mean after what my idiot boss said at the press conference his partner might have thought that we were getting too close for comfort?' Dan asked.

'That's exactly what I think and what about the hibernation drug? We've had no explanation for that yet and, from what we've found so far, it seems that it's almost certainly beyond our friend here. So, where did he get it from? Besides that, Matyas had to work as a cleaner when he first came over to this country so he obviously wasn't rich. So, where's he been getting his money from for the last six months? If he was keeping the girls for three to four weeks where did he keep them and why? We're still no nearer to finding out what all this is really about.'

Mac stopped and looked around.

'And why here, why drive all the way to this particular spot? No, all in all there are just too many unanswered questions for my liking.'

Dan's phone rang. He listened for a while and then wrote something down.

'Thanks Martin. Get Adil and the team over there and, if there's any substance to the call, tell them to get forensics involved straight away.'

Dan turned to Mac and Tommy.

'Someone called in who recognised Matyas as his next-door neighbour and guess where he was calling from? Stevenage. I suppose that might explain why the car was stolen from there. I've sent Adil and the team over to check. Come on, let's see what we can find out at this conference centre.'

As they turned to walk off Andy Smith said, 'I'll let you know if we find anything else.'

They started walking back towards the car then Mac stopped and went back and spoke to Andy. Dan noticed him writing something down.

As they drove off Dan asked, 'What was that all about?'

'I just asked him if he could pass on an important message to whoever is doing the autopsy. I asked them to send a blood sample to Dr. Tereshkova at Luton Hospital. I'd bet a bucket that he's got traces of the hibernation drug in his system and that's probably why there were no signs of violence.'

'Good thinking Mac,' Dan replied. 'Of course, it won't absolutely disprove that it isn't suicide but it might help if we can find more evidence indicating murder.'

Although the conference centre was only ten minutes away by foot it took the same amount of time to get to it by car as they had to drive half a mile down the main road before turning right and then driving even further back on themselves.

The building was a massive early nineteenth century stately home set in gardens that were beautiful even at this time of the year. Inside the huge ornate lobby Andy asked at the reception desk and they were told to wait.

Dan noticed Mac's face fall. His normal expression was replaced by a combination of annoyance and exasperation. Before Dan could find out why, an elegantly dressed man with the name badge 'Stephen' on his lapel approached them.

'I'm the conference facilitator Stephen Harkover,' he said giving them all a sparkling facilitator's smile. 'How can I help?'

'We're investigating a death that happened not far from here last night,' Dan said. 'A man has been found dead in his car. We're just checking in case there might be some connection as you're quite close to where it happened.'

'Oh dear, how unfortunate,' Stephen said, his smile not slipping a notch. 'I doubt very much that it has anything to do with our clientele though.'

Dan noticed Mac nodding his head towards something. He looked around to see a large poster that said 'BIOMED – Europe's biggest biomedical conference.' According to the dates displayed the conference lasted three days and it only started yesterday.

Dan pointed towards the poster.

'How many people are attending the conference?'

'Just over two hundred and fifty,' Stephen replied.

'That many!' Dan exclaimed. 'Do any of them stay overnight?'

'Yes, quite a few actually. Some of our clients have travelled from Europe and a few from as far away as America and Japan,' he said with some pride.

'Did anything unusual happen yesterday?'

Stephen shook his head.

'No for once everything went smoothly, which is exactly how I like it.'

Dan wrote down an email address. Out of the corner of his eye he saw Mac walking slowly towards the exit.

'Can you send us the details of all attendees, names, home and company addresses, everything you've got.'

'Of course, but I'll need a formal data request before I can do that.'

Dan looked around just as Mac left the building.

'That's no problem, I'll arrange it now.'

He rang Martin and gave him Stephen Harkover's contact details. Dan and Tommy went outside where they saw Mac sitting on a low wall.

'What's up?' Dan asked.

'Our man, he's taking the piss,' Mac stated glumly.

'Tell me why you think that,' Dan asked.

'Well, we've had one question answered anyway. Remember I asked why here? Why this particular spot? Well now we know. Our man's having a laugh that's what. He stages the suicide and, just in case we suspect that Matyas has a partner in crime who works in biomed, he does it in a spot that gives us two hundred and fifty suspects on a plate. We'd be looking for a needle in a haystack except there's no bloody needle is there?' Mac said with feeling.

'You don't think that anyone attending the conference is likely to be our man?' Tommy asked.

'I'd bet a year's wages on it. No as I said he's taking the piss, giving us a shed load of work to do and probably laughing up his sleeve at us.'

Dan's expression mirrored Mac's.

'I agree. Come on, we're just wasting our time here. Let's go to Stevenage and see what Adil's found.'

As they drove out of Ashridge Mac thought of Matyas' research into pharmaceutical companies and wondered if choosing to live in Stevenage was just a coincidence. He remembered there was a plant belonging to one of the world's top pharmaceutical companies near one of the motorway exits. He made a mental note to ask Martin to find out if there were any more companies in the area.

The flat was in a sought after part of the town near the hospital and formed part of a development based around a much older house. Adil met them at the entrance.

'You're sure that it's definitely our man?' Dan asked. When Adil nodded he continued, 'Have you found anything yet?'

'Forensics have just about finished but they haven't found much as yet. They've only found one person's fingerprints, presumably our man's, and nothing else out of the ordinary. We've had a quick look around too and either this guy was into extreme minimalism or someone got there before us.'

'What, not even a passport?' Dan asked.

'Nothing,' Adil replied.

'I'd have expected to find a stack of them,' Dan said. 'Do we have a name yet?'

'Not yet. The neighbours all agree that it was definitely Matyas who lived here but none of them even knew his first name let alone his surname.'

Mac glanced around.

'This looks like it's quite an expensive place to live. Was there any CCTV?'

'No, apparently the people who bought their flats in advance didn't like the idea,' Adil said.

'It makes you wonder what they get up to, doesn't it?' Dan surmised. 'Anything at all from the neighbours?'

'Again, absolutely nothing. Apart from saying the occasional 'Hello' in the communal areas he never spoke to any of his neighbours. They all said he was quiet and no trouble.'

'Yes, the perfect bloody neighbour,' Dan said. 'Do you know if he bought this flat or if he was renting?'

'He was renting and I'm expecting someone from the letting agency any minute. They said that they'd photocopy all the documents they had and bring them over.'

'I noticed that there's a car park attached to the development. Did our man have a car?' Dan asked.

'Yes, a silver BMW according to one of his neighbours. We don't know the registration but we checked the car park and it's not there.'

'We know where it is,' Dan said. 'It's up in Ashridge, it's the car he died in.'

'So that's why it wasn't reported stolen,' Tommy said, 'it was his own car.'

'Come on, show us around,' Dan said to Adil.

Adil led them into the lobby and up a flight of stairs. Mac took it very carefully and was soon trailing well behind the others. A door opened and a woman's head popped out looking at the backs of the group of policemen as they walked on towards the end of the hallway.

She jumped when Mac said, 'Police.'

He flashed his warrant card.

'And you are?'

The woman had a silk dressing gown on which she pulled tightly around her. She was in her late forties and, although it was only noon, there was a strong smell of alcohol on her breath.

'I'm Mrs. Stella Lewis-Browne,' she said grandly.

'I see you pay attention to what goes on around here. Do you know anything about the gentleman who lives down the end of the hall?'

'The young foreign man? I've already been asked and no, I don't know a thing about him. We were like ships that pass in the night.'

She seemed quite struck by her metaphor and went silent.

Mac had to prompt her.

'Has anything strange happened recently? Anything different?'

She thought for a quite a time.

'Now that's a question that no-one's asked me yet and yes, there was something strange. Yesterday I saw a stranger in the hallway, a tall man, I only saw him from the back. We don't get many strangers visiting normally.'

'You opened the door just as you did now?'

She nodded.

'And was he going towards the young man's apartment?' Mac asked.

'He could have been, or Barbara's or possibly Mr. Abraham's, they're all down that end of the hallway. I didn't see where he went, my programme came on the TV so I had to pop back inside.'

'Is there anything else that you can remember about this man apart from the fact that he was tall?'

'He had dark clothes on and a baseball cap. The baseball cap was an odd colour though, it didn't go with the rest of his clothes. That's it really.'

'What time was this?' Mac asked.

'It was eleven o'clock exactly, my programme started at eleven so that's how I know.'

'Thank you, you've been most helpful.'

'So, the young foreign man, what's he done?' she asked.

Mac could see from her expression that she was hoping that there would be lots of salacious details. He decided to disappoint her.

'Nothing, it's just a routine enquiry.'

Mac walked down to the end of the corridor and walked in through the open door. The flat was large and well furnished. A big picture window overlooked a well-manicured garden.

'Bloody hell, this must have cost a bob or two,' Mac said. 'And he certainly wasn't keeping the girls here, was he?'

'That's just what we were saying,' Dan said. 'There's no evidence of course but it looks like some-one's beat us to it. It's all too clean and tidy, there's nothing here that might help us; no laptop, no phone, no personal papers, not even any supermarket receipts. I just don't buy it. If I'm going to kill myself why would I care what state I left my flat in?'

'A woman down the hall, Mrs. Lewis-Browne, said she saw a strange man in the corridor around eleven last night, a tall man with a baseball cap. He had to be going to one of the three flats towards the end of the hallway. The other two flats belonged to a Barbara someone and a Mr. Abraham. Is it okay if I check with them?'

'Go ahead,' Dan said.

Mac tried the flat on his left first and soon heard the sound of the door being unlocked. A woman in her thirties opened the door. She had her coat on and was obviously just about to go out.

Mac showed her his warrant card.

'I'm with the police and your name is?'

'Barbara Townsend but I've already spoken to one of your officers.'

'I've just got one further question. Were you at home around eleven o'clock last night?'

'No, I was out with friends until well after twelve.'

'And you live alone?'

'I do and I thank God every day for it,' she said with real sincerity.

'Might someone have tried to visit you last night, a tall man?'

'No, there's only my creepy ex-boyfriend but no-one in their right mind would describe him as tall. Anyway, I've heard that he's gone abroad for some sun with his latest floozie. I just hope the bastard drowns in the swimming pool.'

Mac hoped for better luck as he knocked as he rang the door of the other flat but no-one answered.

Barbara Townsend came out of her flat.

'You won't have much luck there. Jason's been away for a few weeks now. He's in America on business and he won't be back for another month or so.'

She walked off.

Dan and the team appeared in the hallway and walked towards Mac.

'Any luck?' Dan asked.

'Well, it doesn't look as if our stranger was visiting Barbara Townsend and Mr. Abraham here is apparently in America. It looks likely that our stranger might have been heading to our man's flat after all.'

'Sod them!' Dan said with some anger.

'Who?' Mac asked.

'The idiots who voted against CCTV. It might have made our job a bit easier.'

'I'm not so sure,' Mac said. 'Our man was wearing a baseball cap, now what does that tell you?'

'He wasn't sure if there were cameras. A baseball cap, peak pulled down, will cover your face nicely.'

A young lady clutching a large brown envelope approached them.

'DS Thakkar?' she asked hesitantly.

'Are you the young lady from the lettings agency?' Adil asked.

She nodded and Adil showed her his warrant card.

She passed him a large brown envelope and said, 'My card's in there too if you need anything else.'

'Before you go can tell me how the rent was paid?' Dan asked.

'By cash, monthly,' she replied.

'Isn't that unusual?'

'I suppose so,' she said with a shrug, 'but it does happen from time to time.'

Dan thanked her.

Adil passed the envelope to Dan who pulled out some of the documents and quickly scanned them.

'According to this our man's name is, guess what, Mark Brody and yes, here's a photocopy of his passport which is Hungarian. Mark Brody, that doesn't exactly sound like a Hungarian name does it? He paid a deposit of three thousand in cash just over eight months ago and he was paying just over thirteen hundred a month also in cash. I'll get Martin to see if there are any bank accounts in that name but I won't be holding my breath.'

He replaced the documents back in the envelope and said, 'Come on, we're not getting anywhere standing around here.'

They walked down the stairs and the team assembled around Dan in the car park.

'Everyone get yourselves back to the station. I need to update the boss so grab a bite to eat and we'll meet up at two o'clock.'

On the way back Mac commented, 'It's a strange name for a Hungarian passport isn't it? Tommy can you get the number of the food shop for me?'

A few minutes later Mac found himself once again talking to Mr. Meszaros.

When he'd finished Dan asked, 'Well?'

'Surprisingly Mark Brody is actually a Hungarian name too. I guess he picked it because it sounds like a British name as well, so it works for both countries.'

Back at the station Mac and Tommy headed for the canteen. Dan went off to debrief his boss.

'What do you think we'll do next?' Tommy asked.

Mac gave it some thought.

'Personally, I'm certain that the suicide was staged. Beyond that the main evidence that our man wasn't in this alone is the hibernation drug, then there's the tall man in the hallway and the fact that the flat was cleaned out. We still don't know where the girls were kept and why they were abducted in the first place. We also don't know where Matyas was getting his money from. He certainly didn't make anywhere near enough to rent such a stylish flat when he first visited the UK, so who was paying him and what were they paying him to do? He was also researching pharmaceutical companies and I know that there's at least one very big one in Stevenage and probably more. Perhaps he was working with one of those. Anyway, there are more than enough grey areas to warrant continuing the investigation.'

Tommy, struck by what Mac had said, stopped eating for a moment.

'Do you really think that there's a chance that the investigation might be stopped?'

'Only a small one hopefully.'

'But why?' Tommy seemed mystified.

'Solving seven murders at one go will sure make the figures look better.'

'I never thought of it that way,' Tommy said.

'I'm just hoping that Dan's boss doesn't think of it in that way too,' Mac said feeling more than a little worried.

The team waited silently for Dan at the appointed hour. As soon as he walked in the room, they all knew from his face that it was bad news.

'The boss is suspending the investigation as of now. He's happy that our man was solely responsible for the murders and, of course, the improved crime figures have nothing to do with it. Sorry team, there's no point in having a discussion, the boss has made it crystal clear that his decision won't be changed unless something truly earth shattering turns up in the forensics reports. It's been a long few days, go home and get some rest and I'll give you your new assignments on Monday. Have a good weekend or what's left of it.'

The team disappointedly shuffled out.

Dan came over and shook hands.

'So that's it?' Mac said.

'Yes, that's it. Apparently, there are some high-profile burglaries that need looking into.'

'Burglaries?' Mac's face clearly showed his disdain.

'Probably some of his golf chums. I'm sorry that I've got such a short-sighted boss Mac but I've really enjoyed working with you.'

'Me too, Dan. It's been a real pleasure.'

Dan turned to walk away but then turned back again.

'Mac, if you think of anything let me know, especially if it might help me to re-open the case.'

'You sound as if you haven't totally given up then?'

Dan shrugged his shoulders.

'I still want to crack this case, Mac, no matter what my boss says. Keep in touch.'

'I will,' Mac promised.

Dan looked at his watch.

'Guess what? I'm just in time to go shopping with the wife,' he said suddenly looking grumpy again.

As he drove back Mac found himself feeling a little sad. When he got home, he phoned Tim and arranged for an evening session at the Magnets. He felt as though the sudden end to the investigation had left him dangling and he just didn't know what to do next. Oh well, he thought, a few pints, a foot-long hotdog and Tim's company might help to cheer him up.

Chapter Seventeen

Sunday 11th January

Mac was immersed in a strange dream in which he was running after a police car. It was an old police car, a panda car they used to call them, and he hadn't seen one since his childhood. He'd catch up and would be almost within touching distance of the back of the car when it would move away from him again. But he found that he didn't mind that at all. He revelled in the fact that he was running, the swift confident movement of his limbs and the feeling of the wind on his face. It was the feeling of freedom.

Then he woke up.

He lay there for a moment, trying as hard as he could to hold on to that feeling for just a little while longer but it all too quickly melted away. His legs felt numb and useless. With a deep sadness he knew he'd never run again. He slowly sat up and then stood up waiting for the bolt of pain which thankfully didn't come. He looked over at his little alarm clock. It was just after ten o'clock. He felt a little hung over and remembered his session with Tim. After all of his disappointment over the investigation ending in the way it did, he was surprised that they'd had such a good night.

But now it was a Sunday and he had nothing to do. While he made coffee, he remembered that Tim had told him that he'd fixed him up with a client. He said that she'd be at his office at ten o'clock on Monday morning. Mac had tried to get Tim to tell him more and had failed miserably so he knew he'd just have to wait until tomorrow.

He glanced out the window into the garden and noticed that the bird feeders were empty. Nora would never have allowed that. Mac got the bag of bird seed and fat balls out and went outside. It was cold and he started shaking as he filled up the receptacles. He then scattered some seed on the ground as Nora always said that some birds preferred it that way. By the time he'd made it back inside to the warmth of the kitchen a cheeky red robin was already pecking away at the scattered seed. It made Mac smile.

He watched more birds assemble around the feeders while he drank his coffee. Without him even thinking about it his mind started ranging over the case. A sudden thought occurred to him. There was after all at least one thing he could do today.

The drive to Luton was easy in the Sunday traffic. The hospital ward wasn't quite as frenetic as it had been last time he'd visited. He looked at the patients' names on the white board and couldn't see Hetty's anywhere. Mac had a very bad feeling for a moment until he asked a nurse. She assured him that Hetty was alright, she'd improved and had been moved to another ward.

The ward was unfortunately quite a walk away. When Mac looked through the glass panel in the door, he could see Janet Lewinton sitting by the side of a bed reading aloud from a book. He really admired her determination.

'Mrs. Lewinton?' Mac said as he approached the bed.

'Why it's Mr. Maguire. How are you?' she asked with a smile.

Mac thought that she looked tired.

'Never mind me, how's Hetty doing?'

'Getting better I believe. They say that she's slowly coming around but they're still not sure how much damage has been done.'

Mac looked down at Hetty. She looked very pretty and had a childlike quality about her as she slept. He had to admit that she looked better than he'd expected.

'There's still hope then?'

'Yes, there's still hope Mr. Maguire, there's always hope.'

'I take it you heard that we found the man who we think did this to Hetty? That he's dead?'

'Yes, it was on the news but I must admit I can't get angry about him.'

Mac was intrigued.

'Why is that?' he asked.

'When I saw Hetty on that slab in the morgue it wasn't that much of a surprise. It just happened a bit sooner than I thought it would, that's all. The way she'd been going, the drugs, the life she led, it was inevitable that she'd end up there before long. This way there might be a chance. If she comes back to me then she'll have been off drugs for quite a while and she might have a real chance at leading another life, the one I wanted for her.'

Mac hadn't thought of it that way but he had to admit that she had a point. He left with Janet's promise that she'd let him know if there was any change.

The car almost drove itself to the Europeast food shop. He told himself he should try some of the foods that contributed to such a lovely aroma every time he'd walked into the shop but he knew that he was just kidding himself. He was still on the case. Mr. Meszaros was once again at his station behind the deli counter.

'Good day Mr. Maguire. What can I do for the police?'

'I'm not a policeman today, Mr. Meszaros. Today I've come to buy some of your wonderful looking food. What can you recommend?'

'I can put together a little taster package that I do for people who want to try our food if you like?'

Mac did.

Mr. Meszaros took out a sheet of clear plastic and began assembling slices of sausages, cheese and some other stuff that Mac couldn't identify. He wrapped this up carefully and put it in a bag. He then took a plastic cup and placed three small pickled cucumbers inside and fitted a lid.

He handed them to Mac and said, 'There you go, a snack fit for a king.'

As Mac was paying, he said, 'I suppose you heard about Sandor on the news yesterday?'

'I did. My uncle came running downstairs and he was all breathless. I thought he was having a heart attack or something until I finally got it out of him. A very bad business all round.'

'I don't suppose that you or your uncle have thought of anything new since?'

Mr. Meszaros slowly shook his head.

'I'm sorry, no. My uncle was surprised though when he heard that Sandor was originally from Ukraine. He said he was so sure that he'd been born in Budapest.'

'Yes, he was good at fooling people, wasn't he?'

'So that's over anyway,' Mr. Meszaros observed.

'Yes, that's over.'

Mac only wished it was. He hated unfinished business.

He drove home and tried to think of what he could do for the rest of the day. Unfortunately, Tim had a stall at a market over the other side of Hertfordshire so he'd be unavailable until the evening. As it was the decision was taken out of Mac's hands.

The simple action of stepping out of the car caused a huge spasm of pain to grip his back. He must have blacked out for a moment because he found himself on his hands and knees with no idea how he'd gotten there. The pain receded just long enough for him to get into the house. He had just closed the door behind him when it hit him again. This was the worst of all the types of pain that Mac experienced. It felt as though all the muscles in his lower back were locked in a cramp and it was absolutely unbearable. He had to wait a number of minutes before the pain receded enough for him to make an attempt to get into the kitchen. He found that his face was wet with tears.

He finally made it into the kitchen and threw his shopping in the fridge. He quickly took two little blue pills and put on another pain patch. The blue pills normally took about half an hour to knock him out and he always slept for at least twelve hours afterwards. He desperately hoped that this would be the case today.

He stumbled to his bed and threw his clothes on the floor. He hesitated for a second before lying down, the pain always got worse before it got better. This time was no different but he was still surprised when a loud grunt left his lips. He knew that he just had to hold on and it would soon get better. It was probably his own fault anyway, he told himself. He'd been doing more than he should and, almost every time he did that, there was an inevitable payback. The pain gripped him again but it wasn't quite so bad this time. After what seemed an eternity, he gratefully drifted off into a dream filled sleep.

Chapter Eighteen

Monday 12th January

He awoke and for a while he had no idea what day it was. It was dark outside. He looked over at the alarm clock and the luminous dial told him that it was six thirty but he didn't know whether it was six thirty in the evening or the morning. Then he remembered the pain and said a little prayer that it had gone away.

He lay there for a while knowing that he'd have to move eventually as he desperately needed to pee. He gathered up his courage and slowly sat up, so far so good. He then stood up and checked his pain levels. A remnant was still there but it was only a faint echo of the agonising pain that had stopped him in his tracks.

He stumbled to the toilet, leaning on the wall as he went as his left leg wasn't quite doing as he ordered, and he was more than grateful to release the pressure on his bladder. He wondered if he should go back to bed but he felt so wide awake that he thought he'd at least have a drink before trying. He poured himself a large orange juice and swallowed it in one gulp. He then had to pour some more to wash down his pills. He turned the radio on in the kitchen and was amazed to find that it was Monday morning. The little blue pills had done far more than he'd expected, he must have been asleep for nearly eighteen hours. He figured that, with all the running around he'd been doing recently, he probably needed it.

He took off the oldest patch and made himself a pot of coffee. After he'd had a cup he then showered and shaved. While he was shaving, he thought about the mysterious client he was due to meet in just over three hours and felt glad that he had something to do with his day.

He poured himself another cup of coffee and turned on the TV. The third item on the news was that the Bedfordshire Police had caught a serial killer responsible for at least the death of seven people. Mac saw Dan's boss standing at the microphone thanking the team who had done such wonderful work. One reporter asked him if he thought Oleksandr Shevcheko had committed suicide because he knew the police were hot on his trail. He replied that it was highly likely and, although he had escaped the full punish-ment for his crimes, good solid police work had ensured that he wouldn't kill again. He could see Dan standing behind his boss rolling his eyes heavenwards. He all too obviously didn't agree.

He knew that, unfortunately, he'd be chewing on this case for weeks to come. He'd never been any good with unsolved cases and he was still desperately hoping that he might be able to come up with something that might make Dan's boss open it up again. He took his time drinking his second cup and found it was a quarter to eight when he next looked at the clock. He had an idea.

He remembered seeing it advertised in the Magnets 'Breakfast from 8 a.m.' so he thought why not? He was standing outside when one of the staff opened the pub for business.

It was a barmaid that he knew, she looked a bit bleary eyed.

'You're looking a bit tired this morning Kate,' Mac observed as he waited at the bar to order his meal.

'Yes, I had to fill in last night, they were two staff short. I didn't get to bed until after two,' she explained. 'You're looking quite wide awake though. We don't see you here so early normally.'

'I got to bed after twelve myself, so I've had a few hours more,' he said, not mentioning the fact that it was after twelve noon.

He ordered the big breakfast. He was suddenly hungry as he remembered that he hadn't eaten at all the day before. After he'd eaten, he ordered another coffee to go and it was just before nine o'clock when he opened the door to his office.

He stood at the window and sipped his drink as he looked out at the comings and goings in the large car park at the rear of his building. The day was overcast and grey but at least it wasn't raining. Staff from the council offices were parking up their cars and trudging wearily off into another Monday morning.

He looked at the spot where she'd stood in the rain, frozen with grief as the knowledge of the death of her only child finally hit her. Meeting Janet Lewinton had certainly sent him on an unexpected path and one he'd enjoyed taking for the most. It had showed him how important it was that he kept working. The unsatisfactory ending still galled him though.

Tim said his client wouldn't arrive before ten but he liked being early anyway. He wondered what his client might be like and why Tim wouldn't tell him anything. His thoughts were interrupted by a flash of yellow appearing around the corner. A Porsche sports car, brakes squealing, pulled up abruptly outside his window. A woman got out and, without bothering to lock the car, made her way to his back door. All he could see was her long blonde hair swirling in the breeze. His client was early.

She came in and glanced around the room without making eye contact. She turned her back, stood in the exact spot that Mac had been standing in a few seconds before, and gazed out of the window. He sat down behind his desk and gave her the time that she obviously needed.

He studied her closely. Blonde hair, an expensive cut he'd guess. Designer clothes too, really good quality and made to measure, her slim figure showed them off to advantage. It didn't require any detective skills to figure out that, between the car and the clothes, she must have some serious money.

'You used to be a policeman,' she said without turning.

Her voice was cut-glass English upper class.

'Yes, I used to be a policeman.'

The woman turned around. Mac guessed she was in her late twenties and quite pretty if her face hadn't been contorted by some inner pain. He also noticed that her nails were bitten to the quick.

'You solved some famous murders, I looked you up on the internet last night. I mean, I trust Tim, but I was curious. I read that you had to retire because of ill health,' she said glancing at Mac's crutch balanced in the corner of the room.

'That's true too,' he conceded.

Mac really didn't want to talk about himself so he changed the subject.

'How do you know Tim?' he asked, gesturing for the woman to sit down.

She sat down and said, 'Tim? I've known him since I was young. My father used to employ him to renovate all the antique stuff he bought. Tim's a wizard at restoring old furniture. When I was home from school, he used to let me watch him work and we'd talk about things.'

Mac could well believe that, Tim was a talker all right. Right at that moment the penny dropped. He knew who she was.

'Anyway, we became friends, he still helps me with all the furniture daddy left. Daddy died just over four years ago'.

'Do you miss him?'

209

'How can you miss what was never there?' she said with a shrug. 'I used to come home from school and I'd be all alone in that old house while he'd be off wherever, making yet more money. There was only Tim and one of the servants I could talk to. I've always hated being alone.'

She looked sad for a moment and then realised that she hadn't even told Mac her name.

'I'm so sorry Mr. Maguire, I haven't even introduced myself. My name is Laura de Vesey, my father was Hubert de Vesey.'

He knew who her father was, everyone did. He'd made his money buying up companies cheap and ruthlessly asset stripping them. He'd ended up not quite as rich as the Queen but not far off. If anyone needed an anti-capitalist pantomime villain it was Hubert de Vesey's name that usually cropped up.

Tim had hated her father and not only for his ruthless business tactics. Tim had always wanted children but he and his wife hadn't been that lucky. Laura's mother had died young and the way her father ignored her, when Tim could see how desperate she was for love, had made him really angry.

He remembered Tim saying, 'Some people just don't know what's valuable in life.'

A fleeting sadness went through him as he realised how true this was.

'So, Laura, how can I help you?' Mac asked gently.

She stood up and returned to the window.

With her still back turned she eventually said, 'It's my boyfriend, I'm pretty sure that he's cheating on me. I need you to find out who he's seeing so I can end it.'

He now knew why Tim hadn't told him anything about his client and why she needed his help. Mac Maguire, ex-head of the London Murder Squad, finally reduced to chasing around after wayward boyfriends.

He would bet good money that Tim was gambling on him being unable to refuse a woman in trouble.

He sighed. The trouble with best friends is they end up knowing you all too well.

'Tell me about him,' Mac said now fully resigned to his fate.

She sat down again and smiled, her face lighting up as she remembered better times.

'We met in one of the best salons in London. He was young and beautiful and he really knew how to cut hair. After he'd cut my hair once I never let anyone else near it. I gradually began to get feelings for him and then one day, right out of the blue, he asked me out for dinner. We had such a lovely time, he said he really liked me too and I so wanted to believe him. We became very close, Giorgio quit his job and we travelled the world. God, those days were so much fun, when it was just the two of us. I kept telling myself it was just a thing but, in the end, I couldn't help myself and, against my better judgment, I fell in love with him. I couldn't sleep last night so I had a look at some of the photos we took back then. I was so happy and I thought he was too, but, if I'm honest, I knew in my heart that it had to end someday. It always ends.'

'You've been cheated on before?'

She got up again and went back to the window.

'Yes, Laura de Vesey the walking cash machine, that's me. You know I've heard it said that people envy me but if only they knew, money can be such a curse. Every time I've trusted a man, even my own father, I've been let down. At the end of the day it always turned out that it was the money that mattered most. But Giorgio, I thought he was different, I thought…oh, what does it bloody matter what I thought!' she said angrily.

He suspected that her anger was directed mostly at herself.

211

'Laura, please sit down,' Mac said softly. 'Tell me about Giorgio.'

She did as he asked.

'God, you hear about these rich women falling in love with their hairdressers all the time, how bloody original is that? But it wasn't like that Mr. Maguire, it really wasn't. He's younger than me, but just by a couple of years, and he's the most caring man I've ever met. Giorgio gave me hope, I was sure that he loved me too. Perhaps he did for a while but nothing lasts does it?'

'When did you start suspecting that he was seeing someone else?'

'It was gradual but looking back I suppose he started losing interest in me about six or seven months ago. He didn't want to travel any more, he said fun can only last so long and he needed to be doing something. So now he's 'doing something' while I just sit at home all day.'

'What does he do?'

'He's gone back to hairdressing and in a short time he's built his salon up to become one of the best in London. He's incredibly good at what he does and, if I'm honest, I envy him his success a little. What have I ever done apart from having money?'

'I take it that you provided the funds to start his business off?' Mac asked.

Laura nodded.

'He's a good investment though, I lent him just over a million and he's already paid nearly half of it back.'

Mac saw a despairing look pass over Laura's face.

'And I take it that you're worried that, once it's all paid back, then he won't need you anymore?'

'Yes, why would he? He can make his own money doing something he's good at and loves doing. What else have I got to offer other than money?'

Mac wondered at such a young, elegant and obviously intelligent woman thinking so little of herself.

'So, what specifically makes you think that there's another woman is involved?'

'History I suppose, it always ends that way but there are other things. I'll admit that he's been working hard and he doesn't spend as much time at home as he used to but I feel that there's a distance beginning to build between us. Who knows, perhaps it was already there and it was just my imagination that he cared at all.'

'What makes you think that?'

'I've known him for over a year now and he's never told me much about his life before we met or his family. He let it slip once he has a sister but I've never met her. He's always avoided talking about his family, mention family and he'd change the subject. But I never pressed him, not once, I didn't want to spoil things. I think he must have had an unhappy childhood though. I've seen him quite sad at times but he never tells me anything. If you love someone, aren't you supposed to tell them everything? God, I've been such a bloody fool again, haven't I? I never see it coming. Anyway, that's all I know, he has a sister, who is married and lives in Watford somewhere.'

Mac was intrigued.

'Have you any idea why he never took you to see his sister?'

She shrugged.

'I used to think it was because he was ashamed of her for some reason, I mean Watford, not very upmarket is it?'

'You don't think that now though,' he stated.

'No, no I don't. Last week I picked up the phone. Giorgio must have thought I was out, he was on the extension talking to a woman.'

She glanced at Mac shame-faced.

213

'I know I shouldn't have listened in but I thought at last that this was her, the woman he's been seeing, and I just couldn't help myself. Mr. Maguire, I've been so unhappy.'

He could see the seeds of tears forming in her eyes. He wanted to spare her the indignity of crying in front of a stranger.

'Can I get you a glass of water?'

Laura nodded.

Mac went next door where there was a little kitchen area and gave her a few minutes.

'Thanks,' she said as he gave her the glass.

'You were saying that you overheard Giorgio...'

'God my heart was thumping so hard that I thought I'd pass out but I calmed down when I realised that it was only his sister he was talking to. I'm an only child and I must admit that I was jealous of the way they spoke to each other, so easily and so full of love. It was obvious that he loves every bone in her body.'

'How did she sound?'

'Nice, really nice, like someone I'd like to meet. It didn't take me long to work out that if he wasn't ashamed of her, it must be me that he's ashamed of.'

Mac had no answer to that.

'Have you got a photo?'

She pulled a photo out of her pocket and put it on the desk. Mac glanced at it. Giorgio was young and very good looking but there was something familiar about him, something he couldn't quite put a finger on.

Mac thought that Laura's suspicions were all a bit nebulous so far, so he tried again.

'Is there anything else that makes you suspect Giorgio is having an affair?'

'Yes, every second Friday afternoon he disappears from the salon. None of his staff know where he goes and, when I asked him directly, he made up some story about seeing an old friend. I knew he was lying of course, more like an old flame I'd say. Will you take my case Mr. Maguire?'

He knew he was in a corner. When he'd agreed to try out being a private detective, he hadn't figured on chasing around after unfaithful boyfriends. However, he also knew that he desperately needed to be doing something.

'Yes, I'll take the case.'

He observed her as he said this. Her expression was a mixture of relief and fear.

'Tell me about Giorgio's routine.'

'He leaves the house around six thirty every morning except for Sundays and comes back late, usually around seven or eight. Sometimes it's even later than that and he always says it's because he had a 'special client'. I just don't know what to believe anymore.'

'What does he drive?'

'A black Audi TT.'

'Bought by you?' Mac asked.

Laura nodded.

'Okay Laura, I just need your address and a phone number.'

She rummaged about in her pocket and produced a card.

'It's all on there. Try the mobile number first just in case I'm out. I've put the address of Giorgio's salon on the back.'

'I'll report in when I know something. By the way when's the next 'second Friday'?'

'It's this Friday coming. Thank you, Mr. Maguire, I just need to know the truth, to be put out of my misery. If he is seeing someone, find out who she is so that I can end it. I thought Giorgio wasn't like the rest, I really did, and somewhere in here,' she said holding a hand over her heart, 'I still hope. I still hope Mr. Maguire and it's bloody killing me.'

She was making for the door when he said, 'Don't you want to know what I charge?'

'Charge whatever you like, I've got lots of money, everybody knows that,' she said with a twisted smile and left.

He sighed and picked up the boyfriend's photo again and studied it. Where did he go every second Friday? And why didn't Giorgio want to talk about his previous life and his family? What was he hiding?

Mac was certain he'd seen that face before and, considering his previous line of employment, this didn't bode well for Laura de Vesey.

Chapter Nineteen

Tuesday 13th January

Mac sat motionless as he waited for the Audi to appear. He'd been waiting since before six o'clock. He'd decided to follow Giorgio's car into London just in case he made any side trips on his way in. He'd parked his Almera a hundred yards or so before the huge electric gate behind which, somewhere, stood the De Vesey house.

He'd checked it out yesterday in daylight so he'd be sure of finding the best place to park up, somewhere he wouldn't be seen by a car leaving the house. He'd stopped in front of the gate first and looked down the long drive on the other side. There was no sign of a house. He wondered just how big the grounds were.

He took a sip of coffee from his travel mug and thought of the hundreds of times that he'd pulled observation duty. When he'd been in the force, he knew that many of his colleagues hadn't like going on observation with him as he hardly said a word. He'd always thought it was a good time for reflection and, anyway, he felt he should be actually observing, paying real attention to what was going on outside the car window. He glanced over at the passenger seat and remembered that for a lot of those times his sergeant, Peter Harper, had accompanied him. Silence had suited them both. All that was there now was his crutch, leaning against the passenger door. With a twinge of remorse, he also remembered Peter knocking on his front door not much more than a couple of months ago. He'd hid in the kitchen.

For once he was more than grateful when his thoughts were interrupted by the electric gates gliding silently open. He started his ageing car up and waited for the Audi to appear. The black car, headlights on, eased out of the gates and made towards the main road. Mac followed the red tail lights not worrying if Giorgio spotted him. His old green Nissan was anonymous and wouldn't get a second glance.

The Audi made towards London on the motorway. He had no problem following Giorgio, he was just one in a sea of cars so he kept as close as possible. They were heading towards Central London, a trip that Mac had made almost every day when he'd been working. They went straight down the Edgware Road and, although it was still early, they still hit some traffic. They then went around the side of Hyde Park where the Audi made its way to Belgrave Square before finally pulling up outside a shop down one of the side streets. Giorgio got out, pulled out some keys and opened the front door of the shop.

Mac knew this area fairly well. He'd always called it 'Embassy Land' as there seemed to be at least three or four of them on every street. Mac looked around. The street was signed 'One way only' with parking bays on one side and double yellow lines on the other. He parked on the double yellows in a place where he wouldn't be obstructing traffic and where he could get a good view of the shop front. He thought it ironic that one of the very few perks of being disabled and in constant pain was that he could park virtually anywhere he liked. He got his disabled blue badge and time disc out of the glove, placed them on the dashboard and started earning his money.

He'd only ever come to this part of town before on police business. He could remember at least three cases that involved embassy staff, a pain in the arse every one of them due to having to dance around diplomatic immunity. He looked across the street. The shop Giorgio had just entered was surrounded by expensive restaurants and retailers whose windows had never been coarsened by a price tag.

The shop front was elegant and restrained and the sign above the shop simply said 'Capelli Giorgio'. The lights came on and behind the large plate glass window Mac could see a row of padded chairs and high-tech hair dryers, all coloured white. He got his tablet out and typed the shop's name into Google Translate. It meant 'Hair by George' in Italian. Again, he felt the same tickle in his brain as he had when he'd first seen Giorgio's photo. He felt it should have some significance for him but again it proved elusive. He searched to see if there was a web site and, while the site was elegant and expansive about the business, it revealed nothing about Mr. Lo Bianco that he didn't already know.

A young woman arrived. She was very pretty and she gave Giorgio a wide smile. Was this the love interest Mac wondered? However, Giorgio just gave her a quick hug and a peck on the cheek, hardly the actions of a lover.

She listened intently as Giorgio spoke to her and it was all too obvious who was in charge.

All in all, another four women and three men drifted into the shop over the next half hour. Then, just before nine o'clock, they all gathered around Giorgio who seemed to be giving them a team talk. While he was doing this a Bentley, followed by a Rolls-Royce, pulled up and a very fashionable woman stepped out of each. Mac figured that Capelli Giorgio must be good if such well-heeled women as this were prepared to get out of bed so early in the day to get their hair done.

After a quick look around Giorgio opened the shop door and the women swanned in. Within five minutes Mac saw three more Rolls-Royces, an Aston Martin, a Lamborghini and a Bugatti pull up. The cars might have cost a fortune but he guessed that the women who got out of them might be a tad more expensive. He wondered idly how much a haircut might cost at Capelli Giorgio.

The team were hard at it all morning, especially Giorgio. If he wasn't cutting hair he was meeting and greeting customers and keeping a careful eye on the rest of the team. Mac had wondered about the amount of money Laura had given Giorgio but, this being such an expensive area, he guessed that a million to fit out a business like this might be just about right.

Mac sat up. Giorgio was on the move. He retrieved his crutch and got out of the car. A sudden bolt of pain shot through him as he straightened his back but thankfully it disappeared as quickly as it had come. He followed Giorgio, being careful to stay on the other side of the street, and was grateful that he only went around the corner to a smart coffee shop and delicatessen. He could see Giorgio reading his order out from a piece of paper.

He followed him back to the shop where Giorgio went straight back to work. Mac was surprised at the way these hairdressers kept at it, he felt tired just watching them. About half an hour later a man arrived with coffees and sandwiches. He realised that he was getting hungry too. While Giorgio was busy eating, he decided to get a sandwich and, hopefully, some information as well.

He went to the counter of the coffee house and ordered a cheese sandwich and coffee to go. The young man behind the counter offered him six types of bread, eight types of cheese and an even greater range of different coffees to choose from. Mac found the amount of choices confusing so he just ordered cheddar on white and a cappuccino to go. While he waiting for his sandwich, he decided to see what the young man knew about Giorgio.

'I was thinking of booking my daughter in for an appointment at the hairdresser's around the corner. Is he any good?'

The young man looked Mac up and down.

'Come into money, have we?' he said archly. 'Sorry, just my little joke, don't mind me. Is Giorgio any good? He's the best. You want to see some of the women who go in there, God they are so gorgeous! Not that I'm interested in them in that way of course. No, I definitely picked the wrong profession. So, here I am serving coffee and sandwiches while next door the beautiful Giorgio is getting up to twenty thousand for a haircut.'

'Twenty thousand!' Mac exclaimed in disbelief.

'Oh yes and not that long ago he got flown out to Los Angeles to do her hair for the Oscars. Oh, who was it now? Gerald, darling!' he shouted over his shoulder.

A tall man in his late thirties came out and presented a paper bag to Mac on a little silver platter.

'You called, dearest?' he said, draping his arm proprietorially over the young man's shoulder.

'Who was that actress? The one Giorgio went all the way to LA to do her hair for the Oscars?'

Gerald gave them a name that even Mac knew.

'After that they all wanted him to do their hair. He is really good though and so good looking too. I love you, sugar,' Gerald said as he turned to the young man, 'but he is fantastic eye candy.'

They both nodded dreamily in unison.

He went back to his car and ate his sandwich. It cost twice as much as a dinner at The Magnets would have but he had to admit that it was good. He made sure that he'd gotten a receipt though.

Twenty thousand for a haircut, he thought in wonder.

He felt there was something deeply wrong about that. He knew some people had shed loads of money but still, twenty thousand for something that would need doing again a few weeks later? Some coppers starting off didn't get much more than that in a year.

Giorgio was still hard at work even after the salon closed at six. He and the young woman who had arrived first, obviously his assistant, were looking at what Mac thought might be an appointment book and some other papers. She left around six thirty and was met at the door by another woman who hugged her and gave her a lover's kiss full on the lips. They walked off down the street hand in hand.

Definitely not the love interest then, Mac thought.

Giorgio locked up a few minutes later and Mac followed him all the way back to the electric gates of the de Vesey house.

Chapter Twenty

Friday 16th January

On Wednesday and Thursday Mac had gone through exactly the same routine. He wasn't bored though. It was work and he always found observation interesting. He thought of it as being like a sort of microscope and looking at the minutiae of someone's daily life can tell you a lot about them. He found that he was warming to Giorgio who was a real worker and seemed to be well liked by his team.

His new duties also gave him quite a lot of time to turn over the facts of the unsolved case in his head but, for all the effort he put in, it got him exactly nowhere.

It was the 'second Friday' and Mac waited expectantly for the afternoon to come. If Laura was right, he might find out a bit more about the mysterious Giorgio. Sure enough, just before one o'clock he said goodbye to his team and got into the Audi. Mac followed him through the busy London streets feeling the excitement mount. Instead of carrying straight on, the Audi turned right. Giorgio definitely wasn't heading towards home then.

He found himself on the A10 heading north and he was surprised when Giorgio turned left and headed towards Haringey. What would a hairdresser to the stars want in this part of town? Giorgio quickly turned left and right down residential side streets until Mac wasn't quite sure where he was. He even began to wonder if Giorgio had spotted his Nissan and was trying to lose him. Eventually the Audi pulled up outside a nondescript nineteen-sixties council house. Mac drove straight past the parked car but Giorgio never even gave him a glance. Mac turned the car around at the top of the road and parked where he could get a good view of the house.

The area had definitely seen better days. The street was strewn with litter, shop windows were boarded up and he was pretty sure that the twelve year old hanging about on the corner wasn't selling newspapers.

A few minutes later someone in the house pulled back the curtains and Mac got out of the car and walked down the street for a closer look. He could see inside the front room of the house. An old lady was sitting in a chair with a towel around her shoulders. She smiled broadly as Giorgio started to cut her hair. She then turned her head and Mac got a good view of her profile.

'Christ almighty!' he said out loud.

He knew who she was and he knew who Giorgio was. He looked at the house number, 192. It was the same house and then suddenly it was sixteen years ago. The memories came flooding back again as if it were only yesterday.

He knew that Giorgio had looked familiar the minute he'd seen his photo. He'd been just plain Georgy White when Mac knew him. He rolled his eyes upwards in disbelief. Giorgio Lo Bianco is, of course, George White in Italian but he'd never twigged. Of course, it had all happened a long time ago and Georgy had changed a hell of a lot, however, he found that he was still surprised that he hadn't recognised him. It had been such a bad business, a case that he could still remember clearly even though sixteen years had gone by.

Mac stood there frozen, uncertain as to what to do next. His heart was telling him to knock on the door but eventually his head won the day and Mac reluctantly went back to his car and drove away from Haringey and the case. At the bottom of the road a burnt-out van stood half on the pavement, half on the road. He slowed down as he passed the van knowing it should mean something to him but he couldn't think what. His brain was in a whirl.

He sighed, yet another case that hadn't exactly proved to be a success. Of course, he'd have to tell Laura that he couldn't carry on following Giorgio around but the real problem was that he wouldn't be able to tell her why. Again, he wondered if he should have knocked on the door and, again, he told himself that he'd made the right decision. He reminded himself that it wasn't up to him.

He gave his name at the electric gates and he could hear a tremor of fear in Laura's voice as she replied. The gates slid open and Mac started down the long drive. The drive went straight on for quite a while and then turned to the left. Only then did he get a view of the De Vesey house. More of a castle than a house, he thought. There must be forty or fifty rooms at least.

Laura was waiting at the front door, arms crossed. He could sense the anxiety from her body language even from a distance away. She led him into a room bigger than the floor space of his entire house and gestured for him to sit down on a delicate looking chair. He hoped it was stronger than it looked.

She sat opposite, her nervousness at what she might learn was all too apparent. All the blood seemed to have drained from her face.

'So, what have you found out?' she eventually asked in a tremulous voice.

He described the salon, the people who worked there and Giorgio's work routine. He had to remind himself not to call him Georgy. He kept his visit to Haringey and what he'd learned there to himself.

Laura looked puzzled.

'There's more to this, I know it. So where is he now? It's a second Friday so why aren't you following him?'

'I'm afraid I won't be able to take the case any further.'

'Any further? What on earth do you mean?'

'I mean that I can't continue with the case. I can't follow Giorgio anymore.'

'Why?'

She looked stunned as she said this.

'I'm afraid that I can't tell you that,' he replied, feeling both deeply embarrassed and deeply sorry for Laura.

'You can't tell me?' Laura said shrilly as she stood up. 'Christ, what have I done to deserve this? I can't even hold on to a bloody private detective.'

She was close to tears and inadvertently gave Mac a clue as to why she might be feeling so desperate. She held her hands over her lower stomach as if she was protecting something. Mac was sure that she was pregnant. This didn't make him feel any better but again he had to remind himself that it wasn't up to him.

'I'm really sorry, Laura,' was all he could say.

'Yes, they're all sorry, they're all so fucking sorry. Daddy's sorry he missed the school play, sorry you're such a wonderful person but I've met someone else, sorry darling but it was always about the money. It's always sorry but it means nothing does it?'

Mac could see she was close to hysteria. All he could think to do was to take her in his arms where she went completely to pieces. After the tears had stopped, she pulled away and apologised.

'I'm...sorry,' she said with a slightly ashamed smile.

'Don't be. Have you thought it might not be as bad as you've been thinking?'

'You mean there might be hope?'

He said a little prayer that he was doing the right thing.

'Yes, there might be. I know I've only been on the case for a few days but I've seen nothing that suggests Giorgio has a lover. All I've seen him doing is working very hard.'

226

'There might be hope?' she repeated again to herself, as though fearing to believe it.

'Will you take my advice? Talk to Giorgio tonight and tell him everything. Tell him how miserable you feel and why. Will you promise me?'

She nodded.

'I will, Mr. Maguire. I've wanted to for ages but I'd always feared...I was so sure...but now you say there might be hope.'

Mac left hoping to God that he had done the right thing. He went back to his office and let the silence wash over him.

Two cases so far, both ending very unsatisfactorily. Mac wondered if being a detective was really the answer. He pulled Tim's present from the drawer and sat looking at the unopened bottle of Jameson's Irish Whiskey.

He wondered how Georgy might react when Laura spoke to him. He hoped to God he was right in giving her hope but he was seriously beginning to doubt his own judgment. He supposed that he should have asked her not to mention his name but for some reason he couldn't. The genie was out of the bottle now and he had no idea how the cards would fall.

He started to open the bottle. He wasn't normally a whisky drinker, although he liked a shot occasionally, but he was now considering downing the lot. He sighed, tightened the cap and put it back in the drawer. He didn't even have the energy to get drunk.

The tiredness was taking over again, weighing him down. The black fatigue which had kept him bedbound for days at a time was washing over him and he almost felt grateful. Right now, all he wanted to do was escape into a dark place where there were no dead girls, no tearful women and no memories.

He was just about to get up and leave the office for his bed when the image of the burnt-out van flashed into his head. His brain was trying to tell him something but what?

He relaxed and tried not to think at all. He shut his eyes and let his mind drift. It took a while but eventually he saw the burnt-out van in his mind except that this time it wasn't a van, it was a BMW car. He had it! His tiredness suddenly evaporated.

He rang Dan Carter and tried to keep the excitement he felt out of his voice.

'Dan, would you mind if I borrowed Tommy and Martin for an hour or two?'

'Have you come up with something?' Dan asked excitedly.

'It's just an idea. I haven't got the faintest idea if it will get us anywhere, but I'd like to give it a go.'

'That's more than okay with me, come now if you want,' Dan said. 'Oh, by the way forensics have confirmed that Matyas, or Oleksandr Shevchenko as I should call him now, was definitely our man. His DNA and shoe prints are a match for the professor's murder and his car was definitely the one that was used to run over and kill Stelios Andreou. That news pleased my boss no end. Interestingly we've also heard from Dr. Tereshkova and she's confirmed that he had the same drug in his system as Hetty Lewinton. It was just as you suspected.'

This last part of Dan's news made Mac even more certain that Matyas had an accomplice.

Less than an hour later he found himself once again in the incident room with Tommy and Martin who were sitting like schoolboys paying keen attention to what he was saying.

'It was when I saw a burnt-out van that I got the idea. Our man stole cars to ferry girls back to Luton and pick up new girls but what happened to the cars afterwards? We know he was careful, there were no prints or anything else in the car that Hetty Lewinton was

228

found in, but the girls might very well have left some forensic evidence behind inside the car or in the boot. If he was really careful, he'd have set them on fire when he was finished with them, wouldn't he?'

Tommy and Martin looked at each other and then nodded.

'If we assume that he did indeed burn out the cars then they must be on our records somewhere but unfortunately buried in the statistics along with a mass of other car crimes.'

'So, what can we do?' Tommy asked.

'We've got dates and we know the make of car he prefers. It's a long shot but, if we can identify the locations of the cars he stole, that might tell us something about where the girls were kept after they were abducted.'

'We could probably most of the information we need about burnt-out BMWs from the data bases,' Martin said.

'Okay but then we'd need to contact the local stations to narrow it down a bit by asking if any were found in unusual locations.'

'Why unusual locations?' Tommy asked.

'I doubt that our man would know where the local joy riders usually ditch their cars,' Mac answered, 'plus we also need to rule out any insurance frauds. The local police might be able to identify some of those for us.'

'Okay,' Tommy said. 'Where do we start?'

'I think we should start with Luton and then fan out towards the east,' Martin suggested. 'It was on the east side of Luton that the collision happened and where we found Hetty Lewinton in the car boot.'

'That sounds good to me,' Mac said rubbing his hands together.

Martin printed out reams of phone numbers and they started phoning. By five thirty they'd only covered

Bedfordshire and had gotten no good candidates. Mac told them that they might as well call it a day.

'See you tomorrow,' Tommy said on his way out.

Martin said the same before he disappeared.

'But its Saturday tomorrow,' Mac said to the empty room.

He couldn't stop himself from smiling.

Chapter Twenty One

Saturday January 17th

Mac was back in the station well before eight o'clock. He couldn't wait to get on with it. Martin arrived just after eight thirty and Tommy a few minutes later.

After sandwiches and coffee, they got to work. It was nine thirty before they got their first good candidate and, by eleven thirty, they'd gotten good candidates for all five dates. Martin marked the locations on a map and then printed off a large version. Mac pinned it to a board and they all looked hard at it.

In all they'd gotten nine candidates that corresponded with the dates and type of car so four had to somehow be discounted. Mac couldn't see any pattern at first.

'It's strange, I had it in my head that he was working with a pharmaceutical company and that's why he lived in Stevenage but none of these are even in Hertfordshire.'

'There are hundreds of pharmaceutical and life science companies in Cambridge though,' Tommy said.

Mac suddenly thought of something.

'Good boy!' he exclaimed. 'Can you print off this same map but with the train stations on it?'

'No problem,' Martin replied.

He pinned the new map to the board.

'See, look at these five here.'

Mac pointed them out.

'Yes, they're all quite close to train stations, aren't they?' Tommy commented.

'Martin, can you print off the locations where the cars were stolen from?'

They checked and those too were fairly close to train stations.

'So, what does it mean?' Tommy asked.

'Unfortunately, it doesn't bolster our case for more than one man being involved. It looks as if our man ditched the cars near train stations so he could get back home again. All of the locations are near stations on the main line to Stevenage.'

'Why not use a bus?' Martin asked.

'Buses have drivers,' Mac replied. 'You might be remembered but train stations are a lot more anonymous, especially if you don't have to buy a ticket.'

'I'll check for any season tickets in the name of Mark Brody then,' Martin said with a grin.

'Good idea,' Mac said as he looked hard at the map again. 'So, if we get rid of these four, which aren't near a station then...' Mac crossed them off with a pen and, as he did, the pattern jumped out at him.

'It's Cambridge, look!'

All five locations were within twenty miles of Cambridge and they formed a sort of rough circle around the city.

'So, it looks like this pharmaceutical company might be in Cambridge after all then,' Tommy said.

'Yes, I think our man thought he was being clever by varying the location of where he disposed the cars but all he's done is draw a big bullseye on the map for us. As you said there are hundreds of companies in that area but it still narrows it down a bit and that's always helpful.'

Tommy looked at the clock and cursed under his breath. He took his phone out and turned it on.

'Expecting a call?' Mac asked.

For some reason Tommy gave Mac an evasive look.

'No, why should I be expecting a call? I just thought that I'd turn it on, that's all.'

Tommy was hiding something but Mac didn't have a chance to find out what it was.

It was Mac's phone that went off first. It was a text message and all it said was –

'See JD ASAP Mr. C'

'Come on Tommy we've got to go and see someone and I hope to God that it isn't what I'm thinking it is.'

Martin gave him the address from the case file. On the way there, Tommy asked more than once where they were going and why but Mac was deep in thought and didn't answer.

Tommy pulled up behind the Porsche four by four.

'You have to tell me something Mac,' he implored.

'I'm sorry Tommy, I was thinking. Okay this Jay Dee is a pimp, the bottom of the food chain, but I've been getting some information from the very top of the food chain.'

A picture of Mr. C as a Great White Shark came into his mind and it seemed fitting somehow.

'This is where I got all the information on the missing girls in the first place. The text message just told me to go and see this Jay Dee but it didn't say why.'

As they walked to the front door Tommy persisted, 'What do you fear it might be then?'

Mac didn't answer. He said a silent prayer as he rapped loudly on the door. A few seconds later the door opened a couple of inches and Mac could see the pale, fearful face of Jay Dee peeking out. He seemed relieved that it was only the police at the door. They followed him into the living room where Mac could see that a few more pizza boxes and beer cans had been added to the pile.

'What is it?' Mac asked bluntly.

'You got a message from...?'

Jay Dee's face showed his distress and Mac had to remind himself that he was a scummy pimp.

'Yes, I got a message and someone isn't happy. Tell me,' Mac ordered sternly.

'I only knew for sure when I went around there this morning. Please tell him that it wasn't my fault,' Jay Dee pleaded.

'Tell him yourself, I just need to know what you know.'

'I went around there yesterday and her bed hadn't been slept in. When she didn't turn up for work last night, I asked around but no-one's seen her. I checked again this morning and found that her bed hadn't been slept in. That's when I phoned my boss.'

Mac was certain that Mr. C wouldn't take the delay in letting him know kindly.

'You've managed to lose another girl?' Mac asked.

Jay Dee nodded.

'I didn't tell anyone straight away, I was still hoping she'd turn up, I mean all her clothes and stuff are still there. Anyway, the guy who was killing all the girls is dead, isn't he?'

'What's her name?' Mac asked brusquely.

'It's Chanelle, Chanelle Burdon.'

For some reason Mac had been praying that it wasn't her. Mac could picture her clearly in his mind, a young pretty girl who said she'd had bad luck. She feared that something bad was about to happen to her and it was beginning to look as if she'd been right.

'Who saw her last?' Mac asked.

'She was working with a new girl called Kate, she moved in after Kayla....after Kayla went.'

'She's staying at Chanelle's? Is she there now?'

'Yes, I just rang her. I was still hoping that Chanelle might have turned up.'

'Is there anything else?' Mac asked.

'No, I'm sorry but that's all I know. Please tell him that I did my best, it wasn't my fault.'

Mac could hear the desperation in his voice but he reminded himself that Jay Dee wasn't his problem. He turned to go, stopped and then turned back again.

'Where are your family from originally?' he asked.

'From Andra Pradesh in India,' Jay Dee replied, looking puzzled.

'Do you still have family there?'

Jay Dee nodded.

'If I were you, I'd pay them an immediate visit. A very, very long visit, do you understand?'

Jay Dee understood all right. He raced upstairs to pack.

Back out on the pavement Tommy said, 'God he was frightened to death, wasn't he?'

'He was and with good reason too. He was figuring that the guy he works for might think that one girl going missing might be an accident but two...'

'Might be carelessness?' Tommy suggested.

'No. I'm thinking that it might be more like a death sentence. His boss is not the forgiving kind.'

'Bloody hell! Remind me never to take up pimping for a living,' Tommy observed.

'Mr. Jay Dee might well be wishing someone had reminded him of that too if they catch him before he makes his flight. Anyway, he's not our problem. We've got a young girl missing, let's concentrate on that.'

Mac could just about remember the way to Chanelle's house. The door was open when they arrived and they surprised a young blonde-haired girl who was standing behind it. Mac could see a couple of suitcases in the hallway. Tommy showed her his warrant card.

'I'm sorry, I thought you were the taxi man,' she said in heavily accented English.

'We're investigating the disappearance of Chanelle Burdon and we believe that you were the last person to see her. Can we go inside?' Mac asked.

'But the taxi?'

'You can order another one, this is important.'

She reluctantly led them into the living room.

'I can't tell you much,' she said defensively.

'Just tell us what you know,' Mac said gently.

The door knocked and Mac gestured for Tommy to go and deal with the taxi driver.

'Okay, the night before the last one, we were on our street corner and around nine thirty I got a job. I had to leave Chanelle by herself. When I got back, she was gone. At first I thought that she'd got a job too but, when she didn't turn up again that night, I told Jay Dee. That's it.'

'Did you see anyone hanging around where you work, perhaps a car parked down the road?'

'No nothing like that, honestly I saw nothing.'

'I take it you're going somewhere?'

Kate crinkled her face in disgust.

'As far away from here as I possibly can. I'll be in Warsaw in a couple of hours. I thought coming here would be a great adventure but it's just a pig sty. We have those too in Poland but at least its home and girls don't just disappear.'

Tommy came back in.

'He's waiting for you.'

'Can I go now?' she asked sullenly.

'Yes, but we'll need your name and address in Poland before you go.'

'Okay but you won't let Jay Dee know?' she asked nervously.

Mac reassured her that Jay Dee would never know and Tommy dutifully wrote the details down.

Outside they watched the taxi disappear.

'Did you get anything?' Tommy asked hopefully.

'No, nothing. Come on let's go back to the station. Dan will want to hear about this.'

Back at the station Dan was busy catching up on paperwork when Mac and Tommy burst into his office and told him the news. Dan got up from behind his desk and started walking up and down as he thought through what he'd been told.

'Okay, Tommy I know it's Saturday but call around and get the team together and bring them up to date. I'm going to tell the boss that we're opening this case up again whether he likes it or not.'

Mac grinned as Dan strode determinedly out of the door. Tommy and Martin phoned around the team. Within half an hour they were all assembled and seemingly excited about being on the case again. Dan strode in looking serious but his face broke out into a smile as he addressed his team.

'Game on,' he said. 'Okay Martin get me a print out of all the pharmaceutical companies in the Cambridge area, Mary and Buddy, I want you to go and interview all the girls we have addresses for and then interview anyone else who's plying their trade that evening. Someone must have seen something. Adil...'

Dan's words were interrupted by Tommy's phone going off.

So, he got his call at last, Mac thought.

He was surprised when Tommy passed the phone to him. There was a text message on the screen –

'Coming in HRA at three have poss got some info Sammy N'

Bloody hell, Sammy Newell! Mac had nearly forgotten all about him.

'Dan, I'm sorry but I think Tommy and I might have a lead. That medical researcher I told you about is coming back from holiday. He'll be landing in Heathrow Airport in a couple of hours.'

Dan grinned broadly.

'Well, what are you waiting for then?'

'Get a fast car with a siren,' Mac ordered as they walked to the car park. 'I've got a feeling this is going to be a good day.'

Tommy drove them straight on to the M1 motorway and then into the mad dash of the M25. Even on a Saturday afternoon the traffic slowed them down forcing Tommy to put on the siren from time to time. While they drove, Mac contacted the airport police on Tommy's phone and requested help in getting Sammy off the plane as quickly as possible. They kept asking if he was a suspect of some sort and Mac had to assure them several times that he wasn't a terrorist but a medical witness in an important case. They eventually got the message.

In no time at all they were in the arrivals lounge waiting for Sammy Newell to appear. They didn't have to wait long. An electric buggy approached with a policeman holding a sub-machine gun sitting in the back seat. A sandy haired man in his early thirties with a huge grin on his face was sitting in the passenger seat. His face said thirty but his expression said twelve.

Mac introduced himself and Tommy to Sammy Newell.

'God that was absolutely awesome,' Sammy said enthusiastically. 'Less than ten minutes it took. Whoosh through passports and security, bags waiting for me. You guys can pick me up any time you like.'

Tommy helped Sammy with his bags to the police car which was parked on double yellows right outside Arrivals. Mac was just about to get in the front passenger seat when he saw a look of keen disappointment on Sammy's face.

'Are we going to have sirens?' he asked.

Mac smiled and let Sammy sit in the front. He decided that he was definitely thirty going on twelve.

'Take me to the Royal Free, driver,' Sammy excitedly ordered.

Tommy gave Mac an amused glance and they set off.

'What have you got for us Sammy?' Mac asked.

Mr. Newell seemed a bit formal in his case.

'Can we please not talk about it?' Sammy pleaded. 'It's just a tickle at the back of my mind at the moment and if I try and think about it too hard it might disappear. I need to get back to my computer at the hospital, that's where I do my best thinking.'

Mac said no more. In a funny sort of way, he knew what Sammy meant. Sometimes memories can be so elusive that they need to quietly sidled up to rather than chased after head on. The traffic going into London wasn't that bad and Mac wasn't sure if they really needed to have the siren on quite so often. However, both Tommy and Sammy seemed to enjoying themselves.

Tommy parked right outside the front doors and they followed Sammy into the hospital. They went up to the fourth floor and Sammy unlocked the office next to the one they'd interviewed Dr. Olsen in.

'There she is, isn't she gorgeous?' Sammy asked.

He waved in the direction of a desk that had two very large monitor screens, a keyboard, and some games controllers. Mac couldn't figure out what Sammy was referring to until Sammy started lovingly stroking a clear plastic box full of technology that was positioned on the far right of the desk.

'Bloody hell what have you got in there?' Tommy asked.

'Made it myself, this is one of the most powerful babies you'll ever come across,' Sammy replied as he pressed a button on the computer. He then exchanged some computer jargon with Tommy that meant absolutely nothing to Mac.

Tommy just said, 'Wow!'

'I'd be grateful if you could leave me to it gents. I'll text you if I come up with something,' Sammy said.

As they waited for the lift Mac said, 'You looked quite impressed by that box. I must admit it didn't look that fantastic to me.'

'It's not the box, it's what's inside it. I've heard of people building their own computers, mostly for gaming, and some of them are insanely powerful but that's the best I've ever actually seen. God I'd love to have a go on it.'

Mac looked up to the heavens. Boys and their toys, he thought.

'Come on, stop dribbling and let's go and get a coffee.'

As they walked towards the café Mac noticed that Tommy kept looking around as if he was hoping that he'd see someone.

'She only works every second Saturday,' Mac said.

'And is this a second...' Tommy stopped himself in mid-sentence, his face reddening as he realised that he'd been rumbled.

'I take it that phone call you've been waiting for was from my daughter.'

Tommy nodded.

'Well I rang her, just to see if she'd remembered anything and I just mentioned that perhaps we could discuss it over dinner if she liked. Thankfully she didn't say no but, unfortunately, she didn't say yes either. She said that she'd have to check her work rota first.'

'If you go and get us some sandwiches I'll try and put you out of your misery.'

Mac got out his phone and called his daughter. The phone rang for a while before a sleepy sounding Bridget answered.

'Sorry love, did I wake you?' Mac asked.

'It's alright Dad, we had some emergencies yesterday and I had to work late. Where are you?'

'I'm at the hospital, back on the case. Sammy texted us that he was on his way back and we picked him up from Heath Row. We're just waiting for him to come up with something.'

'Sammy's back then? Good, if anyone will have an idea about this hibernation drug then it will be him,' Bridget said. There was a slight pause before she continued, 'You said 'we'?'

'Yes, Tommy's with me.'

'Oh good,' she said sounding a bit strange. 'Can you put him on?'

Tommy arrived with a tray of sandwiches and coffees.

'She wants to speak to you,' Mac said.

'Really?' he said in a strangled voice.

Now it was Tommy's turn to sound strange.

'I need the loo,' Mac said diplomatically.

He went to the toilet and peeked around the door before coming out to make sure Tommy had finished talking. He had. Mac could tell that it had gone well because when he got back to the table Tommy was sitting there as if in some sort of dream with a big, sloppy smile on his face.

'I take it that your call went well then?' Mac asked.

Tommy shook his head in disbelief.

'She said yes, I mean it's only dinner, but...Oh sorry Mac, I mean she's your daughter and all.'

'Don't worry, Bridget is like her mother, nothing I could ever say would change her mind. Anyway, I think she could do a lot worse,' he said as he tucked into a cheese sandwich.

'Do you really mean that Mac?' Tommy asked.

Mac nodded.

'I think that's the nicest thing you've ever said to me.'

'Well...' Mac was interrupted by Tommy's phone. Tommy took a look and then showed it to Mac.

'*Got it S*'

'Come on then, what are we waiting for?' Mac said, wrapping the remaining half of his sandwich in a paper napkin.

Chapter Twenty Two

Sammy was busy blowing up spaceships on two screens when they made it back to his office. Mac turned around and saw Tommy standing behind him with his mouth open and eyes glazed.

'Wow!' Tommy said again.

Mac looked up to the heavens.

'Mr. Newell, Sammy, you said you found something?' he said, raising his voice so he might be heard above the sound of exploding metal.

Sammy tore himself away from his game and a picture of a handsome, grey haired man in his fifties appeared on the screen.

'Sorry, it took me a while to locate the memory. This is the guy who mentioned a hibernation drug. It was after a seminar and we'd all had quite a few beers. He said he'd actually seen it in action in a lab somewhere, Eastern Europe I think he said it was.'

Mac and Tommy exchanged looks.

'Who is he?' Mac asked.

'His name is Professor Bartholomew Moran but I think people call him Barry.'

'How do you know him?'

'We've corresponded a fair bit over the web, as we're more or less in the same field, but I only ever met him the once,' Sammy explained. 'It was at a seminar in Los Angeles a couple of years ago and, when someone mentioned hibernation, he told us this story about how he'd seen the drug in action on mice. It had some bad side effects, if I remember right, but he was quite astounded that it had worked at all.'

'Is he based in the US?' Mac asked.

'No, no. He works at the Life Sciences department at UCL. He's a director or something.'

'The UCL here in London?' Mac asked hopefully.

'Yes, it's somewhere on the Tottenham Court Road I think.'

'Can you get me his number?' Tommy interjected.

A couple of seconds later a number appeared on the screen. Mac looked at his watch. It had just gone four thirty. He thought that they'd be lucky to get him at his office at this time on a Saturday but it was worth a try. Tommy rang the number and got the professor's secretary. They were lucky.

'This is Saturday young man, and the professor sees no-one on a Saturday,' she said starchily.

Tommy explained the urgency of the situation and a few seconds later a man answered. He had a soft Irish voice.

'I'm sorry,' the Professor said, 'my secretary is very protective of me. I've been away for a while and it's my day to catch up on things. How can I help?'

Tommy explained again.

'Can we come and see you right now?' he asked.

'Of course,' the Professor replied and gave an address and directions to his office.

'Okay Mac, let's go,' Tommy said.

They both thanked Sammy who had already resumed playing his game.

On their way out, Tommy stopped and turned.

'You're not one of the Free Wizards by any chance, are you?' he asked.

'You bet,' Sammy replied without turning.

'I'm thoroughly impressed. It's really nice to have met you.'

Sammy replied with a raised fist without missing a move.

As they walked back to the car Mac asked, 'What was all that about Free Wizards?'

'They're a gaming team, one of the best. They play other teams over the web. They're really cool.'

Mac frowned.

'Can we get back to business please?'

Even with some traffic they made it to UCL in just over twenty minutes. They found the professor's office on the second floor just where he said it was. A woman in her forties opened the door and it was clear from her expression that she disapproved of their very existence. She led them to the professor's room and left them with a sour look.

The professor, however, seemed quite grateful for the interruption.

'I hate these catch up Saturdays,' he confided, 'even though I know that the work has to be done. How exactly can I help?'

Mac explained the bare bones of the case and why the hibernation drug might be crucial in solving several murders.

The professor thought on that for a moment.

'Yes, I remember now,' he said with a smile. 'It was Rika who showed me the drug in action. Let me tell you the whole story. I was presenting at a seminar in Budapest and, as it was the last night, a large group of us decided to go for a drink afterwards. God but they really know how to drink in Hungary! Anyway, we were talking about this and that, all work related of course, when someone started talking about the possibility of a hibernation drug and how useful it would be in treating major trauma victims. Rika was there, she was a graduate student at the time, and she spoke very good English too. She mentioned that the lab she worked for part time had come up with something along those lines. The rest either didn't hear or dismissed her but I was interested. So, she took me to the lab and showed me the drug in action. It was amazing, the mice looked more or less dead, yet they were still alive.'

'Sammy mentioned something about side effects?' Mac asked.

He crossed his fingers as he thought of Hetty Lewinton lying in her hospital bed.

'Yes, they were quite bad unfortunately as they'd caused brain damage and memory loss in a lot of the mice. Some were so badly damaged that they couldn't even remember how to eat. Unfortunately for the lab it looked like the drug was going to be a non-starter but Rika said they were trying to find similar compounds that might not have the same disastrous side effects.'

Mac said a little prayer for Hetty. It didn't look good for her.

'Did you see anyone else when you were at the lab?' Mac asked.

'No, it was very late, it was just Rika and me. I must remember to call her sometime and see how she is,' the Professor said with another smile.

Mac had an idea that more had gone on between the Professor and this Rika than just looking at mice. Then another thought struck him.

'You still have her number?' he asked excitedly.

'Yes, somewhere. Maggie?' he called loudly.

The secretary came back in. She looked as if she'd just lunched on lemons.

'Can you see if we have the contact details for a Rika somebody. Wait, yes, Rika Kovacs, that's the name.'

She left to do her duty.

'Is there anything else you can tell us Professor, perhaps about the lab where Rika worked?'

'I'm sorry but I can't remember its name or even exactly where it was. Rika drove me there. It was late at night and I don't know Budapest that well anyway. There was something she said about the guy who ran the lab though, he was English, a tall Englishman, Rika said. She didn't like him but I'm not exactly sure why.'

'She didn't give you a name?' Mac asked hopefully.

The Professor shook his head.

'I'm sorry, if she did then I don't remember it.'

The secretary came back with a post-it note with a phone number on and gave them a look which told them that it was time to leave.

Tommy gave the professor a card.

'Please call me if you remember anything else.'

The secretary accompanied them to the door, making sure that they actually left. She gave them the thinnest of smiles as she closed the door behind them.

'God, she was a bundle of laughs,' Tommy said.

'Ring the number,' Mac said excitedly.

Tommy did. All he got was a Hungarian woman at the other end who couldn't speak a word of English.

'What now?'

'Get me Martin,' Mac ordered.

Tommy rang the number and handed the phone over.

'Martin, this is top priority. We've got the name for a woman in Budapest, Rika Kovacs, and a phone number.'

Mac gave him the number.

'She used to be a graduate student at the university. I'm afraid that's all we've got to go on. This woman worked at the lab in Budapest that developed the hibernation drug. Can you get onto your friend Maria and see if she can track her down? Tell Dan that we're on our way back.'

Mac looked at his watch as they drove off. It was now coming up to five. He felt a familiar tingle of excitement, the investigation had finally reached the tipping point. With a bit of luck, they would soon know exactly who the tall Englishman was. Even though Tommy used the siren it was after six by the time they got back to the station.

The incident room was buzzing when they got there, all of the team were busy doing things. Mac could sense the same excitement in the air he'd felt himself earlier.

'Okay team!' Dan shouted as he stood by the white board. 'Now that Mac and Tommy are back let's catch up. Martin.'

Martin reluctantly took Dan's place.

In a low voice he said, 'Mac provided me with a name and phone number of a woman in Budapest who said she'd worked at a lab that had developed a hibernation drug. The phone number was a dud unfortunately as she no longer lives at that address. However, my friend Maria managed to get the phone numbers and addresses of three Rika Kovacs who used to be graduate students at the Faculty of Science at the university. Kovacs is apparently a common name there. She tried all the numbers and only one of the women spoke English. She confirmed that she'd worked at a lab and also that she'd met Professor Moran after a seminar. She's awaiting our call now.'

'Okay then, let's see what she's got to say,' Dan said.

Mac crossed his fingers and said another little prayer. The whole case might hang on what happened in the next few minutes.

'Hello, is that Miss Kovacs?' Dan asked.

Dan had the call on speaker and the whole team crowded around.

'It is. Who am I talking to please?'

'My name is Detective Inspector Dan Carter of the Bedfordshire Police in England. I believe you might have some information that could be crucial to a criminal case we're investigating.'

'Yes, the policewoman here said it was about the lab that I used to work in. Is that correct?'

'Yes, that's right,' Dan confirmed. 'We're invest-igating a case here of a woman who was found in a state of profound hibernation and we believe that you might know something about a drug that could cause such a state. Is that right?'

There was silence at the other end for a few seconds.

'I'm almost not surprised. I always thought he was a...,' she hesitated over the word, 'yes, a slimy bastard. He always smiled too much.'

'Who is 'he'?'

'He was the guy who owned the lab. He set it up in Hungary because it would be cheaper to run there. He was looking for a breakthrough drug, something that would make him famous. For a while he thought he had it with the hibernation drug or HDE 1078 as we called it. He was so happy, already preparing for the press interviews in his head, I guess. He was a narcissist if ever I met one. Then the bad news came. Autopsies on some of the mice clearly showed brain damage in the memory centres. Although the drug might have been saved many people's lives, I must admit that I was almost glad. I couldn't work with him after that, he was too weird, and so I left.'

'What's his name?' Dan asked.

Mac could sense that the team was holding its collective breath.

'Jonty Hart-Tolliver.'

Mac was surprised that names like that really existed outside of Jeeves books.

'Jonty Hart-Tolliver? Are you sure?' Dan asked looking over at Martin.

Martin was already banging away at his laptop.

'Yes, of course I'm sure.'

'Is there anything else you can tell me about this Jonty or the lab?'

'Not really but there was something going on, I'm sure of it, but I never found out exactly what. Jonty had a buddy, Sandor his name was, but I never found out exactly what his role was. A translator Jonty said but I think he did a lot more than that.'

'What do you mean?' Dan asked.

'Once, when I was working late, I saw Sandor bring a prostitute into Jonty's office. They didn't see me. They were disgusting, Jonty and his little pimp.'

Mac thought that she'd been very lucky. If they had found out that she'd seen them she might not be around now to tell the story.

'Is that Oleksandr Shevchenko you're talking about?'

'Yes, that's him. They made a right pair, tall and short we called them, but there was something really creepy about both of them.'

'What was the name of the lab?' Dan asked.

'It was called JHT Magyarpharm but I don't think it exists anymore.'

'Thank you very much Miss Kovacs. If you think of anything else please let us know.'

Dan put the receiver back and punched the air.

'At last we've got something to go on. Martin have you got anything on this Hart-Tolliver yet?'

'There's a Jonty Hart-Tolliver who is listed as the main shareholder for HDE Pharma UK. The company was started up just over a year ago.'

'HDE? That's what the drug was called wasn't it? HDE 1078. Where is it?' Mac asked.

'That's right and it looks like you were right about something else too Mac,' Martin said. 'The company's in Cambridge, in one of the old industrial sites that's being redeveloped as a science park.'

'It all fits. Okay, I need to call the boss,' Dan said.

Dan explained the new evidence to the DCS over the phone and his raised fist indicated success to the team well before he'd finished his conversation.

'He's at the golf club, of course, nineteenth hole, but he said yes, we have enough to raid HDE Pharma's premises.'

'When are we going to go ahead with the raid?' Adil asked.

Dan gave it some serious thought.

'There's a girl missing and God knows how much time we've got. I'm not waiting until morning, we go as soon as possible. Adil get the Support Unit organised and get them here as soon as they can make it. Mary can you alert forensics and let them know that we'll need a team tonight. Martin get us all the photos and maps of the target site you can. I'll get on to Cambridge Police and get them to pick up Mr. Hart-Tolliver and escort him to the company's site. The rest of you meet me here in half an hour.'

'Come on,' Mac said to Tommy, 'I've just realised we haven't eaten since the hospital. It might be a long night so sausage and egg sandwiches are definitely in order.'

As they quickly ate their sandwiches Tommy looked excitedly at Mac and said, 'I can't believe it! I can't believe that we might be close to solving the case.'

'Well, we can't count our chickens just yet but I agree that we could be close.'

Inside Mac felt as excited as Tommy looked. He really felt that this might finally be it.

It took them just under an hour to make it to the science park. Half of the 'park' was filled with gleaming new high-tech buildings while the other half consisted of neglected nineteen sixties industrial units. Some were still in use but many had windows broken and weeds growing from the brickwork where wind-blown dirt had gathered.

HDE Pharma had one of the glitziest buildings on the site, all glass and steel, angles and curves. Mac looked at the site next door, an old steel fabrication firm from what he could see of the fading name painted on the wall. It clearly hadn't been used in years. A large 'For Sale' sign lay flat on the ground.

The two police cars and the van containing the Support Unit parked up. They only had to wait for a couple of minutes for another police car to pull up. Three policemen and a very tall, loose limbed man with blond hair got out. The man approached the waiting group with a broad smile as though they were old friends he hadn't seen for a while. He held his hand out.

Dan stepped forward and shook his hand.

'Mr. Hart-Tolliver?' he asked.

'For my sins yes,' the tall man replied. 'How can I help the police?'

Dan introduced himself and flashed his warrant card.

'We'd like to search your premises if that's alright.'

Mac noticed that Jonty hesitated for a split second and that the smile dropped ever so slightly. Then normal service was resumed.

'Of course, anything I can do to help the police. Let me open up for you.'

He produced a set of keys and opened the main door. Then he walked quickly into the lobby and disarmed the burglar alarm. Dan gestured for Adil to follow him in.

As he did this Dan turned to Mac and asked, 'What do you think?'

'He's our man alright. Did you notice that he didn't even ask what it was all about? I must admit that I'm a bit worried though. He's letting us look around too easily and that makes me feel as if he's fairly sure that we won't find anything.'

A van pulled up in the car park and three men in white suits got out.

'Good, forensics are here. Now we can start,' Dan said.

Mac turned to look and he felt something click in his lower back.

'Bugger it!' he exclaimed as a spasm of pain gripped his back.

'Are you alright Mac?' Dan asked with some concern.

All the colour had drained out of Mac's face and it suddenly become contorted.

'Unfortunately, no,' Mac replied, angry at his body. 'Of all the bloody times!'

Dan called Tommy over.

'Can you take Mac back home, he's in a lot of pain.'

'No, no,' Mac protested. 'It could be just a temporary thing. All I'll need is a few minutes in the car, lying down with the seat flat. Please.'

Dan nodded at Tommy and he helped Mac stumble to the car. He adjusted the back of the seat so it was as flat as possible and Mac gratefully lay down.

'Let me know if anything happens,' Mac asked.

'Of course, just rest now,' Tommy said.

Mac lay back and was grateful when, after five or six minutes, the pain backed off a bit. He looked at his watch, it was a quarter past eight. He closed his eyes and suddenly felt very tired. He drifted off into a light sleep punctuated by bizarre dreams.

When he opened his eyes, he checked his watch again. It was nearly nine. They obviously hadn't found anything yet. Water droplets covered the windscreen, it had been raining while he'd been asleep. Mac gazed idly out of the window and found his eyes had focussed on something. The car had been parked at the edge of the car park and, from where he sat, he gazed over a strip of unkempt grass that lay between the gleaming glass building and the disused factory next door. He suddenly sat up and looked again.

Ignoring the pain, he got out of the car and looked intently at the patch of grass. He was still looking when Dan arrived.

'You were right, bloody nothing so far,' Dan said grumpily. 'Are you okay Mac?'

'Can you see what I'm seeing?' Mac asked.

'No, what are you looking at?'

'See just there,' Mac pointed with his finger.

The angle of the light from the pharmaceutical building illuminated the raindrops on the blades of grass. A clear straight line could be seen cutting through the grass, a path.

'Someone's been going into the disused factory next door,' Mac said.

Dan instantly lost his grumpiness and got his phone out.

'Martin I'm looking at a disused factory to the right of HDE Pharma. It looks like it was old steel fabrication factory. Can you find out who owns it? As quickly as possible please.'

Dan turned to Mac, 'Come on, let's go and have a look.'

They strode through the wet grass getting the bottom of their trousers wet but neither of them even noticed. The angle of the path pointed towards a little annex built on the side of the factory, possibly for offices Mac thought. As they got closer Mac's blood started racing. For a disused site the annex had a pretty sturdy door and a massive padlock holding it shut tight.

Dan's phone rang.

'Yes Martin.'

'That site, it was bought eight months ago by HDE Holdings Limited, sole director Emilia Hart-Tolliver. She's Jonty's wife.'

'Thanks Martin and bloody well done.'

Dan rang off and turned to Mac.

'It's him alright, the site's owned by his wife. Wait here, it looks like the Support Unit will have something to do tonight after all.'

He returned a couple of minutes later with two uniformed officers one of who was carrying what looked like a massive pair of bolt cutters. As big as the lock was it was lying on the floor two minutes later. Dan opened the door and tried a light switch. A hall with several doors leading off it was instantly illuminated. He ran ahead opening each of the doors in turn. Mac glanced inside each room as he passed by. Old desks, broken chairs and files littered the rooms.

Dan opened the last door, the door facing them at the end of the hallway, and then he stopped dead.

'We've found her Mac, we've found her,' he said softly.

Chapter Twenty Three

Dan turned away from the door and leant against the wall. He looked mournfully at Mac and slowly shook his head.

'Too late Mac,' he said sadly. 'We're too bloody late.'

Mac looked into the room. It was warm, Mac could see a heater in the corner but it was the bed in the centre of the room that drew his eyes. The bed was an old steel model, possibly ex-Army Mac thought, and it had been bolted to the floor. On it lay Chanelle Burdon. She had chains on her arms and legs and she was naked. Her back was arched as though is some spasm and the expression on her face, frozen by death, was etched with pain. Mac checked her pulse just in case but there was nothing.

'Come on Mac, let's leave it to forensics,' Dan said in a low voice.

As they walked out Dan angrily exclaimed, 'Christ, I've seen some things in this job but the look on that poor girl's face!'

Mac could only agree. He followed Dan back into the clean modernity of the HDE building.

'Where is he?' Dan asked Adil.

Mac could sense that Dan's shock had quickly turned to an ice-cold anger.

'Mr. Hart-Tolliver? He's in his office. It's that one there,' Adil said pointing with his finger. 'You've found something, haven't you?'

'Follow us,' Dan ordered tersely.

Dan flung open the door and found Jonty behind his desk tapping away at his laptop.

'Ah, DI Carter. As you haven't found anything can I go home now? We've got friends for dinner and I'm already late.'

The smile widened.

'Mr. Hart-Tolliver, you might just have to miss that dinner. We've just had a look in the disused factory next door and guess what we found?'

Jonty's smile disappeared. Without the smile his face looked quite mean and sinister.

'Take him to the station,' Dan said to Adil. 'And get Mary and Buddy to pick up his wife. Let's see what she knows.'

Jonty stood up and Mac wondered if he might give them some problems but he allowed the handcuffs to go on and meekly followed Adil out of the room.

'I wanted to catch the bastard but I'd hoped...' Dan left the sentence hanging.

'You'd hoped to find her alive. I know, me too.'

Mac tried to picture her pretty face but her contorted death mask was all he could see.

Just over an hour later Mac was once again seated in the interview room with Dan. On the other side of the table sat Jonty and his solicitor. Jonty wasn't smiling.

Dan stated the time and date and then said, 'Interview regarding the death of Chanelle Burdon. Attending DI Dan Carter, consultant ex-DCS Mac Maguire, Mr. Jonty Hart-Tolliver and Mr. Marcus Powell, solicitor for Mr. Hart-Tolliver.'

'You can call me Jonty,' Jonty said, the smile returning.

Dan read him his rights and then, ignoring Jonty's request, said, 'Mr. Hart-Tolliver, what can you tell us about the death of Miss Chanelle Burdon whose body was found...'

Jonty interrupted. 'Listen, can we do a deal?'

'A deal? What kind of deal?' Dan said as he looked suspiciously at Jonty.

'You've got my wife here, she's nothing to do with…all this. Let her go and I'll tell you everything.'

'Everything?'

Jonty nodded.

Dan gave it some thought.

'She's not been questioned yet, so I can't let her go, but I promise that, if you tell us what we need to know, I'll keep the questions to a minimum and send her home in a police car.'

'Okay, that's near enough. Old Marcus here doesn't want me to tell you anything but I honestly can't see the point. Your forensics people aren't idiots, they'll know soon enough that it was me in that room with the girl. My prints are all over the place and they'll probably find some semen too.'

'Semen?' Dan asked, looking even more appalled.

Jonty nodded again and the smile widened, 'Well she was a pretty little thing and I'm only human after all.'

Mac somehow doubted that last part of the statement.

'So, what do I say now? You've got me bang to rights guv'nor or something along those lines?'

Dan stared at him as if he had two heads and had just landed from another planet. His solicitor buried his head in his hands.

'Carry on. No, start from when you were in Budapest,' Dan ordered.

'A nice city, and a very cheap one too. I had an idea about a revolutionary new drug but not as much money as I would have liked so Hungary seemed like a good option. I was so happy when we discovered HDE 1078, I thought that I'd found a wonder drug, which of course is what it was, but we just couldn't get rid of the side effects. Then we found HDE 1134 and, while it wasn't anywhere near as potent as 1078 it did lower blood pressure very effectively and it didn't seem to have any of the adverse side effects. However, animals could only tell us so much as the effects in humans might be subtler but still severe enough to make the drug more or less unusable. I mean no-one wants Alzheimer's as a side effect, now do they?'

He smiled as though they were all having a friendly cup of tea together.

'Anyway, I knew that we only had one shot with the drug as I was running out of money so I decided that we needed some guinea pigs. I persuaded Sandor to get me some girls. He wasn't too keen at first but he soon got into the swing of it, especially as he got some perks out of it, lots of free sex. We kept them in a cellar under the lab and very convenient it was too. Sandor also didn't want to be involved with disposing of them afterwards, he was a bit of a wimp really. I had to bully him a bit to get him to inject the first one with heroin but he seemed to get the hang of it afterwards. The trials went very well and I was sure that when it came to the real tests that the drug would go through with flying colours.'

'How many?' Dan asked tersely.

'How many what?'

'Girls.'

'Oh them, seven in all. I'd worked it all out. We needed six to test the side effects at various doses.'

'And the seventh?'

Jonty's smile never left his face as he said, 'Oh! that was to test for the lethal dose. It only provided a ballpark figure of course but it was still bloody useful information.'

Mac felt his blood run cold as he said those words.

'Anyway, the drug was a big hit. High blood pressure is an epidemic at the moment, over sixty million in America alone. It's probably saved thousands of lives,' Jonty said trying to look sincere. He just looked grotesque.

Mac also guessed it had made him a lot of money.

'So, I moved back to the UK and started a new company, with new premises. I was really going somewhere but we needed another hit drug to be sure of keeping it all afloat. And we did, HDE 1265. In animal tests it slowed heart rate down dramatically, not hibernation but part of the way there, and with apparently no side effects. Again, as the side effects might be subtle, I decided that we needed to run more trials.'

He made it sound so matter of fact, Mac thought, when what he was really talking about was the kidnapping and murder of young girls.

'Sandor helped me out again. He got the girls from Luton, as he knew the town well, and all was fine until he had that stupid collision, the prat!'

'The collision wasn't really his fault,' Dan said flatly. 'Someone ran into him.'

Jonty shrugged his shoulders.

'Whatever. I knew that I had to get rid of him and so I told him that, once he got rid of the last girl, I was going to get him out of the country, get him some-where safe and he believed me. However, I didn't plan on him settling some old scores before he left. When he told me about killing that professor and the taxi driver, I knew I had to get rid of him immediately and so I shot him full of HDE 1078 and staged his suicide. Quite good it was too. Did you like the touch about the biomed conference? Lots of suspects there for you to be getting on with.'

His grin widened and Mac was rapidly reaching the conclusion that Mr. Hart-Tolliver was barking mad.

'So that was that, except that I needed a girl for the lethal dose test. I suppose I could have left that one out, I was fairly certain I knew anyway, but it bugged me so much that I thought why not? Getting a girl was far easier than I thought it would be, to be honest it made me wonder what I'd been paying Sandor all that money for. The only problem was that she didn't die when I thought she would, it took two days longer at the end of which you, unfortunately, turned up. If you'd left it until tomorrow then I'd have been fine.'

Jonty smiled a rueful smile.

'What do you mean?' Dan asked.

'I was going to torch the place tonight. I'd bought the factory so we could expand, we'd need the extra space for the new drug. So, torching it would not only get rid of the evidence but also clear the site for the new buildings and I'd get a bit of a pay out from the insurance to boot.'

'How come?'

'Well I was going to stage it so it looked like squatters were using the place, junkie squatters. I'd already mentioned to some people at the company that I thought someone was squatting there, just to set the scene. I'd carefully place some drug paraphernalia around the place and there's lot of cardboard still in the building so it would burn very nicely.'

'Is that how you originally planned to dispose of Sandor?' Mac asked.

Jonty laughed.

'You're very perceptive, yes that was the plan. Sandor would go in with the last girl and they'd both burn nicely together, poor little junkie lovers. Unfortunately, he jumped the gun.'

'Okay that's enough for now,' Dan stood up. 'Jonty Hart-Tolliver I'm charging you with the murder of Chanelle Burdon. You will be questioned further and other charges will follow in due course. You'll be kept in custody until any court hearing takes place.'

Dan turned off the recorder and then ordered a uniform to take Jonty to the cells. He picked up the phone to tell his DCS the news.

Mac went into the corridor and saw the back of Jonty Hart-Tolliver as he walked towards a lifetime behind bars. Dan came out of the interview room a minute later. He jumped up and punched the air. The look on Dan's face told Mac that it wasn't done in celebration but out of absolute frustration.

'I so wanted to smash that bastard's smile right down his throat!' Dan exploded.

Mac knew exactly what he meant.

'You know I used to see all those programmes on the TV about the Nazi death camps in the Second World War, about how they experimented on people and all of the terrible things they did. I often used to wonder what type of human being could do such a thing. I think we've just met one of them tonight.'

Dan nodded grimly.

Mac laid his hand on Dan's shoulder and said, 'It's a win Dan, a real result. You've just caught a serial killer, one of the most cold-blooded ones I've ever come across, and you've taken him off the streets. If it hadn't been for your decision to go tonight, we'd have lost him but you chose right Dan. It's a win, a bloody massive gold-plated win.'

A wide smile slowly broke over Dan's face.

'Yes, it is a win, isn't it? Come on, let's go tell the team.'

Dan told the assembled team that Jonty had confessed everything. They all stood up and app-lauded loudly.

'Now all of you get down the pub and start getting drunk,' Dan ordered. 'I'll be along later.'

He turned to Mac.

'I'm off to see the boss now. He'll want to hold a press conference as soon as possible so he can tell everyone how he cracked the case. Oh well, I'll see you down the pub.'

Mac shook his head.

262

'I'm sorry Dan but I won't be going. I have to drive home plus, if I'm honest, I'm deathly tired and in need of my bed. However, I would like to meet your boss.'

Dan looked puzzled at Mac's request.

'If you're sure you really want to. He's not exactly a bundle of laughs.'

The DCS was straightening his tie and looking himself over in the mirror when they walked in.

'Bloody good work, well done Dan. The conference is arranged for an hour from now, nice timing for the evening news. This will really show us in our best light. Who's this?'

'Boss, let me introduce you to Mac Maguire, who used to be DCS Maguire from the London Murder Squad. We wouldn't have cracked the case without him.'

The DCS limply shook Mac's hand.

'Really nice to meet you at last and thanks for all your help. I'll bet that you've done hundreds of these press conferences but unfortunately we don't get the chance so often out here in the sticks.'

'Yes, I must have done hundreds I suppose but I never liked doing them that much. However, I must admit that I think you're being very brave,' Mac said with a wide smile.

The DCS stopped fiddling with his tie and turned around.

'Brave, how?' he asked with a concerned look.

'Well, you gave another conference not that long ago more or less saying that you'd got the man who'd carried out the murders. Now you're going to have to say that there was someone else involved and that someone actually ran the operation. If I know the press, they'll pounce on that and all of the questions will be about how come you told us one thing then and you're telling us another now. I know we've all had to do it at times but it's really not nice is it? The press, they're like a pack of wolves when they get going. As I said it takes a brave man to turn up and take a savaging like that and on prime-time news too. You have my admiration.'

The DCS gave this some serious thought.

'Er...Dan, I think that perhaps on balance you should take the conference. I mean after all it was you who caught the perpetrator so perhaps you should get the credit.'

The DCS limply shook Mac's hand again and said conspiratorially, 'Many thanks Mac, we people at the top should always look out for one another.'

'Absolutely,' Mac replied as he gave him a wink.

In the hallway outside Dan and Mac looked at each other and laughed.

'You have my total admiration!' Dan exclaimed. 'You cunning devil, you persuade him out of heading the most important press conference this station will see for years and then he thanks you for it. God but it's been a bloody pleasure working with you Mac.'

'Me too.'

They shook hands firmly and with feeling.

'If I need you again, would you?' Dan asked.

'You've got my card,' Mac replied with a wink.

'Yes, yes I have.'

Dan laughed again as he thought of their first meeting.

Mac went by the incident room and said his goodbyes to the team, although he had a feeling that he'd be seeing Tommy again before too long and all too probably in the company of his daughter. He did indeed feel dog tired and was glad when he reached home. He made himself a cup of coffee and sat down in front of the television and turned on the news.

A few minutes later the announcer said, 'We have some breaking news. A press conference is being held at Luton Police Station and we're going over there right now.'

Mac could see Dan standing in front of a microphone. He spoke clearly and simply and Mac thought that he did exceptionally well. He was glad that it would be Dan's face on all the newspapers tomorrow, he deserved it. When the conference ended Mac washed his cup and gratefully slipped in between the sheets. His sleep was deep and dreamless.

Chapter Twenty Four

Sunday January 18th

Mac awoke in stages, finally drifting into a state where he knew he was awake rather than wanting to be awake. Eventually he got out of bed, checked his pain levels and found them tolerable. He stepped into the hallway and immediately noticed a white rectangle lying near the doormat by the front door. He picked up the envelope and looked at it.

There was no stamp on it and no address. There were just two neatly handwritten words on the front, 'Mister Mac'.

His heart started thumping wildly. He left it on the table in the living room unopened while he went to the toilet, washed and then made coffee. He wondered if it had been delivered that morning but he thought it was just as likely that it could have been there on the mat when he came in the night before. He'd been so tired that he probably wouldn't have noticed.

He kept glancing at the envelope while he tried to get enough courage up to open it. Eventually, and with a huge sigh, he tore the top off and pulled out a single sheet of paper. The printed header said 'Dempsey's Electricals' and gave an address and phone number. His pulse was still racing as he read -

Dear Mr. Maguire,

I hope you don't mind me contacting you. I wonder if you remember me as it's been a long time since we last met.

Laura has told me about hiring you to follow Georgy. I'd be really grateful if you could contact me by phone but only if you want to. I'll understand if you don't want to contact me and will make no further contact if that is your wish.

Yours in hope,
Pauline Dempsey (nee White)

Mac found himself picking up the phone and dialling the number without consciously thinking about it. He held his breath as the phone at the other end rang.

'Hello, Dempsey's Electricals, how can I help?' a woman said in an attractive sing-song tone.

Mac found he couldn't speak for a few seconds.

'Hello, is that Pauline?' he asked at last.

Silence fell at the other end too.

Eventually a tremulous voice said, 'Is that you Mr. Maguire?'

'It is Pauline. Can I come and see you?'

'When?'

'Now would be good, I've waited so long.'

'Yes, come now,' she said and that was that.

He looked at the clock, surprised that it had already gone noon. He showered and had toast and more coffee and was just about to set off when the doorbell rang. It was Tim. Mac let him in.

'I saw the press conference this morning on the news and, when you didn't call, I thought I'd see how you are. How are you?' Tim asked, concerned as ever about his friend.

'I'm not too sure to be honest, something's happened.'

'To do with the case?'

'No, no, something from the past.'

Tim could see a bemused look on Mac's face and he had to know more.

'Tell me about it.'

Mac poured Tim a cup of coffee and said, 'Okay let me quickly tell you the story...

One Saturday in November over sixteen years ago my team had gotten a call. I remember that it had been cold and drizzling for days and that somehow set an appropriately sombre backdrop for what was to follow. In a working-class street in Haringey a neighbour had called on a Mrs. Diana White and found that the front door was open. She went in calling Mrs. White's name but there was no reply. She found out why when she went into the kitchen at the back of the house. Mrs. White was lying spread-eagled on the floor and there was blood everywhere. The neighbour called 999 and we turned up fifteen minutes later.

I've never seen a scene like it before or since, blood was sprayed all over the kitchen cabinets, the work surfaces, the sink, the cooker, it was like an abattoir. You'd never think a single human being could hold that much blood. We found out later that she'd been stabbed seventeen times and had also had her throat cut. It had been a frenzied, brutal attack.

The neighbour kept going on about 'the kids'. When we calmed her down, she told us that Mrs. White had two children, Pauline, who was fourteen, and Georgy, who was eleven, and that they were both missing. Also missing was Mrs. White's boyfriend, a man called Michael Jeremiah. The neighbour was certain that it was the boyfriend who'd killed Mrs. White, adding that she'd seen Mrs. White with black eyes and bruises all too often recently.

Criminal Records told us that she was probably right. Michael Jeremiah had a hefty criminal history, mostly for violence against women. It turned out later that he'd been sexually abusing Pauline for quite a while as well. Her mother had found out and she'd confronted Jeremiah. Unfortunately, all she achieved by this was making him angry enough to kill her. Not long afterwards someone who knew the family came forward and told us that they'd seen Pauline and

Georgy running for a bus along the High Street. They just made it, jumping onto the platform as the bus took off. They also saw a man running after the bus who fitted the description of Michael Jeremiah. Luckily, he was too late to jump on the platform and tried to run alongside the bus. Fortunately for Pauline and Georgy he collided with a bicycle and lost them.

We now knew that we were in a race, a race for the two children's lives. It was likely that they'd witnessed the murder and that was why the boyfriend was after them. We worked non-stop for a day and a half following every ghost of a lead but there was still no sign of Pauline and Georgy or the boyfriend. We were doing everything we could think of and I was getting really worried that we might have already lost the race.

We got our break when I was interviewing Diana White's mother, Elsie, one more time.

I'd finished the interview when she said, 'Those poor kids. They were only happy when their Dad was alive. I'm afraid my poor Diana wasn't much of a mother.'

This gave me an idea. I asked her where they used to live when Pauline's father was alive and she gave me an address only a few streets away. She also told me that all the houses there were being demolished. I thought that it could be somewhere that Pauline might go, as it was a place that she'd once felt safe in. So, my Sergeant and I ran to the car, I could actually run in those days although I didn't make a habit of it. We ran into a block of terraced houses that were half demolished and looked for the number Elsie had given me. Unfortunately, none of the houses had numbers left on them so we just took a flying guess and went into the nearest house.

That's when we heard the scream. It was coming from somewhere upstairs. Luckily the stairs were still fairly solid so we raced up them and then we saw them.

Pauline was in the far corner of the building which was like huge shell upstairs as all the partitioning walls between the houses had been knocked through. She was protecting Georgy, who was hiding behind her, as Michael Jeremiah closed in. He was no more than ten feet away from them when we arrived on the scene. He was holding a long kitchen knife, the same knife that he'd used to kill Diana White.

We went towards them but a large section of the floor had caved in between us and them meaning that there was no way that we could physically get to the children in time. Then Jeremiah turned and saw us. He looked down at the hole in the floor and gave me an evil smile. He knew that we couldn't stop him and I knew at that moment that he was going to kill Pauline and Georgy right in front of our eyes. I don't think he cared about the consequences. He'd already killed so what more could we do to him?

Luckily, knowing how violent Jeremiah could be, I had my Sergeant sign out a pistol. He'd joined the force after leaving the Army and he'd always got top marks at firearm training. This was just as well as I couldn't hit a barn from five feet. Anyway, once he saw that smile, he didn't hesitate, he pulled out the gun and fired. The bullet went in Jeremiah's right temple and it must have scrambled his brains immediately because he dropped to the floor like a puppet whose strings had been cut. We ran back down the stairs on to the street and then up the stairs of the house two doors up and we found that Pauline hadn't moved an inch. She just stood there squashed into the corner. She was shaking violently and little Georgy behind her still had his eyes tightly shut. What could I do? I swept them both up in my arms and told them that everything was going to be alright. I gave them a hug and they clung to me like little limpets. I had to sit with them in the back of the car because they wouldn't let go, especially

Georgy who had taken a liking to my coat and was gripping it tightly.

I knew they probably hadn't eaten for quite a while so, when we were back at the station, I took them to the canteen first and they wolfed down some sausages and beans. I remember that Georgy ate one handed as he still wouldn't let go of my coat. It was getting to be late evening by then so I decided that I'd leave calling the social worker until the morning. I had a fold up bed in my office and I put them in it top to tail. I had to put my coat over Georgy as a blanket because he still wouldn't let go of it. However, they were both absolutely exhausted and went straight to sleep.

Together with a woman constable I looked over them that night. I tried to catch up on my paperwork but I found myself just watching them as they slept. Twice in the night Pauline sat bolt upright with a look of abject terror on her face. I tried to assure her that everything was alright and that both she and Georgy were safe. Both times she went straight back to sleep.

In the morning I got them a good breakfast and Pauline asked me my name. I told her that it was Mac and Georgy immediately piped up calling me 'Mister Mac' and the name stuck. I was really sad when I had to hand them over to the social worker but I visited them in the children's home as often as I could and I saw them during the inquest but not afterwards. I've been curious ever since to see how those kids turned out and today, I'm going to find out. I'm going to see Pauline White and I'm not sure what I'm going to find when I do.'

'Fancy little Laura's boyfriend being involved in an old case of yours. How come you left it so long to see them though? Why didn't you go and see Pauline and Georgy after the inquest?' Tim asked.

271

'That's been a bone of contention with me ever since if I'm honest. After the legalities were done the social worker took me to one side and suggested that it would be a good idea if I didn't see the children again. I must admit it really upset me but she said it would be best for Pauline and Georgy. She said that seeing me would keep reminding them about the horrible ordeal they'd gone through.'

'And you believed her?'

'No, I didn't, or perhaps I didn't want to, but Nora persuaded me that she might be right. I did try to contact them once or twice but the social worker more or less told me off saying that I should wait for them to contact me. It's taken Pauline White sixteen years but she's contacted me at last and now I'm going to see her.'

Tim wished him luck when he went. Mac thought he might need it.

The satnav told him that he was going to Watford and that it would take an hour. After just under an hour the satnav said 'You have now reached your destination' as he pulled up outside a large, prosperous looking house on the outskirts of the town. There was enough space in the driveway for five or six cars but there were only one two vehicles parked there, a Range Rover and a small van with 'Dempsey's Electricals' on the side.

As he got out of the car, he could see a woman standing in the doorway and, even sixteen years later, he knew immediately who she was.

He was wondering if it was going to be an awkward meeting but then Pauline came towards him and gave him a huge hug.

'Come on in, I'm just making some tea.'

Mac followed her inside. The house inside was even larger than he'd thought but it was comfortable, a real home. Mac watched Pauline as she made the tea. She'd must be nearly thirty now Mac thought, little Pauline White all grown up.

'There you go', she said handing him a mug of tea. 'I'd have used the china but I reckoned that you're probably like my husband Mick. He won't drink out of anything except a mug'.

'You're right there, I hate those little, fiddly cups.'

Mac suddenly thought of his Nora and the special porcelain cups she'd only bring out when guests were in the house.

'I need to ask you a question. Do you mind?' Pauline asked.

'No, ask anything,' Mac replied.

'Why didn't you come and see us after the inquest? We looked out for you for weeks afterwards.'

'Didn't she tell you, the social worker?'

'No, she never said anything.'

Mac's heart suddenly felt heavy.

'Well, straight after it was all done and dusted, she took me to one side and asked me not to visit you or Georgy again. She said it would just keep 'reminding the children of their trauma' and that you both needed to forget for a while. She said that I should wait for you to contact me. I asked her if I could say goodbye but she said that you were already in the car and that she'd pass my goodbyes on. Obviously, she forgot. I must admit that I wasn't very happy about it and I said so to my wife. She was the wise one out of the two of us though. She just reminded me that the social worker might actually have been right. She asked me how I'd feel if I kept seeing you and Georgy and then one or both of you ended up psychologically damaged. I couldn't argue with that so in the end I just waited. I never forgot you and Georgy though.'

'You never tried to find out what happened to us?' she asked.

'I tried to arrange a visit and got rapped on the knuckles by the social worker. So, I discussed whether or not I should just ignore the social worker with my wife and she advised against it. When I mentioned that I could always keep an eye on you from a distance she advised against that too. She knew I wouldn't be able to stop at that, she knew I'd end up wanting to meet you. In the end I reluctantly had to agree. After all, I couldn't be absolutely certain that the social worker wasn't right when she said that further contact might cause you and Georgy some damage. Even when I saw Georgy in Haringey cutting your grandmother's hair and I realised who he was, what she said came back to me. I was sorely tempted to knock on the door but then I thought about it and decided not to. He's still a young man and he's doing so well for himself. I wasn't sure if seeing me might bring it all back and perhaps cause him some harm. That's why I dropped Laura's case so quickly. I never forgot you Pauline. There wasn't a year went by that that I didn't wonder where you both were and what you might have been doing but I need to know, the social worker, was she right?'

Pauline was quiet and reflective for a time.

'I think she probably was, thinking about it now. Perhaps we did need to forget for a while. I know it's all in the past but what you've said makes me feel much better somehow. We knew how busy your life was, we thought that you'd just forgotten all about us.'

'What happened to you after the inquest?' Mac asked, hungry for the details.

'Well, we were both placed in a children's home and it was okay. It wasn't one of those places you keep hearing about in the news with the abuse and all. It was good for us, a safe place. It was where Georgy learned how to cut hair after all. That was all a bit of an accident actually. He was just following a girl he fancied at the time who was taking hairdressing

274

classes and then he found that he was really good at it. It's also where I met my Mick.'

'Tell me about Mick.'

Pauline smiled.

'My lump of a husband? He's the best thing that ever happened to me but I didn't realise that at first. He was already in the home when Georgy and I arrived and he took it on himself to show me around and kind of look after me. We really hit it off but just as good friends. I used to call him 'my big brother' sometimes just to tease him. He was a year older than me, an abused kid too, but there was a centre to him that I didn't have. He knew what he was going to do with his life. He was going to complete his apprenticeship and get a job and then, once he knew enough, he was going to start up his own business and be his own boss. Me, I was a mess, I hadn't a clue who I was or what I wanted in life. When I left the home, I had a room in a shared house and got a job stacking shelves in a supermarket. I didn't care about anything those days and, if I'm honest, I went a bit wild. I'd go out and get totally pissed at the drop of a hat and sometimes when I woke the day after with a blinding hangover there would be Mick with tea and toast.'

Her smile broadened at the memory.

'Then one day I seemed to see him differently, perhaps it was the hangover, but it was like I was seeing him clearly for the first time. Here was a young, good looking man with prospects in life and I wondered what the hell he was he was doing with a waste of space like me. I plucked up my courage and asked him.

Mick simply said, 'I'm here because I love you.'

I was shocked, I mean really shocked. When you know you're unlovable and then someone says they love you, and you know they mean it, your whole world kind of turns upside down. My world turned upside down at that moment and in the best possible way. We started dating, I mean really dating, dressing up, going out to restaurants, flowers and chocolates, the whole thing. I was still in some sort of a daze when one night I asked him to stay.'

Pauline pulled a face and Mac could see the little girl again.

'I was scared stiff. I'd always avoided any intimacy, after what had happened, but I took a chance. I'm so glad I did, it was lovely, not fireworks and all that, but lovely and safe and warm. I told Mick I loved him too that night and not long after that we got married. I had no dreams of my own so I borrowed his. I learned accountancy and business management and between the two of us we've built up a business that employs over fifty people but his greatest gift was giving me the optimism to have children. I've got two now and they've made us complete.'

Mac felt a deep sense of relief wash over him.

'So, life has turned out good for you. I prayed that it would.'

'I still have the nightmares and get a bit down at times but you're right, it's turned out better than I could have ever hoped. You know what helps though when I'm having the bad dreams?'

Mac shook his head.

'I remember you, when we were at the police station and I woke up in the night. Your voice was so soothing and when you said we were safe that I believed you. It still helps me now. When I have a bad dream, I picture your face.'

Mac was really touched. Picturing the two of them on the little put up bed he suddenly remembered.

'What about Georgy? What happened with him and Laura?' Mac asked amazed that he hadn't asked earlier.

'Well, you'll be glad to hear that Laura did exactly as you suggested and confronted Georgy. He rang me and said that it was time we talked. It's funny, that's all he said but I knew exactly what he meant. I've told Mick everything that's happened to me and I've even told some of my clients. I'm a counsellor in my spare time and mostly work with people who've been abused when they were kids but some bereavement counselling too. I tell them so they know I'm not just some middle-class do-gooder, that I've been there and I know what it's like. The strange thing is that me and Georgy have never talked about it, not once. We've skirted around it many times but we've never talked properly. Isn't that strange?'

'Perhaps you were just trying to protect each other,' Mac suggested.

'Yes, I think you're right, I think we were both scared of somehow bringing it all back for the other one. Anyway, we had to talk about it now. Georgy and Laura came over and we told her all about it, every detail. We were all in bits, crying and that, and I'll be honest, it was much more painful than I thought it could ever be. After telling her all about his childhood I think Georgy half expected Laura to walk out but she didn't, she clung to him and let him know how much she cared. When we'd all calmed down, she asked Georgy why he hadn't told her about this before. He said that he was ashamed of his past and was afraid that if she found out she might think less of him. I think she understood how hard it had been to talk about it when she realised that this was the first time that we'd talked to each other about it in over sixteen years and we were brother and sister. So, then Georgy tells her that what he really wants is what me and Mick have, a house, kids and a proper life together. A life with her. She told us about her life then. About the mother she loved who died young and the father who totally ignored her and about her living virtually alone in that big house.'

277

She gave Mac a sad smile.

'It was clear that she was terrified of being lonely again. I realised then that she felt she was unlovable too, just like I had, and that was why she was so quick to assume that there must be another woman. For all her money it turned out that she was just another abused kid too. Anyway, Laura then asked Georgy if he was sure he really wanted kids. When he said he did and she told him that his first one was already on the way, well we all went to bits again but in a really nice way. Mick got out a couple of bottles of wine. Laura only had half a glass of course but the rest of us made up for her. It turned out to be a really good night in the end.'

'I'm so relieved. I was really worried that my coming on the scene might have caused you some pain,' Mac said.

'Luckily, both Georgy and me are in a good place now. I've learned through my counselling that you can't forget the bad stuff forever. At some point you have to remember, to look it straight in the face or else it festers. It was the right time for us.'

There was a sound of a key at the door.

'Watch out, here they come,' Pauline said.

Mac heard the raised voices of two young boys before he saw them.

'You pushed me...'

'No, I didn't it was your fault, you fell...'

'No, I didn't...'

'Yes, you did...'

Two boys dressed in Judo outfits stopped in mid-stream when they saw Mac. They looked over at their mother with a question on their faces.

'You can have your milk and cookies upstairs and only one hour on the X Box and then in the bath. Your dad will be back in a couple of hours and we're going out for tea this evening. Before you go, I want you to introduce yourselves to an old friend of mine, Mr. Maguire. Politely now, both of you.'

The younger of the two stepped forward.

'Hello, my name's Michael and I'm eight.'

'Oi, you!' the other one protested. 'I'm older, I should go first.'

'Calm down,' Pauline said, 'and introduce yourself nicely.'

'Hello, my name's Dennis and I'm ten, well nearly ten.'

She ruffled their hair and gave them both a hug each.

'Okay, upstairs both of you,' she ordered.

Mac had a question on his face as the children raced off.

'Yes, we named him after you. We couldn't exactly call him 'Mac' now could we?'

He somehow kept it together until he heard the door upstairs slam and then he had no choice but to let it all go. She'd called her son after him. It punched a big hole in the dam of his emotions and they all came flooding out. He burst into huge, racking sobs and Pauline held him until it subsided. She gave him some towel roll to dry his tears.

'I'm so sorry, so sorry. I'm just a stupid old fool.'

'No, you're not. You're just human like the rest of us, that's all. Tell me is that the first time you've cried since your wife died?'

He nodded.

'It's not right is it, when you can't cry for someone you've spent your whole life with?'

'I'd say it was absolutely normal.'

'Really?' he said with some surprise.

'Sometimes grief runs too deeply for tears. Has it been bad for you since your wife died?'

'I haven't known who or where I was a lot of the time and the pain of losing her was so great, much greater than anything physical I've ever felt.'

'It's the price we pay for having loved. How many good years did you have together?'

'Just over thirty. Amazing isn't it, that someone could stand me for thirty years. I met her when I was twenty and I'd not long joined the police. I remember I went along with a friend of mine to a youth club, under protest as I thought I was too old for all of that. Anyway, my friend was interested in a girl who went there and so I went along to keep him company. I saw Nora the minute I walked in the room and I couldn't take my eyes off her. I was a bit shy in those days and no good at all with the chat up and all that. But that evening I went straight over to her and we talked and it was so easy to talk to her. We arranged to meet again but I knew from the first moment I saw her that she was the one. Luckily she felt the same and less than six months later we were married.'

It was Mac's turn to give a sad smile.

'We lived in Birmingham at the time but a few years later I got the chance of a job at the Met and I was so desperate to work in the London Murder Squad. Nora was happy to move but I found out then that she'd always had this dream of living in the country. We'd been trying for a baby for some time with no luck and she was convinced that living in the country would help in some way. So, we looked and looked for somewhere to live outside London but anything we liked was too expensive on a detective's salary.

Then one lucky day we drove to Letchworth and Nora loved it immediately. I could tell from her face as we drove around that this was the place she'd dreamed about. We tried the council and went on the waiting list for a while. We were living in a pokey little flat near Paddington Green at the time which Nora absolutely hated. Anyway, she kept plugging away at the council and eventually we got an offer.

I remember how excited she was as we drove out to look at the house. It was only a couple of minutes walk from the countryside but, if I'm honest, I was a bit disappointed. It was one of those post-war pre-fabs and it needed a bit of doing up. It did have its good points though, it was all on one level and it was much bigger inside than I'd have thought. However, Nora didn't care about any of that, she only had eyes for the back garden. It was huge with a massive lawn, fruit trees and hedges. Like the house it needed looking after but Nora fell in love with it instantly. I agreed to move there with the idea that we'd find something nicer later on but we never did.

We did up the house and I must admit I was quite surprised at how nice it turned out. 'Nora's shed' we used to call it. Nora worked on her garden and made it beautiful. She'd been right about something else too because within a year we had our little addition, my daughter Bridget. Then later, when I broached the subject of moving, Nora made it clear to me that the only way she'd leave that house was in a box. Unfortunately for me she was right about that too.'

Mac paused as the emotion welled up once again. Pauline gave his hand a little squeeze

'Sorry, where was I? Yes, anyway we'd been talking for ages about me taking some serious time off and going on a cruise. I'd even taken the time to go to a travel agency and I was going to surprise her with the brochures but that night the surprises were all hers. I knew that there was something wrong the minute I saw her face. She sat me down and handed me a letter, it was from our local hospital. The word 'malignant' jumped out and punched me in the stomach. I didn't know how happy I'd been until I read that letter. She lasted less than three months. Everyone said that she'd have only been in pain but it was far too quick for me. I'd have given my life for another half an hour with her.

Anyway, I'd been suffering from back pain for a couple of years but now it got much worse, I just didn't have the resources to fight it any more. I couldn't keep it a secret and soon after returning to duty they made me take a medical and that was the end of my police career. The MRI scan showed damage to my lower spine and they told me and my daughter Bridget that it was most likely secondary bone cancer.

Poor Bridget was so upset. They said that I might only have three months left too. So, I started sorting out the insurances and stuff like that. At least Bridget would get enough from the police insurance to put towards a house and so I was resigned. Then I had a CT scan, to pinpoint exactly where the cancer was, but they couldn't find anything. I remember Bridget was so happy, she wasn't going to be an orphan after all.'

'And what about you?'

'What do you mean?' he asked.

'What was worse, losing your job or being told that you were going to live?'

Mac's head snapped up. He gave it a few minutes thought before he spoke.

'I hadn't thought about it quite like that but you're right. The worst thing was being told I was going to live. If it had been cancer then it was all out of my hands. I'd be in pain of course, which I am anyway, but it would soon be over, no more pain, no more grief. Yes, I'll be honest, I wanted to die but I couldn't admit it, even to myself'.

'Why?'

'My wife's last words, she said 'Live for me'. I've not done a very good job of that, have I?' Mac said.

'You will Mac, you will. The world needs you. Those kids upstairs wouldn't exist if it wasn't for you. So, what are you going to do now?'

'I don't know, work has always been my crutch in a way. I'll try my best as a private detective I suppose.'

'But you've been a policeman for so long, you must have learned so much. Isn't there some way you can pass on what you know?'

Mac thought of young Tommy who was so eager to learn.

Pauline continued, 'The police force has been your life and leaving it has obviously hurt you. If you go into training you can connect with the police again, you can be of use.'

'In all that's happened you know I never thought of that. You're very wise and, in that, you remind me of someone'.

'What will you do now?' she asked.

'I don't know, I'll think hard on what you've said to me for one thing. I've been pushing people away ever since Nora died and I don't want to do that anymore. I've got a lot of catching up to do and I think I'd like to start right away. I've got a sister who lives in Birmingham, her name's Roisin and we were always very close. She's been to see me two or three times since the funeral but it's like I wasn't there, like I was a ghost. I think I should start with her. Oh, I was nearly forgetting that it's my birthday in a couple of days too. It would be nice to spend it with Roisin and my old friends.'

Pauline smiled and squeezed his hand again.

'I think you'll be alright, Mac. I think you'll be just fine.'

'You know I still haven't met Georgy properly. I'd love to see Laura again and meet your Mick too, he sounds like someone I'd really like. Are you doing anything the Saturday after next?'

'No, nothing as far as I know.'

'How would you like to come down to Letchworth then? If you come down on the afternoon, I could show you the sights, such as they are. I could book you a couple of rooms in the hotel, the boys could have their own room. They do a nice dinner at the hotel and Georgy and Laura could join us. It would be my treat. If it would be okay, I'd like to invite my daughter Bridget and my friend Tim too. I've spoken to them about you and Georgy and I know they'd both love to meet you.'

'I'd love to meet them too,' Pauline said with a warm smile.

'I'll get the hotel to send you the all the details then. I'm looking forward to it already.'

Mac said his goodbyes to Pauline knowing he'd be seeing her again soon. He felt quite light headed as he drove home.

Chapter Twenty Five

He quickly packed a bag and decided that he was going to catch the train rather than drive. He hadn't been on a train in ages. He was lucky and found a window seat free. He knew that he was like a big kid in that respect but a train journey just wasn't the same if he couldn't look out of the window at the world going by.

At the next station stop a man sat down beside him and immediately got out his laptop and headphones. He started looking at the BBC News page and then Mac had a surreal moment as he watched Dan again at the news conference. The man noticed him looking over his shoulder and sniffily turned the laptop around so he couldn't see the screen.

He started to get excited as familiar names and places went by; Rugby, Coventry, Birmingham Airport and then finally the streets of Birmingham itself speeding past. As they neared the city centre, he found that he could still put a name to most of those streets, after all he'd played in them, roamed them as a teenager and then patrolled them as a policeman. He'd lived almost as much of his life outside Birmingham as he had in it but it was still home.

He waited until everyone had gotten out before he moved from his seat. While he'd been waiting for the train, he'd made his calls to Bridget and Tim, letting them know where he was going, and finally one to his sister Roisin. She said she'd be a bit late picking him up so he was in no hurry.

He stood on the platform and breathed in the air of his childhood home. He was really looking forward to seeing his sister again and, not forgetting his friend Blue, who she'd married. He was hoping that he could get at least one night out with Blue and his other old friend Liam. They'd grown up on the same street and they were part of his earliest memories, part of himself. He hadn't seen them since the funeral but then again, he hadn't seen anyone since the funeral, not really. He had a lot of catching up to do.

He made his way to the pickup point and from there he could see the landscape of Birmingham spread out before him. Some didn't think it was exactly the greatest city in the world but Mac didn't mind, it was his first love and you never forget your first love.

A few minutes later a bright blue Mini pulled up and a woman got out and ran towards him. It was his little sister Roisin. It still startled him to see her in a dress, for years she'd been a nurse and had lived in the uniform.

She gave him a huge hug and them cupped his face in her hands and looked deeply into his eyes. He soon saw her shoulders slump and her body relax.

She gave him a brilliant smile and then said, 'Denny, it's so good to have you back again.'

Three months later

Mac rang the doorbell. Janet Lewinton gave him a big smile as she opened the door.

'Mac, how nice of you to visit us again.'

Mac could see Hetty. She was peeking at him from behind her mother as young children do, being both curious and a little frightened. She looked at her mother's face. When it told her there was nothing to fear she jumped out and did a little twirl.

'Hello, I'm Hetty,' she said brightly.

'How are you today, Hetty?' Mac asked.

She thought about this for a moment and then said excitedly, 'We're making cupcakes today!'

Her mother smiled and ruffled her hair.

'Well remembered Hetty. Oh, look your cartoons are on now.'

Hetty gave another little twirl and said, 'I love cartoons' and disappeared.

Janet gave Mac a slightly rueful smile.

'She looks well enough and she seems a little sharper than the last time I saw her,' Mac said.

'Yes, the doctors say she's making some progress but they keep warning me not to expect too much. They say that there's been some damage but they don't seem to know exactly what that might mean. They even think there's a chance it might be partly psychological, her retreating into childhood to escape the memories of what was done to her.'

'You're doing very well,' Mac commented.

'I have to now I'm a mother again. I know she's been through so much and I'd never have wished it on anyone but there are times when I'm so glad I've got my little girl back. We have such fun together but then

I feel so guilty about it afterwards,' she said with a frown.

'You shouldn't. If it is psychological then I dare say that having some fun might help her adjust. If it's not, well, if it's not then you've got your young daughter back again and she deserves every bit of happiness that you can give her.'

'Thanks Mac, I think I needed to hear that. Yes, I've got my little Hetty back, she's just the same as she was when she was nine and when her father was alive. That was the last time that we were all happy. She still talks about her daddy sometimes and asks me when he's going to come home.'

A fleeting sadness passed over her face.

'You know it's strange but I never knew how much I still missed him until Hetty came home. I'd decorated her bedroom and made it as comfortable as I could for when she came out of hospital but that first night she came into my room and said that she'd had a bad dream. I took her into my bed and we cuddled up together. She's slept there ever since. I can't tell you of the comfort of waking in the middle of the night and finding another warm body close to you.'

'You know when my daughter Bridget became a teenager and started moving away from us, becoming more independent, my wife said that it's a pity we can't keep a smaller version of them as well. She was so right. They're so trusting and loving at a young age. I really miss that you know.'

Janet was thoughtful.

'Yes, I should say a prayer of thanks every day for having my young daughter back again and it's not so bad. If she does recover then she'll have been free of drugs for ages and there'll at least be a chance that she can have the life I wished for her. If not, well if not then I have enough money to make sure that she'll be well provided for after I'm gone. So, no, it's not so bad.'

When he'd finished his visit, he paused before getting into his car. He could hear the sound of laughter coming from the side of the house. He went and had a look. The window was open and he could see Janet and Hetty in the kitchen mixing something in a big bowl. Janet stuck her finger in the bowl and put a blob of cake mixture on the end of Hetty's nose and they both laughed again. Hetty tried to lick it off with her tongue and the faces she pulled trying had her mother in near hysterics.

Mac felt a little hand in his and he looked down and could almost, almost see little Bridget looking up at him, a smile on her face and trust in her eyes.

For a moment he felt an intense sadness and said, 'No, not so bad at all.'

THE END

If you enjoyed this book then please leave a review.

You can learn more about me and my books by
visiting my author website -
https://patrickcwalshauthor.wordpress.com

Manufactured by Amazon.ca
Bolton, ON

31405638R00173